and Other Stories by South Asian Women
in Canada and the United States

Her Mother's Ashes

and Other Stories by South Asian Women
in Canada and the United States

edited by

Nurjehan Aziz

TSAR
Toronto
Cardiff
1994

TSAR Publications
P. O. Box 6996, Station A
Toronto, Ontario
M5W 1X7 Canada

The publishers acknowledge generous assistance
from the Ontario Arts Council and the Canada Council.

"Free and Equal" was published previously in *The Massachusetts Review*
(Winter 1988-89); "A Child Departs" in *The Toronto South Asian Review*
(Summer 1990); "Her Mother's Ashes" in *The Toronto South Asian Review*
(Summer 1992). The excerpt by Agha Shahid Ali on page 162 is from his
book *The Half-Inch Himalayas*, published by Wesleyan University Press,
1987.

Cover art: *Conversation* by Rossitza Skortcheva Penney

Canadian Cataloguing in Publication Data

Main entry under title:

Her mother's ashes, and other stories by South
    Asian women in Canada and the United States

ISBN 0-920661-40-8

1. Short stories, Canadian (English) - Women authors.*
2. Short stories, Canadian (English) - South Asian-
Canadian authors.* 3. Short stories, American - Women
authors. 4. Short stories, American - South Asian
American authors. 5. Canadian fiction (English) -
20th century.* 6. American fiction - 20th century.
I. Aziz, Nurjehan.

PS8329.H47   1994   C813'.01089287   C94-931692-X
PR9197.33.W65H47   1994

Printed and bound in Canada

Contents

Preface

This collection of stories was conceived on the premise that South Asian women, despite all their differences, possess enough in common to make the enterprise of collecting their works in a single volume a meaningful one; and moreover that this commonality among them supersedes national boundaries, at least in North America, as Arun Mukherjee's introduction makes abundantly clear. Calls were sent out for the stories, and word of mouth spread. There was no resistance by any author to being included only among women, or among South Asians, or to deleting the boundary between the two countries. The final result is this anthology. The equal numbers in it of stories from Canada and the United States is almost an accident.

Whether and to what degree the stories bear the trademarks of the two countries in which their authors make their homes is for readers to judge and critics to debate over. They were all written in English by experienced women writers who are first-generation North American, arriving there from the countries of South Asia, Africa and the Caribbean. They amply demonstrate the volume, quality and breadth—perhaps unprecedented—of dedicated creative writing currently being produced by immigrants to North America, and women in particular.

I would like to acknowledge and thank M G Vassanji—friend, husband, critic and a writer himself—for his help in editing some of the stories; his comments, suggestions and tips from the very start of the project have been invaluable. I am also indebted to Roshni Rustomji-Kerns for introducing some of the American writers to me. Thanks are also due to the authors for their cooperation and patience during the long stages of the production of this book.
                                                      —Nurjehan Aziz

Introduction

ARUN PRABHA MUKHERJEE

The publication of *Her Mother's Ashes*, an anthology of short stories by South Asian women of Canada and the United States, is a pioneering event. Usually anthologies observe national boundaries. Unstated nationalist assumptions of teachers, theorists, and publishers of literature ensure that literary boundaries do not transgress the political boundaries that modern-day nation states created through war, colonialism, outright theft, and only rarely through consensus. And then these same arbiters of literary boundaries propose that essentialized national identities can be deciphered from the literature of a nation. Much ink is wasted on both sides of the Forty-ninth Parallel discussing how "Americans" are different from "Canadians," those discussing this well-worn subject being inevitably white.

Those of us who are defined as ethnics find such exercises somewhat problematic. As American and Canadian aboriginal women writers have already demonstrated, through anthologies such as *A Gathering of Spirit* and *The Colour of Resistance*, lines on the map denoting national boundaries are artificial constructs as far as the cultural and historical realities of native people of the continent are concerned. The South Asian community, similarly, cuts across these border lines, with ties of kinship, custom, ritual and religion. While South Asians have been trotting the globe since antiquity, the last two hundred years saw them moving as indentured workers, railway workers and as traders to several corners of the British empire. They went to the Caribbean, Fiji, Mauritius and East and South Africa during the nineteenth and early twentieth centuries, as sugar and agricultural workers, artisans, technicians, teachers, lawyers and doctors and petty traders. Although they did trickle into the United States and Canada as agricultural workers and lumbermen during the late nineteenth century, their numbers on this continent began to grow only after the mid sixties, after these countries amended their racist immigration policies directed against the South Asians.

What is most interesting for me is the ability of South Asians to assimilate in the host culture without letting go of their South Asian identity. There is, of course, no South Asian essence being posited here. These short stories by South Asian women, reporting on different geographic, cultural and historical aspects of the South Asian experience, make the diversity of South Asian communities quite apparent. First, we who live in North America are different from those who live on the Indian subcontinent, and then there are differences among us North American South Asians, depending on our ethnic, geographic, linguistic, religious and national affiliations.

In fact, the term "South Asian" is as inadequate in expressing our diversities as "European" would be for English, Welsh, Scottish or Irish ones. Thus, while I am South Asian or East Indian to the average Canadian, I am a Bengali to those South Asian Canadians who have arrived from India. And yet, when a Bengali tries to speak to me in Bengali, fooled by my surname, I fumble and stutter because I am actually a Punjabi, my Punjabi ethnicity covered over by my married name. That is to say that amongst ourselves we are Gujarati, Marathi, Tamil, Telugu, Malayali, Punjabi, Bengali, Goan, Parsi, Sikh, Hindu, Muslim and Christian, etc., and not South Asian, a term that is only a bureaucratic invention.

And yet we need that term because despite our ethnic, religious, linguistic and national diversities, we *are* bound together by all kinds of subtle bonds. As long as the term South Asian does not get used to compress our specificities into a homogenized blob, it does serve the legitimate purpose of denoting the fact that South Asians do have what Wittgenstein might have called family resemblances.

We must guard against the homogenizing tendencies of much Western scholarship which speaks of "the third world woman" or "the South Asian woman" as though these terms denoted actual, existing entities whose characteristics could be quantified and differentiated. Those of us who come from areas known collectively as "the third world" or "South Asia" know how reductive such generalizations can become.

If only those who call us "the third world woman" or "the South Asian woman" could come to understand that these terms describe only two among several of our identities, there would be no problem. If only we could explain to the outside world that we as South Asian women are also third world women, Punjabi, Bengali and Goan women, Sikh or Muslim women, Indo-Caribbean or African Asian women, and, yes, working-class or bourgeois women. But our specificities don't stop there. For Hindus are divided among castes and subcastes and Muslims among sects.

Let me explain what all this has to do with the reading of the South Asian women's short stories. In Perviz Walji's story, "A Child Departs," a shopkeeper named Mr Yusuf spits "You Khoja" at the child narrator who tells him "You Punjabi." Now the bitterness of that exchange will remain indecipherable to those who are cultural outsiders unless they are told that "Khojas" are considered a heretical sect by orthodox Muslims. The child narrator, instead of shouting back the name of the Muslim shopkeeper's sect, calls him by the name denoting his geographic and linguistic identity, she herself being a Gujarati, information that will remain inaccessible to those who cannot decode the ethnicity and religious-affiliation clues buried in the author's and her characters' names.

As someone who teaches South Asian and South Asian Canadian literature, I have come to realize how much prior knowledge I bring to South Asian texts that my Canadian students cannot unless I help them. For instance, I begin my class by telling my students about the gender, caste and religious markers buried in my name so that when a South Asian from a similar background sees it printed somewhere, she or he can immediately figure out four things about me: that I am a woman and a Hindu of Brahmin caste and I come from Bengal. When the fellow South Asian finds out that I am only married to a Bengali, she then surmises that mine must have been a "love marriage," since most marriages in India still happen to be within caste.

This is my way of introducing to my students the ethnic, religious, linguistic and caste identities of the authors I am teaching. These identities need to be understood before the interpretation of the text can proceed. To return to "A Child Departs," Aunt Fatma loses her child when she is pressured into remarrying because the child belongs to the father's family according to Muslim law, not that personal accomodations are never made. A Hindu widow, on the other hand, has faced religious and social sanctions against remarriage. Even to this day, a Hindu widow remarrying is an exception rather than the norm, such is the level of social disapproval, despite all the efforts of social reformers of the turn of the century.

The importance of names as the capsule carriers of identity and as signifiers of that identity to those in the know becomes evident in Roshni Rustomji-Kerns's story, "A Memory of Names," where Katy Cooper learns of her Parsi identity upon her trip to Devinagar in search of her roots. And that is why Devika Bardhan's transformation into Debbie Barton in Himani Bannerji's story "On a Cold Day" marks a loss as final as death, even though Devika does not die a physical death.

Of course, not all readers will pick up this anthology with the same amount of prior knowledge. A Punjabi Hindu South Asian like myself does not need to be told about Alakshmi, the goddess of bad luck, in Chitra Divakaruni's "Bad Luck Woman." The short story draws from the reservoir of culture that I was brought up in. On the other hand, the Parsi agiari, or the fire temple, and the Parsi rituals of death are things that I know only at second remove. To give another example, Surjeet Kalsey's title, "Crossing the Threshold," reverberates for me with the weight of traditional wisdom in the same way as "till death do us part" might to a Christian, believer or not. Both phrases are imbued with an aura of cultural authority. Hindu women of the north hear the injunction about crossing their marital home's threshold only in death even before they step out of the cradle, or so it seems to me. They use it to persuade themselves not to when they are tempted to cross it. Kalsey's Chetna has struggled with its admonitory power for twenty-two years before she gathers the courage to leave the abusive marital household.

I comprehend the full weight of Chetna's decision because I retranslate "Crossing the Threshold" into Hindi and Punjabi: "dehli na langhna, bitia." I heard those words spoken in my ears by umpteen elderly women in real life and in literary and filmic representations as I was growing up. But what about readers who don't know the injunctional nature of those words?

As Himani Bannerji has said, in an essay entitled "The Sound Barrier: Translating Ourselves in Language and Experience," she often finds herself "caught up in a massive translation project of experiences, languages, cultures, accents and nuances" (30). She reminds the reader that a South Asian writer's text "is a text with holes for the Western reader. It needs extensive footnotes, glossaries, comments, etc.—otherwise it has gaps in meaning, missing edges" (33). Texts made up of "fragments of language, memories, textual allusions, cultural signs and symbols" (29) need readers who are either already familiar with these aspects or are willing to learn about them.

Too often in feminist criticism an assumption is made that women can understand each other cross-culturally just because they are women. As Chandra Mohanty suggests, this is a gesture of "ethnocentric universalism" (63) that reduces the "other"'s heterogeneity in order to appropriate and subsume the "other" into the self that has the power to define itself as the norm. That has been the mode in which Western literary criticism, including feminist literary criticism, has studied South Asian and other non-Western literatures.

However, to study non-Western texts in the mode of ethnocentric universalism, by imposing eurocentric social, cultural and religious values, is rather like seeing one's own face in the mirror than really encountering the other. Real knowing, instead, takes place in the form of a dialogue. As Mini Adola Freeman, an Inuk Canadian puts it, "We do not sit with each other long enough to understand each other. We do not educate each other enough to understand each other's cultures" (188). Instead of sitting with the other, "ethnocentric universalism" erases the other because the speaking self, or the self who has been given the power to speak, assumes that everyone else is a carbon copy of him- or herself.

"Sitting with each other" is the mode, I believe, where true learning can take place. Reading this anthology will require homework on the part of the reader, somewhat less for a South Asian reader, a bit more for non-South Asian readers. To quote Bannerji again, these stories will leave "gaps" and "holes" in the reader's comprehension as they are full of cultural, political, historical and textual references to South Asian experience.

Some people may feel that I am making it all seem so hard. That literature is universal and its meaning accessible to anyone who takes the trouble to pick up a book. Of course it is an "anyone" who has taken literature at college and learned how to decode things such as characterization, structure, symbolism, allusions, tone and so on. Unfortunately, all this technical information has been provided through the teaching of only a limited set of Western books called the classics or the canon. The fact is that all the above-mentioned categories are culture-specific. A writer's notion of character and a reader's notion of character depend a lot on their acculturation and possibilities of action provided by the society. And as these stories suggest, people do not leave their histories and cultures behind when they migrate. So Geeta Kothari's protagonist, Lally, born and brought up in the United States, nevertheless goes back to India to immerse her mother's ashes in the holy river Ganges. And she remembers her mother's stories of the 1947 partition of the country as she spins her own stories in a 1980s daycare centre. Similarly, Lakshmi Gill's Magdalene works harder at attaining her PhD despite having to take care of three children and an uncooperative husband, as though to compensate for her father who quit his studies because "the British had to be ousted." Again, many readers will perhaps need help with that reference. For South Asian readers of my age and for readers who are well acquainted with Indian history and literature, that little reference alludes to Gandhi's call to Indian youth to quit the educational institutions of colonial India and devote themselves to throwing out the British colonizer.

There is a tendency among North American literary critics to categorize the writings of non-aboriginal minorities as "ethnic" and/or "immigrant." There are set responses to this so-called ethnic or immigrant writing. The critics responding to this work often use terms such as nostalgia for homes left behind, the pain of pulling up roots, the problem of assimilation in the host society. If the work deals with non-Canadian settings, the mainstream Canadian critics have tended to dismiss it as non-Canadian. Even such an astute critic as Frank Davey dispenses with M G Vassanji's *The Gunny Sack* and Rohinton Mistry's *Such a Long Journey* in one footnote in his book *Post-National Arguments* because they "contain few if any significations of Canada or of Canadian polity" (7). He does not even mention Farida Karodia's *Daughters of the Twilight*, perhaps because few Canadians know that Karodia has lived and written in Canada since 1970.

The predominance of nationalist assumptions in Canadian criticism has prevented a wider dissemination of writings of Canadian minority writers. Big publishing houses have been reluctant to publish them and teachers in Canadian schools and universities have tended to avoid teaching them. The nationalist literary theory has excluded them as "new" or "not-yet-Canadian-enough," the assumption being that we who are "new" will become "Canadians" when we have fully assimilated, that is, forgotten our language, religions, history, literature, cuisine, habiliments.

The trouble is that history shows us otherwise. Ethnicity is a tenacious thing. As the short stories about the Parsi characters by Bapsi Sidhwa, Feroza Jussawalla and Roshni Rustomji-Kerns, all Parsis themselves, show, Parsis have succeeded in maintaining their identity as a community over the thirteen centuries they have spent in India after they fled Persia under the threat of religious persecution. The South Asians who have migrated to Canada after a hundred and fifty to two hundred years in East

Africa and South Africa have also managed to preserve their identity. And so have the Indo-Caribbeans. One can, of course, never predict the future and it is always possible that South Asians in North America will forget and assimilate. However, to understand their present, non-South Asians will have to pay attention to the not-yet-forgotten elements.

Reading a literature or understanding a people, I believe, requires a willingness to learn and an innate curiosity. During the five hundred years of colonialism, Western culture has looked down upon non-Westerners, called us barbaric, superstitious, lazy, ignorant and many other things. Actually, we are just different. And not just different in a binary way, what Mohanty calls "the third world difference" (63). No, we are different from the West but we are also different among ourselves. The Indian subcontinent has been home to multiple ethnic groups, religions, cultures, languages, and lifestyles. We who originated there know too well that difference is not always easy to live with and often minorities pay with their lives for their difference from the majority. If there is anything we South Asians know it is that difference is not just a trendy postmodern critical category but something that people live and die for.

As I see it, the world faces a bleak future unless we learn to live with our neighbours' differences, whether it be as individuals or as nations. And learning to live with differences means learning to know what they are. To repeat Mini Adola Freeman's words, "we need to sit with each other long enough" to hear each other's stories and to learn each other's recipes.

I have been teaching South Asian and South Asian Canadian literatures for the last three years at York University and my classroom is full of young and old eager learners. Some of the most moving moments for me have been the times when students recount, both inside and outside the classroom, how they go about filling the "gaps" and "holes" in their knowledge of South Asian cultures. They ask their friends and their family members! Thus an Italian Canadian student was helped in the preparation of her seminar by a Bengali friend who could tell her what the name of the heroine of a particular novel signified, and who, of course, asked her parents. Recently, a South Asian Canadian student brought her mother's prayer book to share with the class so they could look at a picture of Goddess Kali, alluded to in some poems of Surjeet Kalsey. There have been times when some students brought in, as part of their presentation, a particular food to share with the class that was mentioned in the day's text. Such collaborative learning exhilarates me.

I look forward to teaching this anthology in a similar collaborative manner. I hope that the stories will be augmented by stories the students will tell of their own experiences, of similarities *and* differences. We will discuss the meanings of the multiple ethnicities, languages, religions and points of origin embedded in the stories. We will discuss the meaning of the 1947 partition of India, as Canada once again prepares for a separatist surge in Quebec. We will discuss the ramifications of South Asian patriarchy as it oppresses these fictionalized women's lives. (And when we discuss it, I will make sure that we do not automatically think of arranged marriages and the joint family as causes of their oppression as some Western feminists are prone to do. They are and they aren't.) And we will discuss colonialism and racism as legacies that continue to determine South Asian Canadian and American women's lives in the last decade of the twentieth century.

We will explore whether the short-story genre, as deployed by South Asian women, is the same as the one codified by writers like Henry James or whether they have brought in their own inflections. I will only say here that the word for short story in many South Asian languages simply means "telling."

This anthology, then, is not about simple nostalgia, the word too often used to pathologize "immigrants." Instead, it is about memory, history, and the material realities of South Asian women's lives. It is about who we are and where we came from and why. Our lives and experiences are part of North American history just as they are part of world history. Cross-cutting both, our stories and our lives testify to the fact that national identities and national boundaries are somewhat recent inventions whose meaning needs to be interrogated continually.

Works Cited

1. Bannerji, Himani. "The Sound Barrier," *in Language in Her Eye: Views on Writing and Gender by Canadian Women Writing in English.* Ed. Libby Scheier, Sarah Sheard and Eleanor Wachtel. Toronto: Coach House Press, 1990. 26-40.
2. Brant, Beth. Ed. *A Gathering of Spirit: A Collection by North American Indian Women.* Toronto: Women's Press, 1984, 1988.
3. Davey, Frank. *Post-National Arguments: The Politics of the Anglo-*

phone-Canadian Novel since 1967. Toronto: University of Toronto Press, 1993.

4. Fife, Connie. *The Colour of Resistance: A Contemporary Collection of Writing by Aboriginal Women*. Toronto: Sister Vision, 1993.

5. Freeman, Mini Adola. "Dear Leaders of the World," in *Sharing Our Experience*. Ed. Arun Mukherjee. Ottawa: Canadian Advisory Council on the Status of Women, 1993. 186-90.

6. Mohanty, Chandra. "Under Western Eyes: Feminist Scholarship and Colonial Discourses." *Feminist Review*, 30 (Autumn 1988): 60-88.

"Why Am I Doing This?"

HEMA NAIR

It lay in the middle of the plain blue bedspread like a voice shouting shrilly in a quiet church. A pale pink slip with a peach-edged lace border. From under its fluffy cloudiness, the stiff white price tag, printed in black, stuck out like a slyly jeering tongue. Vijaya turned away with a suppressed sob. It wasn't even her size. She wore size 6 and the slip was 12.

But it wasn't the wearing she had craved.

It was the grasping, the slipping into her coat pocket, the swift walking away, past the cashier where there was a small queue of people waiting to pay, and getting inside her car and driving home in one, practically unbroken stride that had drawn her to that lingerie sale. She had come in and flung the thing on her bed and sat down with a crash of creaking wood on her rocking chair. Her feet, still demurely covered by the black shoes with pointed toes and silver buckles which she always wore for work, began automatically to rock the chair backward and forward.

"You take what is not yours and you know where God sends you? To burn in hell! Remember that."

Vijaya could see her grandmother's face as vividly as though she had spoken the words that very morning—sitting with her back against the warmed brick verandah, with the carved nutcracker, splicing betel nut into brown slivers to be savoured slowly in her toothless mouth over the afternoon. How she had loved to sit and watch her grandmother take a smooth, coffee-brown supari, place it in the centre of the fork between the two prongs, and at just the right moment bring the two ends together in one swift rush. *Crr-unch!* Vijaya winced at the memory of that sharp splintering. It had always seemed to her that granny chose that shattering moment

1

to deliver some fierce code of behaviour. Countless times she had wagged her stiff, arthritic finger at Vijaya and admonished her not to steal, not to lie, not to kill, not to answer back while all the time breaking supari after supari into chewable bits.

If granny could see her now. But granny had died, alone one night far away in her red-tiled house in the village and Vijaya had grown up, graduated and got married, ready to travel life's well-laid path. And now here she was, thirty-two years old, working in a bustling small town in the United States and living in her two-bedroom apartment, paid for by her earnings as a physical therapist. And spending her evenings stealing things from the mall.

Every time Vijaya returned with some stolen bit—a skirt, a pendant from a jewelry shop, a small, sequined evening purse—she would stare at the object in the neat order of her bedroom and wonder why she had taken it. It was not for lack of money. Today, for instance, that slip had cost less than four dollars and she had had over three hundred dollars in cash, inside her wallet, apart from her checkbook and credit cards.

I'm going mad, she told herself cruelly. I must be. Why would I do such a silly, unnecessary thing? Especially when I never seem to use any of those useless things. It always astonished her to see how rapidly and completely they lost all value and attraction once they were in the safety of her own room. That slip this evening had seemed the most stunning, most yearned-for object in the world and yet, now, Vijaya thought how cheap and tawdry it looked. One wash and it will be limp, faded history, she thought contemptuously.

But why am I doing this? she screamed silently, getting up and striding around the small room with rising panic. Why do I walk away without paying for things I don't need? The question signalled the start of a tidal wave of helplessness that terrified her with its power and she quickly brought her mind back from the edge of that abyss. It's nothing, she told herself. Nothing. Nothing to worry about. I just won't do it any more. The next time I have the urge to slip something into my pocket I'll just . . . walk away. Or I'll take it and pay for it. Like a soothing glass of warm milk at bedtime, Vijaya's repeated words drove her panic away. Slowly, there came in her a gratified sense of pride at her own self-control. She had conquered it. This was the last time.

Later, as she switched off the lamp and pulled the blue and white flowered quilt around her, Vijaya ignored a small voice reminding her that

2

this was not the first time she had convinced herself that it was the last time.

She woke up late next morning and lay in bed for another hour wondering what she would do with her day. The hours on Saturdays had to be helped and heaved to move along. The Indian store was of course a good possibility. But then she remembered her visit last week. Hadn't there been a distinct look of suspicion on Mrs Nagar's face when Vijaya returned from the spice counter? For a second, Vijaya had become almost paralysed with fear. Had Mrs Nagar seen her slipping that fennel packet into the bag? She had been swept away by a sudden irresistible urge upon seeing the tempting plastic packets of spice strewn around. Vijaya had paid for her pita bread and packets of dals and snacks and quickly run out. I won't go there for some weeks, Vijaya thought now resentfully. How dare she look at me like that? It's all their fault. Why do they put all their goods around so carelessly? Next time I go I'll just pay for that stupid packet in a casual, spontaneous way.

"Oh, by the way Mrs Nagar, before you ring up my bill, would you put in a bill for 2.99? I think there was a packet of fennel in my bag some weeks ago and I didn't see the price for it on my bill."

How nice and confident that sounded. Vijaya could see herself, leaning on the counter with a relaxed smile on her face. In these imaginary situations that her mind played out like a mini-movie, Vijaya was always vocal, unshy and totally in control. That'll teach that Mrs Nagar to look at me like that, she thought with a pleased smile. Also, it would make Mrs Nagar feel it was her fault for not putting the price on the bill. But not today, she decided. Today she would visit that new Indian store that had opened a few months ago at the shopping centre in Cedar Park. What was it called? Spice Land?

Happily, she threw back the covers and went off to the bathroom. Dressed in her black stirrup pants and a maroon shirt, Vijaya made herself a cup of coffee. She opened the fridge and stared at the small dishes covered in smooth veils of plastic. No, she didn't feel like eating anything. It was while she was rinsing her cup that Vijaya happened to glance at the clock. Was it only eight? Two hours before the shops opened! She put the wet cup on the rack and wandered back to the living room. It had a matching set of golden brown sofa and chair with a glass-topped rectangle coffee table in between. The floor had a beige rug that also covered the floors of the rest of the apartment. From behind the sofa a gleaming brass halogen lamp spread its white light discreetly over the small room. It was a spotlessly clean room, looking as if it had been realized that very minute from the pages of a furniture catalogue. Vijaya straightened a perfectly straight table and went and looked out of the window.

Outside was a round, flower-edged lawn. Further away stood a row of grey and white apartments similar to hers. The American couple who had sold her the apartment had told Vijaya with smiling emphasis that living in Green Woods was like living in the country but with the convenience of a modern flat.

"On a quiet summer morning, I've actually seen deer walking across that grass patch," Peter Watts had said, shaking his head in disbelief or awe at the memory.

Vijaya had barely listened. She was too busy taking in the spartan beauty of the rooms and trying to assimilate the fact that she could actually afford the mortgage. She had agreed to take the place at once, and when the Wattses, who were moving to New England to help Peter's mother run an inn, offered the entire furniture and draperies for another 3,000 dollars, Vijaya had paid without hesitation. Later, the others at the hospital had expressed disapproval at that.

"You could have at least tried to bring the price down a bit," Margy, a tall blonde physical therapist from Germany, had said.

"They expect you to," Nina Wang had nodded. She was Chinese and concealed a dynamo of strength and savvy under her fragile, childlike face.

But Vijaya had just shaken her head and said she was very happy to get a fully furnished house.

"I don't have to wait for months to get my flat organized," she had said softly. "I have saved myself the bother."

"But I would have thought you'd want to decorate it yourself," Margy said in surprise.

Leaning against the cool, slippery windowpane, Vijaya wondered how Margy's party had gone off yesterday. Actually it had been the story of that party that had sent Vijaya off to the mall in that furious, desperate search. Margy and Vijaya had planned to have dinner and see a movie. But on Friday afternoon, Margy's boyfriend, Chris, had suddenly called up to say that he had met a long-lost friend from Holland and he wanted Margy to throw a party in his honour. Margy, who was madly in love with the good-looking Chris, who was five years younger than her, did not even stop to think before she agreed. She had come over to Vijaya's desk and stuttered out a sheepish apology.

4

After Margy left, loudly planning a dinner menu she could quickly arrange, Vijaya sat for a long time staring at the unread sheets of her patients' progress reports. She had been thrilled when Margy casually asked her to see the film with her and later on go eat somewhere. Despite having worked at the hospital for five years, Vijaya had few friends. Margy said we girls could get together anytime, Vijaya thought resentfully. But Margy was always busy. She was going off to the beach with Chris, or away on a hiking trip or sailing with some of his numerous friends. Listening to Margy's breathless descriptions of her weekend fun made Vijaya's eyes grow dull with envy. It didn't seem to matter to Nina Wang. But then Nina Wang had a huge umbrella of relatives to visit, shop and eat with.

When she drove out of the hospital parking lot, the car had seemed to turn towards the mall as if it had been programmed. Vijaya sensed a momentary surprise at seeing the familiar fortresslike buildings at the end of the road. She rarely went to the mall on a weekday . . .

Jerking herself out of her recollection of last night's experience Vijaya tried to gaze at the placid view laid out before her. If only she could sit awhile on that white-painted wooden bench, placed so picturesquely next to the wide semicircle of flowers. In the first few months after she had moved, Vijaya had kept promising herself a quiet afternoon there but somehow, whenever the opportunity came up, she began to feel hesitant. No one ever sat there, she told herself finally. It would look so conspicuous if she went and perched there in full view of the two rows of apartments. If only she could one day catch sight of someone sitting there! That would give her the signal to go there also. It was always better in this country to wait and see.

She turned away from the sterile scenery of the window and went to the second bedroom. A small, cherry-wood desk stood next to a lacey white-draped window, and so she called it her den. Maybe she could write a letter home. Slowly she pulled up her chair and took out the topmost letter from a small pile in one of the front drawers. It had come last week.

"It was good to hear that you are healthy and doing well in your job," said the shaky script of her father. "Every day your mother and I visit the Krishna temple in the morning and pray that your life will continue in its prosperous course. You deserve every happiness, for I know only your hard striving in a strange country enabled you to study and find yourself a good job and your own apartment. My heart swells with pride. God is really great . . . " Vijaya thrust the flimsy airmail into the drawer and slammed it shut.

5

If they knew! For them she was the most successful of the children, the one they talked about glowingly at family gatherings. And I am the most successful, she told herself fiercely. Of course I am.

Those early days of coming to America. How stupid she had been. How ignorant. She didn't even know then how to take a bath in a tub. The first day when she came out after a refreshing shower, the floor and walls had been splashed wet and Madhuri Aunty had made such a face as she went about mopping up.

"Over here we don't like getting the floor wet," she had explained.

Vijaya had been puzzled. Not get the floor wet? Why, in their small, white-tiled bathroom in Bangalore, the floor and the walls were constantly wet all morning till the family had finished their baths. Wasn't the bathroom supposed to get splashed? Questions had thronged her mind but something in her aunt's disgusted expression kept Vijaya from asking them. She had crept into the tub after that and timidly opened the shower to a trickle and wet herself in a quick, guilty way for a few minutes. When she stepped out, she would spend a feverish fifteen minutes wiping the tub, the walls and even the floor where her damp feet had stood, with the dry end of her towel.

And the language! So many strange words and so many strange pronunciations of familiar words. She still remembered the time she had mispronounced UPS. When the uniformed man handed her a parcel and asked for a signature, Vijaya had run into the family room and informed Vinny, her ten-year-old cousin who was watching a video film with an American girl from her class, that the ups man was at the door.

" 'Ups'? What do you mean 'ups'?" Vinny said, looking very surprised.

"Why, there is a van outside . . . it's got 'ups' written on it . . . he has a parcel," Vijaya stammered incoherently.

Vinny followed her to the door and saw the man, and she burst into uncontrollable laughter. In between shouting for her mother, Vinny had roared.

"Why Veejaya, don't you even know how to say 'UPS'? It's not 'ups,' It's U P S. United Parcel Service. Ups!"

Vinny had rushed back and repeated it to her friend, saying, "Have you ever heard anything more dumb!"

Vijaya heard giggling each time she passed the room. The sound made Vijaya feel as if her skin was being slowly peeled. In the darkness of her room at night, Vijaya had squirmed with shame. She and her silly tongue. Why hadn't she been able to understand what that man had been telling her? For days she had avoided Vinny, hating to see the contempt that she was sure she would find in her cousin's eyes. If only she could go back. But her father's words at the airport had been so definite.

"Go to the US and make your own life there, Vijaya. You are fortunate that my brother has agreed to sponsor you. There is nothing for you here. How long can you stay with us? Your mother and I are old, and after we are gone do you want to live at the mercy of your brother's wife?"

There had been no mistaking the meaning in her father's words. He had no money to give her. Whatever he could had been already spent for the jewelry, the gifts and the dowry . . . Vijaya had touched her father's feet and followed the straggling line of people into the long gleaming aircraft.

She had longed for the day she could leave her uncle's house and live on her own. Away from Vinny's sniggers and her sullen-faced aunt. Yet, weeks after she had moved into her rented apartment, Vijaya had been homesick for her uncle's home. She missed the noise, the talk at the dining table. She missed going to sleep knowing that everybody was just a door away. She even missed washing the enormous amount of dishes, forks, spoons and glasses after dinner. That had been her task. It had been Aunty's idea and for the three months that Vijaya had stayed there, she had washed up every night.

She had never stayed alone in her life. Coming back home was something Vijaya dreaded. Switching on the lamp and inhaling the dustless symmetry of her room made the tiredness take root in her bones and she drooped in her house. The evening hours between six and nine stretched out like a limp rubberband that had lost its elasticity. At first, Vijaya tried to make the long hours pass by writing long letters home. It gave her day some meaning and gave a purpose to the following day. But soon, her letters made her feel as if she was talking to herself, for she received very few replies. Her father wrote that the cost of airmail had gone up and he could not afford to write once a month.

Vijaya had even gone to the public library near her apartment and borrowed a few books. But they lay in a neat pile on her table. She could never work up the enthusiasm to open them. She had never been a great reader anyway. Her mother had frowned upon girls reading novels or any form of fiction and Vijaya had always plenty to do around the house.

"I don't want you to get spoiled just because you are an only daughter," was a frequent comment from her mother. And so Vijaya learned to be a good housewife. She swept, washed, cleaned and cooked diligently, and equally diligently she worked at her school exams. When she passed with a first-class degree her parents had been quite pleased and proud. But at her whispered voicing of a desire to enrol in medical school, her father's beaming smile had vanished.

"A doctor? You want to be a doctor? What for?"

"Do you realize how much money it takes to become a doctor?" Her brother Vikram had enquired, with a frown. "As it is, we are having trouble saving up for your wedding."

"Don't talk like a foolish child," her mother had advised with a shake of her head. "Just join our local college and wait till your elders find a good husband for you."

It had been pure luck that the Little Flower convent college had a three-year course in physical therapy. And despite the open scoffing of her family, who would have liked her to take a degree in history or literature, Vijaya had taken the course. It had been that certificate which had opened the way for a new future for her later, when everything else had crumbled.

Vijaya had got a job in a hospital within two weeks of sending in her resumé to an employment agency that her uncle had taken her to. And from the first day, she had loved her work. Once she was with a patient, on the floor of the exercise room, Vijaya forgot who she was. She was only a voice, a will, a powerful pair of hands, urging the seating, struggling human being before her to straighten a weak back or bring life surging up an atrophied leg. It was like being at the centre of a constant battle.

But Vijaya never really partook of the joy of victory. In fact, whenever a cured patient thanked her for her efforts, Vijaya would return the smiles and shyly accept the warm embrace or handshake. But in her heart she would think, "Why do they call my work on them meaningful? The real effort has been the doctor's. It was the doctor who performed the operation that enabled them to come to the rehab and re-learn skills they knew anyway. They are just being polite in praising me."

Staring down at the polished surface of her desk, Vijaya saw the wide smile Mr Kerr had given yesterday when he came to her desk and placed on it a slip of paper with his *left* hand, the hand which six months ago had hung like a paper cutout against his side.

"We did it, little one," he had grinned, "we did it, Mowgli girl."

Mr Gerald Kerr was a retired policeman with a brood of story-hungry grandchildren, and *Jungle Book*, he informed Vijaya on their first meeting, was one of the favourites. As their exercise sessions continued, Mr Kerr started calling her Mowgli girl. Vijaya greeted her new name silently, but inside, a velvety feeling arose, as if she had just slipped into a warm tub for a soak. One evening, curiosity had finally driven her to rent the *Jungle Book* cassette. Mowgli was just a little boy, she discovered bleakly. Was Mr Kerr poking fun at her? Was he hinting she looked like that skinny, stubborn little orphan? Tears started at the thought of the pleasure she had allowed herself to experience at her nickname. As usual, living in a dream world, she thought Mr Kerr must have had a good laugh when he saw the wide, over-friendly smiles she would greet him with everyday. Mowgli girl, she had thought bitterly.

The bitterness stayed in her throat like vomit surging up. The pent-up feeling became so unbearable that finally Vijaya felt she had to get away from her apartment. She had to go out and breath deeply and expel the choking in her throat. She slipped behind the wheel of her car and decided to drive around aimlessly. In ten minutes she had parked amidst the wide sea of cars outside the mall. I'm going to look around and pass the time, she told herself. But deep down she knew why she was there.

The burgundy leather wallet lying on the counter. The feel of it, butter-smooth. The black-suited back of the saleswoman as she arranged a shelf of briefcases. The breathless walk out of the mall with the feathery thud-thud of the wallet hitting her thigh from the inside of her coat pocket, an echo of her pumping heart.

Vijaya was speeding back home and, next to her, on the seat lay the folded square of calfskin. Unconsciously, she was humming along with the flute concert playing on her tapedeck. The rage, the fear, the anguish would come later. Right now, all she knew was the release of that curdling bitterness.

Who would have believed it? She, Vijaya, the pious, extremely well-behaved and truthful person? Of whom even her mother-in-law, traditionally the most critical voice in a young wife's life, had said, "One thing I can say with conviction, Vijaya would never do anything that would lead to someone pointing an accusing finger at her."

All through the months of that tortuous divorce, her poor father and mother had drawn the feeble warmth of that sentence and wrapped it around them like a thin shawl. Endlessly they would tell the daily congregation of relatives and friends who came to commiserate, "Her own mother-in-law said that. You can see how blameless she is. It was her bad luck that Shyam turned out to be such a bad bargain.''

It was her bad luck that Shyam had continued his affair with his colleague at the bank. Renu Karkaria. Vijaya had met her just once and even that recollection was vague. It had been at the dinner party they had given for Shyam's department after the wedding. There had been ten people and afterwards, when the fact of Shyam's affair and the name of his lover had become a household source of sorrow, Vijaya remembered a thin, brown-haired girl who had kept laughing loudly at every joke that was made. The other women had just smiled or shaken their heads in mock disapproval when the men made particularly bold remarks, but the girl in the purple sari had thrown back her head and shrieked. Her mother-in-law too had noted this and afterwards commented to Shyam, ''Some of your women colleagues seem to have no idea of decent behaviour. I couldn't believe the way that starved-looking girl sitting on the sofa near the window was laughing!''

''Oh that's Renu,'' Shyam had laughed easily. ''Renu Karkaria. She's just a kid and thinks everyone is funny.''

And that was how Vijaya had later remembered the name. Once, in the middle of a bitter confrontation between her father-in-law and Shyam, her father-in-law had pointed at her and asked, ''What's wrong with her? Tell me, what do you find lacking?''

For a second, Shyam and his father's eyes had run over her in a quick, calculating flash and Vijaya, standing petrified against the door, had felt the same uneasy shame as when she caught herself naked in the bathroom mirror. But Shyam had never wanted her for a wife. After six months of living in their house, sleeping in the same bed with him, Shyam had shouted that sentence at her. It had not been Vijaya he had wanted. It had been the fifty-thousand rupees of her dowry. The money that his father needed to expand his business and the money that Renu Karkaria and her widowed mother could never have raised.

She, the unwanted, had finally left when Renu had become pregnant and Shyam had threatened to leave home and live with her. Vijaya's father had been summoned to escort her back. Her father had no hard words for his son-in-law. ''It's fate,'' he had said listlessly. ''Only fate is to be blamed for your ill luck.''

She was a success story now, Vijaya thought with a small smile. A daughter who had whisked her embarrassing presence away and become a comfortable, far-off postal address. Why had she never wanted to return, even for a visit? But go back to what? To the same pitying looks and whispered conversations? "Maybe what you are feeling is right," her father had once agreed. "People here will only rake up that old story again. Better for you to continue with your new life there."

A new life as a thief. Of course not, Vijaya responded instantly to that cruel new voice inside her. Restlessly, she moved across the room straightening a picture, aligning a table, plumping a cushion. The room seemed to have shrunk suddenly. How suffocating this apartment was. If only she could stop that irritating voice inside her. Why was this room waiting like an animal about to pounce?

The car keys fitted into her hand as if they had been carved there. Without even looking at her watch, Vijaya knew it was nearly ten. By the time I reach the mall, it will have opened, she thought, locking the apartment door and pressing the button for the elevator. As she plummeted down, Vijaya told herself, "Just a quick look around the shops and then I'll come home for a nice, quiet afternoon."

The Spouse and the Preacher

BAPSI SIDHWA

Large eyes darting like startled moths, the slender girl in red sari emerged nervously from the doors at Kennedy Airport. She anxiously scanned the row of waiting faces in the arrivals lounge and, the anticipatory smile on her lips fading, felt her eyes begin to smart. The fear that had lurked unacknowledged in her mind during the flight now leapt out like a bolting horse: Nav was not there to receive her.

Roshni hesitated, blinking back tears, and then, yielding to the pressure from behind, self-consciously trundled her heaped cart past the throng of relatives and friends who were effusively greeting the other passengers arriving from Bombay.

Roshni came to a stop and stood at a short distance from them. She felt intimidated by the vast hall in which she found herself and by the crush of people bustling purposefully on all sides. Nav would expect to find her here: that is, if he turned up at all. An Air India stewardess flashed her a smile of recognition, and checking her brisk passage, stopped to ask, "Everything all right?"

Roshni nodded, touched by her concern. "Yes, thanks."

The stewardess had been specially kind to her on the flight. It was amazing how many people on the flight had guessed that she was newly married. It must be her Banarasi silk sari and the festive red glass and gold bangles.

Roshni leaned against her cart. The stewardess's concern had comforted her, and despite her tension she noticed the sheer size of the hall. The illumination, from concealed lights that approximated daylight, the glittering expanse of glass, steel and marble soaked into her consciousness. And it suddenly struck her that she was in America, the fabulous country of her fantasies, of *Newsweek* and rock stars and MTV, the home of her husband, and she was overwhelmed by a surge of excitement.

As the crowd in front of her thinned, Roshni noticed a block of chairs ahead of her. People were lounging in tired postures, their hand luggage strewn about their feet.

Judging that she would be able to keep an eye on the arrivals point from there as well, Roshni pushed her cart towards a dumpy little gray-haired Indian woman sitting in the front row, her slippered feet stretched out to a small bag on her cart.

Smiling timidly, Roshni glanced at the vacant seat next to the woman. The woman made a small accommodating movement in her chair, and said, "Sit, sit. I'm also waiting . . . for my son. Who's coming for you?"

"My husband," Roshni said, shifting to Gujarati. She guessed from the woman's Hindi accent and the drape of her sari that she was from her own home province, Gujarat.

But the rush of blood that ignited her dusky skin, and the way Roshni had said "My husband," caused the woman to lower the dangling heels of her slippers to the floor and turn to her with an indulgent grin. "Acha," she said, employing the versatile word to declare her pleased comprehension, "so you're a brand new bride! How long have you been married?"

"Almost a month."

"Congratulations! Live long. See much-much happiness. Where are you from?"

"Balsar."

"I'm also from Gujarat," the woman announced on a note of triumph, delighted by a coincidence that, given the population explosion of Gujaratis all over the planet, was not surprising. "From Baroda. It's quite close to Balsar," she said, getting specific. "What does your husband do?"

"He's a computer analyst."

The crisp English words imbued Roshni's speech with unintended primness.

"Aachaaa," the woman drawled, dragging the elastic word with a wry but amiable touch of wide-eyed awe. "Then he must be verrry clever."

Roshni smiled in bashful concurrence; and, realizing she might have sounded as if she was putting on airs, compensated for it by chattily volunteering information, "He's just got a job with an American company in upstate New York, in Albany. He's going to show me around New York

13

for a few days and then we'll go to the small town where he's working. He told me that I would like it. But first he would teach me to drive a car.''

The woman studied the girl, her gaze lingering on the wide gold-embroidered sari border, the red bindi on her forehead, the centre parting in her smooth hair. "You know," she said, "I thought at first you were Hindu." Roshni flushed crimson. She thought she sounded exactly like a "Goo-jjoo." In fact Roshni, who was dark for a Parsee and self-conscious about it, had decided during her teens to use her small-featured chocolate looks to advantage the way the South Indian girls did. She took to wearing vividly coloured saris with contrasting borders that complemented her dark beauty, and coiled her long hair in a silken knot at the back.

Dressing this way had changed the way Roshni saw herself, influenced her conduct and attitudes. And her sense of identity with the majority Hindu community had imbued her with a confidence she lacked in the company of her siblings and cousins, brash, lighter-skinned creatures who wore miniskirts and dresses, played the piano, and affected Western mannerisms. Roshni had taken to practising classical Indian ragas on the sitar.

Noting the girl's acute discomfort, the woman shifted ground and made a series of sympathetic clicking noises with her tongue. "It's not right," she said shaking her head reprovingly, "your husband shouldn't keep you waiting like this. But he'll come, don't worry. One has to drive such long distances here. If there's any problem, my son and I will help you. Don't worry."

Roshni looked at her gratefully. After a few minutes she asked, "Could you mind my luggage while I go to the toilet?"

"Go, go," the woman said nodding, "freshen up," and she made a small, understanding sound with her lips.

Roshni had barely returned to her seat when she spotted Nav. She shot up from her chair, and pitching her voice discreetly, called, "Nav, Nav."

Nav's worried face cleared with relief when he saw her. And as he strolled over to her Roshni's heart stilled. He looked so attractively at ease and debonair in his jeans and striped T-shirt. Now that she had the chance to observe him neutrally, without the critical assessment of her relatives and friends who had found him alternately too tongue-tied or too patronizing, too tall or too pale, he looked startlingly handsome. More in his natural element here than he had in dilapidated and dingy old Balsar.

A happy little catch in her lungs stopped her breath.

"Hello," Nav said, and bashful about hugging his wife in public, he

14

lightly touched Roshni's shoulder. Then he placed his hands in a "can-do" businesslike way on the cart.

Roshni glanced at the Gujarati woman with a smile of leave-taking, but the woman, her short legs once again stretched to the cart, was peering at Nav through narrowed and contentious eyes. Clearly she was not about to permit any leave-taking without venting her feelings.

Following the trail of Roshni's disconcerted gaze, Nav also looked at the woman. And, laying in wait for him to do just that, the woman promptly said, "Is this good? Your bride comes all the way to America for the first time, and you make her wait like this? It is shameful!"

Nav's laid-back American pose at once vanished, and he became as polite and contrite as was expected of an Indian youth being chastized by an elderly woman.

From the corners of her eyes Roshni keenly observed the change in Nav's personality as he made his excuses. She was glad the man she had married still cared enough for what people from their part of the world thought of him.

In the taxi Roshni said: "I thought you weren't coming."

"You knew I'd come."

"I was frightened." Roshni sat sullen and huddled in her corner.

"Don't be silly. There were hundreds of people around you. This is New York, not Balsar. You've got to learn to be strong-hearted and independent if you want to survive in America." He made a disgusted noise. "That interfering old Goojjoo woman got you unnecessarily worked up."

"But I *was* frightened." Roshni was emphatic. She sat up, bristling, and looked stonily out the window. A tear trickled down her cheek, and another.

Nav slid across the seat and put his arm round her shoulders. "I'm sorry. I tried my best to be on time. I was longing to see you. I put the alarm on for five o'clock . . . I've had to come a long way, you know."

But Roshni twisted her neck to turn her face further away and became as stiff as a reed broom in his embrace. She sniffed.

Nav twisted his long body awkwardly to dig into his jeans pockets, and handed Roshni a tattered tissue. Then he forcefully drew her to him.

Roshni maintained her taut approximation of a bristly reed broom. But her heart, that Nav had so peremptorily ordered to be strong and independent, fluttered and pounded hopelessly.

Sensing the cause of her agitation, in which dread and confusion mingled with anger, Nav said, "I'm sorry, I didn't mean to be rude or bossy . . . I'm sorry . . . Please, please don't be like this," until Roshni's resistance crumbled. She buried her wet, reproachful face in his ribby chest, and her travel-exhausted body gradually grew languid and trusting.

Nav gently stroked Roshni's back. He kissed her forehead, her fragrant hair and slender neck all the way to the Catholic Seminary on 108th Street and Broadway, where he had booked a room for the duration of their week-long honeymoon in New York.

In the next few days some of Roshni's private trepidations and misgivings regarding her husband, whom she scarcely knew despite their nervously consummated marriage in the small bedroom reeking of whitewash in Balsar, had been replaced by a sense of dependence and trust, and a burgeoning passion. For Nav was as ardent and tender a lover of the sultry body of the exotic girl he had chosen to marry above all others shown to him in Navsari, Surat and Balsar, as he was an instructive and informative guide to her in New York.

They visited the Statue of Liberty, the Zoo at Central Park, and breathed the gusty exhilarating wind that made it difficult for them to hear each other speak atop the Empire State building.

But the bossy aspect of Nav's personality, which had agitated and provoked Roshni in the taxi, kept rearing its aggravating head like a leery squirrel.

Roshni became resigned to the fact that Nav was a compulsive instructor, and there was little she could do about it but accept his particular brand of benevolent guidance.

Always prepared to enlighten the country bumpkin from Balsar, which, he grandiosely assured Roshni, was as removed from worldly ways as it was far, Nav drew upon a reservoir of his experiences and mishaps in the United States to forewarn and forearm his bride.

And if Nav was an indefatigable instructor, his bride was an astute judge of human character. Roshni had it within her realistic and sympathetic grasp to intuit the fragility of Nav's buffeted ego. She registered almost by a process of osmosis the assaults on it, and from her own reaction to certain aspects of the American culture, estimated the prerequisite of shocks demanded of a newcomer to this opulent, opportunity-laden, and at the same time bewildering environment. Roshni realized that Nav's experience shielded her, and she had the native intelligence to bolster his fragile ego in order to strengthen her spouse to their mutual benefit. It was a challenge demanded by the new country. Even though Nav was teaching her to adjust to it, he was also a newcomer to the life outside the university that had sheltered him for four years.

Nav soon discovered within himself a surer strength and was privately thankful for his unexpectedly diligent and, if not appreciative, at least understanding pupil.

On a bright Saturday afternoon Nav proudly paraded his wife, radiant in an emerald shot-silk sari with a plum border, on Madison Avenue. Nav's chest swelled. Strutting beside her he noted the admiring and approving glances she drew their way. And when Roshni had had her fill of gazing at the captivating window displays, and became restive to go into the stores, Nav tactfully navigated her into a bus instead.

While Roshni excitedly looked out the window at the deep gorge the immense buildings made of the road and the cosmopolitan carnival of camera-toting tourists, Nav gazed covertly at the amiable stranger, colourful as a tropical butterfly, who had become his wife. In the lottery of fate that allotted wives, he felt he had picked a winner.

The bus took them all the way down to lower Fifth Avenue and deposited them at Washington Square in Greenwich Village.

Once they entered Washington Square through the gates Roshni took hold of Nav's arm. They sauntered through the throng of holiday-makers, surprised by the range of activities going on, all of them competing for their attention.

They stood before the small tables, watching speed chess and backgammon. "Why don't you try?" Roshni asked, and Nav prudently replied, "I'm not good enough."

His humility took Roshni by surprise. She pressed his arm closer, and the yielding softness of her flesh pulsed through Nav's blood like feathery threads of happiness as they watched skateboard experts show off by jumping over three trash cans set out in a row, and graceful frisbee enthusiasts perform amazing feats with their sailing frisbees.

At first they only heard the preacher.

They drifted closer and Roshni spotted, through a shifting screen of other idle drifters, a respectably-suited, middle-aged preacher, energetically waving a bible and belting out God's Word through a mike attached to two small amplifiers. "He's a Protestant proselytizer." The knowledgeable husband informed his wife. "Let's watch him for a bit. They can be quite funny sometimes."

Roshni lowered her thickly fringed lids and glanced at her spouse from

17

the corners of her dark eyes. At this moment Nav sounded just as insufferably stuffy and patronizing as Roshni's family had been at pains to point out to her in Balsar.

But then they did not know the other, finer aspects of a personality she was in the throes of discovering. The tender, passionate and vulnerable facets that were beginning to shimmer for her like the diamonds carved by the acclaimed artisans of Gujarat.

Meanwhile the man of God appeared to be in a frenzy. The muscles in his face were bunched in tight knots that jumped as he yelled: ''Jesus Saves! I've found the Lord! Repent sinners, repent. The end of the world is coming! Now is the time! The end of the world is coming.''

Roshni stared at him, fascinated. People were ambling past them, and except for a young well-dressed couple who looked like European tourists, and a few children, nobody paid him much attention. The preacher's fierce oratory and obsessive style reminded Roshni of an eccentric priest who occasionally visited Balsar to exhort the twenty-odd bewildered Parsees gathered at Kharegat Hall—for wont of anything better to do—to march straight to the United Nations headquarters in Geneva and wrest back Iran, the land the Parsees had fled fourteen hundred years ago, with their importunate demands.

''Jesus saves! The end of the world is coming!'' roared the preacher.

''He *is* funny,'' Nav said, and Roshni, smiling, concurred.

''Repent! I have found the Lord,'' bellowed the preacher. ''The Lord will find you, sinner!''

And the proselytizer made a smart little turn on his patent leather heels and unexpectedly pointed a long and rebuking finger at Nav.

Thinking that the condemning finger was directed at some unfortunate sinner behind him, Nav glanced swiftly over his shoulder. No one stood behind him. Nav turned his scarlet face to the preacher and said, with commendable calm considering his shock, ''I'm not a sinner.''

''Everyone's a sinner. The Lord knows. Repent! The Lord will show you the Way. Accept Jesus into your heart. He died for your sins. Repent!'' And since great truths bear reiterating, the preacher, tirelessly repeating himself, exhorted: ''The end of the world is coming! The Lord saves!''

''Zarathushtra will take care of my sins, my good man. I'm a Parsee. I believe in my Prophet Zarathushtra!''

Nav sounded very like a fabled uncle, Roshni thought, described by her grandmother, who had irritated a New Yorker two decades ago with his sermon that Zoroastrians didn't smoke because they venerated fire, and thus he couldn't give him the cigarette money he had asked for. The aggravated New Yorker had snarled ''O yeah?'' pulled out a knife, and relieved the uncle of his wallet.

''Thou shall not place false Gods before me!'' boomed the preacher, who had by now turned cherry-red with wrath. ''There is only one path to our Lord. Turn to the Saviour or you'll burn in everlasting hell. Repent before it's too late!''

Nav made a slight, reflexive movement that rippled through his muscles, readying him for battle, and Roshni let go his arm.

''It's fundamentalists like you who are causing all the trouble and violence in our world,'' Nav shouted in a voice as terrible as the proselytizer's and, swiftly glancing at Roshni for approval, continued, ''If you did a decent day's work we'd all be better off.''

''I work in the vineyard of the Lord! I seek lost sheep to return them to the fold. Jesus saves! The end of the world is coming,'' thundered the twin speakers.

Thinking of ways in which to respond, Nav waited for a pause in the preacher's repetitive prattle when he became vaguely conscious of a still and quiet but somehow menacing presence near them. At the periphery of his distracted vision Nav got the impression that the presence had an abnormally bulky scarf wrapped round its neck and shoulders.

And then, saying ''Ho!'' Nav staggered back. He tripped over a stone and, his legs flying out from under him, fell abruptly on his buttocks.

The distracting presence had a thick, eight-foot-long boa constrictor wrapped round his neck and shoulders, and for all Nav had shouted ''Ho!'' and fallen flat, the slight man with the boa remained as still and detached as a statue of Buddha, if one could imagine a Buddha with blue eyes and a sandy moustache.

The attention of the crowd that had gathered round Nav and the preacher during their spirited exchange at once shifted to the stationary figure with the huge constrictor writhing, pleating and slithering round his chest and arms. The boa constrictor, as thick as a man's arm, as splendid in its sophisticated coat as a model, raised its sleek head, flicked out its forked tongue to examine the sandy moustache, and curled around sinuously to explore what was going on in the back.

The preacher, looking distraught at having the rug pulled out from under his act so unfeelingly by the reptilian competition, shifted his attention, and

Nav and Roshni beat a hasty retreat—right into the welcoming arms of a three-card monte game.

A burly black dealer was bent over the three cards he was expertly sliding on an improvised table made up of two cardboard boxes stacked one on top of the other. He was slick, fast, intent, and as he juggled the cards he talked up a storm to attract an audience. "Twenty-dollars twenty-dollars—which is the ace of spades, pick out the ace of spades. Twenty-dollars twenty-dollars—watch the ace of spades, pick out the right card."

A player, so thin and tall and young that he appeared to have outgrown his jeans, fixedly followed the movements of the dealer's quick hands which were, for all their size, as supple as a conjurer's. The skinny young player rubbed his chin and deliberated for some seconds; then he hesitantly picked out a card. It was the ace of spades.

Shouting, "O'rrright!" the youthful winner jubilantly twirled around and waved a little wad of twenty dollar bills high above their heads. His victoriously whirling head was shaved above the ears and abruptly crowned by a flat disk of thick hair.

An alert and admiring spectator, sporting a stylish Afro and a scar that ran from cheek to lip across his otherwise handsome face, shook the winner's hand and thumped his back. The excited young man had obviously had a run of luck and was about to try again.

Nav and Roshni watched the dealer juggle the three cards on the cardboard table. Every short while he would lift up the ace of spades to show its position and busily start sliding the cards face down on the table again. Out of the three games they watched, the skinny youth picked out the ace of spades thrice.

It looked reasonably simple and clearly it was above board. The dealer wasn't wearing a jacket, and he had his shirt sleeves rolled up over his bulging forearms. There was not much chance of his being able to slip a card up his sleeve or indulge in any chicanery without being caught. All one had to do was to watch the dealer's clever hands and fat fingers carefully and outwit them.

Nav moved closer.

The dealer glanced at him briefly out of surprisingly light eyes, and pretending indifference, shouted: "Twenty-dollars twenty-dollars, watch the ace of spades."

Exhilarated by his bout with the proselytizer, and shaken by his humiliating encounter with the boa constrictor and his subsequent fall, Nav felt compelled to match his shrewd eye against the dealer's skill.

"Ten dollars," Nav said, astutely bargaining. He glanced swiftly at Roshni to ascertain that he had impressed her with his shrewdness. "I don't have any more money. Ten dollars."

"Twenty-dollars twenty-dollars, pick out the ace of spades," the dealer said, ignoring Nav and the ten-dollar bill he held between his index and middle fingers.

Meanwhile the Protestant proselytizer had set up house near them.

"Gambling paves the way to hell!" he boomed through his microphone, and to Nav it felt as though the deceptively innocent-looking amplifiers had singled out his ears for their assault.

"Thou shalt not gamble! The end of the world is coming! Repent. Jesus saves!"

"Ten dollars," Nav said, speaking more assertively, and also loud enough to be heard above the din. He wagged his two joined fingers back and forth making the ten-dollar bill flutter.

The dealer glanced about. The excited young winner had turned his long and narrow back on the game and was busy talking to the admiring spectator with the scar and the stylish Afro. Nav appeared to be the only candidate.

The dealer unraveled his massive beige palm saying, "Okay, just this once"—and he pocketed the bill Nav handed him as swiftly as a lizard snapping up a fly on a whitewashed Balsar wall.

Roshni observed the gesture and was struck by its significance. There was as little hope of the bill being recovered by Nav as of the metaphorical fly being stuck back on a wall.

Entranced by the unexpected possibility of her boastfully savvy and perennially instructive husband being diddled, Roshni observed Nav with fascination.

Nav was intent, keen-eyed, alert. And, as his eyes followed the dealer's movements, a smug aspect spread over the spare flesh covering his sharply defined features.

Nav's arm suddenly shot out, and his hand, like a serpent striking, picked out the middle card.

It was the five of hearts. The wrong card.

But hope is an indestructible part of human nature and Roshni could almost feel Nav being suckered into thinking the next time he'd win his money back.

21

Roshni moved closer to warn her husband, but before she could express her misgiving Nav gave the dealer another ten-dollar bill. Roshni stared at Nav as he watched the deft conjurer's hands with hypnotic intensity. The smug aspect was no longer in evidence; it had been replaced by a perplexed frown.

Nav abruptly and triumphantly pounced on the card to the left of the centre—and picked out the seven of clubs. He gawked at it in disbelief.

Almost absently Nav took out another ten-dollar bill from the new lizard-skin wallet Roshni had brought for him as a gift. Again he pounced. Again he lost.

All at once it dawned on Nav that it was real money he was dishing out and losing so fast. The flicker of suspicion that had had no time to manifest itself, now shot into his mind. He had followed the dealer's hands exactly and knew exactly where the ace of spades should have been. Nav was sure the man had somehow changed the card.

"You're cheating," he shouted, mortified and indignant.

The dealer's startling yellow eyes turned muddy and locked on Nav's with a dirty look calculated to turn his feet cold. Nav's toes shriveled into little frozen shrimps inside his woollen socks and gym shoes.

The tall youth in the outgrown jeans who had won so spectacularly earlier, scoffed, saying "Ha!" in an intolerably superior way.

"Call on the Lord for salvation!" the preacher bawled in the course of his own fiery discourse, and inadvertently ignited further sparks in the little scene going on between Nav and the three-card monte set-up.

"I'll call the cops for salvation!" yelled Nav, unconsciously echoing the preacher. "You can't cheat me!"

Nav noticed that the euphoric winner and the admiring spectator with the stylish Afro had closed ranks with the dealer. Too late, he realized they were the shills. He was abashed and outraged at having been so easily taken in.

Now the three swarthy men combined to glower down on Nav with malignant looks calculated to chill his bones.

Nav felt the marrow freeze in his bones.

But thirty dollars is thirty dollars, and it constituted a substantial chunk of his scarce resources as a junior computer analyst in upstate New York. "Give my money back, you bunch of crooks, or I'll have you locked up!" Nav threatened ominously, but the icy shiver that zipped through his spine made his voice quaver.

Not to be outdone, the proselytizer in the course of his unwitting discourse hollered: "The only salvation is the Lord! Lightning shall strike the sinner!"

"Why you dirty little squealer," the dealer hissed. He grabbed hold of Nav by the V-neck of his blue hand-knitted cardigan, and Nav's Adam's apple bobbed up a notch higher.

As if in a nightmarish trance, Roshni saw Nav teetering almost on the tips of his gym-shoed toes. She noticed with a sense of shock how extraordinarily elongated and narrow he looked with the clothes on his chest all crunched up in the dealer's giant hand.

Their fists clenched, the two shills moved on Nav like lightning striking.

Roshni suddenly and instinctively let out a shrill, long, bloodcurdling screech and then, certain that her husband was being maimed and murdered, screamed, "Police, help police! Murder! Murder!"

The dealer lifted his cropped head in surprise, and observing the foreign woman in a sari screaming like a demented trumpet, quickly cast his eyes about. He must have seen something that agitated him because he abruptly let go of Nav and snatched up his cards.

The youthful shill who had scoffed at Nav with such wounding superiority, dismantled the table with a swift kick that sent the cardboard flying.

The dealer and his partners ran in three divergent directions and evaporated among the skateboard acrobats and frisbee enthusiasts before the two cops in navy uniforms sauntered up to the scene of the crime.

His cardigan askew, his shirt half out of his trousers, Nav was too embarrassed to give an account of the scam to the complacent cops.

When Roshni hysterically told them of her husband's losses and how close he had come to being murdered, one of them looked her up and down in her sari and laconically remarked, "Everybody knows those guys always rip you off. Y'guys must be from someplace else. He's lucky he didn't get his pockets picked."

Consumed by curiosity, hanging on to the megaphone and the little Samsonite attache case in which he kept his amplifiers, the preacher had moved closer with his props. His blue eyes bulging, he craned his neck and danced from foot to foot to peek over the heads of the small crowd.

Once he grasped what had happened, the man of God waved his bible, molded his fiery features into a righteous glower and putting his megaphone to his mouth, bellowed: "The wages of sin are death! Thou shalt not gamble! Vengeance is the Lord's!"

23

The policemen winced at the blast to their ears and raised their capped heads. The burlier of the two cops took a few menacing steps towards the preacher. The preacher hastily turned away and belted out God's Word with his back to the crowd. But one could tell from the wobbly note in his thunder that his aggrieved heart was no longer in his sermon.

As they rode the succession of buses to the Seminary, Nav remarked: "Well, my dear, one lives and learns. Remember, one never gets something for nothing in America, and if you're stupid enough to expect to, you'll get ripped off. I hope it's been a lesson to you."

Roshni, who had maintained a suitably sympathetic silence as she observed her husband's bruised face slowly discolour and grow puffy, gave his arm a squeeze. She lay her head on his shoulder, and said: "I'm glad you stood up to that horrible bully!"

The next morning Nav told Roshni that he was taking her out to lunch at a very special place.

She was still in bed. "Let me see your face first," she said, and propped herself on an elbow to examine it.

Nav promptly moved his face to within an inch of her's and grabbed her amorously.

But Roshni's alarm for his wounds was too great to allow for amorous shenanigans. She pushed Nav away with a strength and vehemence that surprised him, and shouted, "I want to see your face. Not your damn cock!"

Nav, shocked by the unexpected words that issued from the naive lips of his bride from Balsar, let go of Roshni. He stood up, looking dazed. Was there to be no end to the surprises this unusual girl was to awe him with?

Roshni got out of bed and holding Nav to a suitable distance by his pajama-suit front, much as the three-card monte dealer had held him the day before, scrutinized his face.

It appeared to be even more puffy and swollen. But in the dingy room with light coming in only from a narrow curtained window, the colours appeared less strident.

Roshni took pains to get all dressed up and added the finishing touch by putting on the delicately dangling ruby earrings given to her by Nav's mother. After grabbing a quick cup of coffee and some doughnuts in the Seminary hall at noon, they rushed off to catch a bus.

Nav escorted Roshni, who was duskily glowing in a navy silk sari with a magenta border that matched her earrings, through the impressive glass doors of the towering World Trade Center. Nav had decked himself out in brown trousers and a brown tweed jacket with leather patches on the elbows for the occasion.

They stood in line for the elevator. When the doors opened to receive them Roshni gingerly stepped into the curved glass cocoon as if she was stepping into the next century.

Although her senses were awash with wonder, Roshni stared impassively at the rapidly receding marble floor, the green incandescence of the atrium dwindling. Nav had cautioned her not to gawk and gush like a tourist: she'd stand a good chance of being mugged if she did.

It seemed to Roshni that every day she discovered something new to enchant her and, her heart throbbing, she absorbed the enchantment quietly, hording it like a secret treasure, as she shot into the sky in the glass and aluminum missile. Roshni could scarcely believe that she, the ugly duckling of her family in Balsar, had stumbled somehow into this magical new world with its blazing lights, rocketing elevators and greenly incandescent indoor gardens with huge overhanging trees. How gladly she'd show off all this splendour to her relatives when they visited. She yearned to see the expressions of wonderment on their faces.

The captain led them to a small table. They sat across each other as the restaurant rotated centimetre by centimetre to give them a privileged-eye view of New York. But Roshni only looked through the glass when Nav pointed out a landmark that was familiar to them. Otherwise the fringed darkness of her eyes, soft with unfathomable emotion, remained on her husband's bruised face.

In the harsh light pouring in from the sky Nav's bruised skin displayed all the colours of the rainbow. And lit also by happiness from within, Nav was radiant. "Do you know," he said, the sweep of his arm embracing Manhattan, "more money changes hands in New York in one hour than in a whole year in Bombay?"

"Really?" Roshni said, leaning forward in her chair and placing her arms, folded one upon the other, on the table. Surrendering to the moment of bliss she looked at her young husband tenderly. "God, you really know so much!"

She knew him well enough by now to decode his speech—
This was their language of love.

25

On a Cold Day

HIMANI BANNERJI

I

The morning Asima jumped from her seventh-storey balcony it was especially cold. The city lay in the grip of a cold wave which made this December an unusually cold one. But the day was not grey or overcast. Instead, a hard white light encased the city in a crystal jar, under which the black bare branches of trees clawed upwards for air, the outlines of houses looked sharply defined and silent, and the smoke from their chimneys, wispy and thin, struggled under a pale blue sky.

The white cold light fell on Asima, as indifferently as on the phone booth, the pizza store and the sequined models in the shop windows. There she lay, sprawled on the sidewalk, quite close to the curb, with red liquid oozing out of the back of her head, and from under her face, which was in profile. This blackish red liquid must have been warm because as it came in contact with cold air, it smoked. The light caught this smoke as well, and Asima's face was visible through its shimmering haze. If she had convulsed a few times immediately after falling, now she was perfectly still, as were all other objects on the sidewalk, for instance the battered coke can that lay very near her outstretched hand, as though she had been sipping it as she fell. The brown hand, with the fingers slightly curled, looked small, helpless and somehow irrelevant, as did her little gold earring in which a strand of hair had got caught.

*

26

II

All morning Asima had been restless. She had wandered from room to room aimlessly. She walked through the small two-bedroom apartment as though it contained miles of road within it, and the road went in circles, and nowhere in particular. It could be said that she was trying to tidy the apartment, or pack up things, or both. For objects such as pieces of clothing, bags, and sandals lay here and there, but unfolded and scattered about. She had also pulled out some letters. The contents of a drawer, including some colour photographs, lay spilled on the floor as well. She had emptied out her bathroom cabinet, and also partially the closet next to it, and the pillows on the beds had cases pulled away from them. It seemed that she had been searching for something, as surely as she had been trying to sort or pack.

Her face had a particularly intent look to it, her movements were both precise and aimless. As she walked from room to room, from corner to corner, object to object, she felt, smelled and eyed them searchingly. She was looking for something that she did not find. In her linear, rectangular living room she sat from time to time on her striped foam couch, or at her kitchen table, with its recipe pad, salt and pepper shakers, bright Woolworth coasters and a half-filled teapot. Certainly Asima could not find what she had been looking for. As she lifted up each object for a close inspection, something seemed to be always missing—a part, a function, a meaning perhaps. Because she could not seem to understand either what they were doing there or meant her to do to them. Their meaning, or even command for action to her, remained implacably sealed under their form and exterior. She broke a fingernail trying to go beneath the hard skin of the coffee cup and did not seem to realize that the cold dregs of tea that lay at its bottom signified a sip, a drink.

Her detachment from the objects in the room, the walls and the space enclosed between them, felt oppressive to her, as if the emptiness of the space was actually a heavy, solid object which kept expanding, pushing her against the wall and choking her.

She looked out through the window onto the sunlit city outside. There was still room out there, she felt, and those things outside were houses where people lived, and down below there were roads where there were people, cars, lights, noises, voices, movements. Whatever it was that she was looking for was out there, in the sunlight, on the road, under the sky and in the outline of houses under the sky. It was as though there was a message there for her, a letter from home speaking a familiar language, it called out to her, to get away from this silent, enclosed, solidly empty space that expanded, squeezing tight against her ribcage.

Asima stood near the window looking out for a while. She put down the photograph she had been scrutinizing, holding up to her ear to hear a voice, and a pair of child's bracelets that she had been clutching with the photograph—gently—on the window sill.

Even before her body found the door to the balcony, her eyes had gone out into the world, they had jumped into the road, milled about with people and cars, and jostled past two dogs on a leash and in red coats, past toy stores and the secondhand clothing store. Now she was surefooted, aimed towards a destination. As she went to the edge of the balcony, the world rose up to her, the road was both horizontal and vertical, on the ground and touching her balcony door. She climbed over the low railing that separated her from it and she stepped on the air. For her it was the firmest of grounds. It moved with the speed of waterfalls, of light, of souls leaving the body on their marvellous flights.

III

Mr Abdul Jalal was taking a sip of the coffee that he had freshly brewed for customer take-out, when he noticed Asima rapidly moving down past his window. The smoking hot coffee missed the aim of his lips and drowned his neatly trimmed butterfly moustache instead, calling forward an exclamation.

"Ya Allah!" said Mr Jalal, checking out with himself. "We have a woman suiciding here? Or maybe she just fell or even got pushed out?"

At this last, his eyes turned inward, as it were, and he could see a pair of hands, and yes, they were male hands, a husband most likely, pushing a woman towards an open balcony door, pushing and shoving her until he got her over the edge. This thought and vision happened instantaneously, and simultaneously gave Mr Jalal a purposive rather than a speculative thought. Putting aside his coffee cup, which had suddenly lost all meaning and become a pointless appendage, he reached for his phone, which lay black and solid next to the tray where baklavas from last week's delivery lay encrusted with drying honey.

To the voice of the operator he explained. "I am calling a cop," he said, "a woman jump down from above. I see her from my window." To whatever it was that the operator said on the other side, he pronounced his

28

gratitude. Putting the receiver down in its cradle, Mr Jalal stepped out from behind the counter. Absentmindedly he wiped his fingers on his corduroy pants, and picked up his coat, scarf and gloves. He dressed himself methodically, as though going out on a visit. He ran his hand across his moustache as he always did on such occasions, opened the glass door of his shop and stepped out onto the sidewalk.

There the woman lay on the sidewalk. He could see her, even though the shocked and curious passersby had partially surrounded her.

To no one in particular he shouted out—"I call the cops already." No one responded to him. He walked a step further. It was bitterly cold. The woman, he noticed, had nothing warm on. A flower-patterned acrylic housecoat, open at the chest, showing part of a gold chain and the top of her left breast; her feet were bare and stiff; and her face was brown-skinned and young. His countrywoman? Mr Jalal wanted to cover her with a blanket, something to keep her warm and cover her shame. "But she is dead," he thought, his hands up in a gesture of prayer. The name of Allah bounced off the cold face of Asima for a few brief seconds, until the howling of the police sirens drowned out Mr Jalal's prayer.

IV

Debbie Barton, or Devika Bardhan, as she was once called in her native Calcutta, was on her way to the office. It was about nine o'clock in the morning, very bitterly cold, and she was a little late. As she stepped out of the warmth of the subway station, Debbie felt the cold hit her in the face like a fist. She was a little breathless from its impact at first, but picked up speed soon enough, drawing the collar of her coat tightly against her throat. Her eyes went instinctively to the huge glass panes of the clothing stores she passed, and there, in one shop window, sprawled between two mannequins, white and blonde, their breasts and crotches thrust out, she saw herself in a flowered nightdress sprawled on the sidewalk! This pulled her up short, and she wheeled around, to view the body of Asima on the sidewalk.

Horrified and fascinated at the same time, she slowly walked towards the body. And as she looked at Asima more closely, this uncanny feeling of resemblance gave way to relief as the feeling of seeing herself reflected in a mirror made room for the recognition of difference. A woman from either India or Pakistan, or Bangladesh or Sri Lanka, or for that matter from

Trinidad or Guyana, or Africa or Fiji—from just about anywhere in the world, of South Asian origin, as the newspapers said, lay in front of her, dead and cold. Yet in that face neither young nor old, she saw something of herself, and even some of her friends. Standing a few feet away from the body, among a gradually increasing circle of passersby, she searched the fragile face in front of her for clues. What, she wondered, could drive her to do this? To die like this, she thought, in this cold country. Coming all the way here to die! The brown face in front of her, the wisps of hair on the face, the gold earrings glistening in the sun—she looked searchingly at each item. Suddenly she felt the impulse to touch the woman lying on the ground, to sit next to her and cradle her head on her lap, to take a coat from the shop window to cover her from the cold. She felt herself go colder when she noticed the purple tinge settling into Asima's lips and cheeks, the brown of the extended arm taking on a grey and the stiffness of hard wood.

A woman from my own country, she thought. Doesn't she have anyone? Why is no one looking for her? A husband, a child, a relative? What is her name? Who is she? The woman lying before her could give no answer.

But even though she gave no direct answers as to her personal identity, the dead woman sent forth a wave of images to Debbie. Her sheer presence on the sidewalk, her black hair and brown Indian face, her feet lightly calloused at the heels, all riveting and obstructing the traffic as though a mango tree in bloom or a palm tree had suddenly sprung up in the middle of this cold concrete. Busy streets of her own city, its warmth, smells, dust and colours overwhelmed Debbie Barton, who now saw herself as she had been only a few years ago, in a starched sari, a braid down her back, carrying her sister's automatic umbrella, waiting at the end of the road near her parents' house for a cycle rickshaw to show up. It was uncanny how she could see herself, as though in a mirror, someone else, from a long time ago. Devika Bardhan of Jadavpur had no idea about the permed, made-up, perfumed Debbie, who changed her name because a counsellor had advised her to, as one of the stocks-in-trade for finding a job.

"Debbie Barton," said the counsellor, whose surface was as shiny as new nail polish. "It's a neat, easy, nice name. Every employer wants to be able to pronounce their employees' names without going to heritage language classes." Debbie thought that was a good idea too. It certainly saved having to coach people or wince every time they mispronounced her name. She had learned the phrase "Can't complain." She said, "Can't complain." She had been working at the cash in a nearby clothing store. She was young, attractive and adaptable. There was a future for her here.

Her mind again drifted to the woman in front of her, she lay like a question mark before her. Debbie had a frantic desire to know her history, at least her name, and of course who pushed her out into the street from such a high place, from the safety of her home. A husband, she thought, maybe he pushed her, or maybe he just left her, alone, in this big city, without a penny, without a future or a past. So she was fed up and just jumped. And yet there was this silence, and of course Debbie would never really know, except maybe tomorrow a little news item would appear in the paper.

But in the middle of the silent space that lay in the cold air between Debbie Barton and the dead woman on the stark grey pavement, the police arrived, their lights flashing, their sirens hooting, their neat blue and black outfits matching the cold air in precision and trimness. Backing off many steps to their curtly ejected order, Debbie saw how healthy and pink these officers of law looked, and how like deaf and blind men, neither seeing nor hearing, with pairs of black gloved hands, they moved various props around onto which with the help of the ambulance men, they placed the cold, stiff remains of the brown woman. As they lifted the stretcher, Debbie's hands went up to her forehead, palms joined in a gesture of both homage and prayer.

Mr Abdul Jalal, whose hands were also uplifted, noticed this gesture. Quietly he moved over to her, they were almost at the door of his grocery and take-out coffee and snack store. Fixing Debbie with his grave eyes, he asked, "You know her? Your countrywoman maybe?"

"No, I don't know her," said Debbie, "but yes, she's from my country." Though the crowd was dispersing now, Debbie stood there, unable to move in any direction. The cold was biting into her bones again, something she had not noticed in the last while. She felt dazed, the idea of right away walking into her workplace quite unnerved her. Where could she go? So, without thinking she turned around and followed Mr Abdul Jalal into his store.

As she sat in a chair at one of two small tables stuck away between two shelves of canned goods, she was still cold and huddled into her coat, her hands and feet tingled as if stimulated by little electric shocks. The big toe of her left foot also hurt somewhat, a symptom she had developed by forcing her feet into closed high-heeled shoes, without which they would not hire her, it seemed.

"A coffee please," she said to Mr Jalal, who had retreated behind his counter now, and was carefully putting away his outer garments under it. The store was small, it sold dry goods of Middle Eastern variety, odds and ends such as brass bowls and scarves, and coffee and sweets for take-out.

Mr Abdul Jalal brought her a coffee, pulled up a chair near her table, and sat down. It seemed as if they had attended a funeral together, and had now achieved a state of courteous intimacy. "Why do you think she did it?" he asked her, as if she had been a sister of the deceased.

"I don't know," said Debbie. "Perhaps she wasn't happy, perhaps someone pushed her."

"Who?" asked Mr Jalal. "Her husband maybe?"

"Maybe," said Debbie rather absentmindedly. She neither felt obliged to talk, nor felt it necessary to avoid his probing. She was just comfortable, with this talkativeness and curiosity about others' affairs. It made her feel she existed, and that the two of them were real persons together.

How different, she thought . . . and she recalled the morning as it had passed before she saw the dead woman . . . It was past seven when she had got up, made herself tea, ate some cereal with a bowl of milk, stared at a set of clothes which felt not like her own but a set of costumes or disguises. She sat in her kitchen for a while, working herself up to get dressed, to put on her makeup, which made her dark brown skin look rather ashen, and to go to work. She had to develop the right motivation and the right attitudes, she thought as she applied a little Cover Girl rouge to her cheeks. She should probably get a diploma in one of the community colleges. While leaving her apartment, one more time she noticed the peeling wall at the top of the radiator, heard the hiss and sputter, and dreaded the cold she would encounter as she bent down to zip up her boots. On her way down she looked in vain for a letter from home. Once on the street she again had this peculiar feeling of unreality, as though she was somewhere where she had no business being, nor knew exactly how she got there.

At the subway station she waited humbly, deferentially at the end of the line. She was going to ask a question today which she had rehearsed in her mind. She shunned any such exercise normally, since the answers came grudgingly and curtly, without her having the courage to get any detail. She got a feeling that she was not quite there, a feeling of invisibility compounded by the fact that a white woman jumped the queue, banging her with her huge shoulder bag, but did not look back once or say "sorry." The same woman, however, bumped into a white young woman and hastily said, ''Sorry, real sorry'' in a penitent voice, while the young woman said, ''You just butted into the line.''

A small agitation followed in the line, white people spoke to each other across her head, face, body, as though she were invisible. Slowly, as she stood there struggling to keep herself from completely disappearing, she looked at the white people, they were losing their faces, sex and details of clothing and becoming one mass of a cold ice colour. This feeling continued with her as she sat in the train, making herself as small as possible, knees straight and together, hands over them, her handbag not exceeding the boundaries of her lap. Two white people sat on either side of her, and they kept expanding, squeezing her out of the very little space that she took. She looked at the passengers across from her seat—a white young male whose legs were aggressively thrust forward with knees jutting out, and a white woman sitting comfortably with a magazine, taking just as much room as she needed. Her purple coat, matching scarf and beautifully groomed hair and shiny skin with a discreet touch of makeup exuded a confidence that Debbie could never have. At the time of leaving the train Debbie inadvertently banged into a white man, and even though she said ''Sorry'' instantly, she heard him mutter something about ''fucking pakis'' under his breath. Then she had come onto the street and seen herself lying on the pavement, reflected in the shop window. It was a nasty shock, but now in Mr Abdul Jalal's store, faced with his questioning, she felt that she was gaining a body and a voice, that someone actually heard and saw her. He even had questions for her.

''What country do you come from? Are you alone here? How long do you live here? Are you married? Why are you alone, a girl should have a husband if she is alone in this country.'' Back in her own country if a shopkeeper asked her these kinds of questions she would not answer him—she would leave the store with some rude or curt reply. But here it was a different matter. Very soon she had told Mr Abdul Jalal about her worries regarding her old parents, her brothers' unemployment and her own ambitions. He in his turn, arranging tins of stuffed grape leaves, tahini and ready-made humus, packets of cardamom and other wares, confided to her his extensive business plans, worries about his relatives in Palestine, his son's misdemeanours. They talked as do refugees who find themselves in the same camp.

Finally she asked him for the time. She was indeed very late for work, but decided to go anyway. She didn't want any pay docked for Christmas, when the girls at the office gave each other presents. Though she was not a Christian, she could not stay away because it brought an air of liveliness to their workplace.

As she made her way to the door she turned around to thank Mr Abdul Jalal. He was still preoccupied with the dead woman. "I wish I knew what her name was so I could offer a prayer," he said.

Debbie could never understand what made her lie at this last moment.

"Actually," she said, "actually I knew her. Not well, just met her at a party. I just didn't want to talk about it. Her husband had just left her and taken away their kid. She didn't have a job, her English wasn't great and she was really down—depressed."

Mr Abdul Jalal turned his heavy gaze at her. "So what was her name?" he asked.

"Oh, Devika. Devika Bardhan," said Debbie.

"What kind of name is that?"

"From India," she replied, "from a city called Calcutta."

"I heard of Calcutta," said Mr Abdul Jalal. "A big Muslim community there too. OK," he said, "I'll offer up a prayer for her when I go to the mosque this evening."

"Thank you," said Debbie, and stepped out into the street and the cold whiteness of the city.

A Child Departs

PERVIZ WALJI

When Mom finally returned from Nyanza, bringing with her Aunt Fatma and Alim, she looked exhausted. I too was exhausted from the long wait and the anticipation.

When the big bus finally rolled to a stop in front of our house, I ran out to meet it. Aunt Fatma greeted me sombrely, cheerlessly, but I was not surprised. Dad had warned me that she would be sad, since Uncle Moez had just died in an accident.

"What a horrible thing to happen to Moez," I had heard Mom telling Dad as I crept outside their bedroom door the night before she left for Nyanza. "To be dragged under a bus—" she broke into a sob.

"It is horrible," Dad replied. "What's to happen to Fatma and her child, Allah knows."

Now, looking at my aunt's face wasted with tears, as she directed the driver to unload her luggage, I realized that whatever was happening to her in her life must be terrible indeed, for it had taken away from her face the serenity that I remembered so well from her previous visits.

Alim, who was two years younger than I, stood on the side of the road surrounded by suitcases, pretending not to see me. As the bus drove away in a cloud of dust, I turned to Alim. I wanted to talk to him but was overcome with shyness and hid behind Mom's skirt.

"Let's all go inside and get washed." Mom took Alim's hand. I clung to her skirt and followed them. Juma, our servant, carried the suitcases.

Alim, I soon realized, was quiet this visit. He was not the boastful boy I remembered from his last visit with his father. He would stare into space or stare at his mother. In the middle of a game of hide-and-seek, for example, he would simply walk away. Mom said that he missed his dad. She said to leave him alone when he was like that. He had a right to be alone when he wanted to. Sometimes I heard Aunt Fatma weeping in her room. Alim would stand outside the door, listening to the sobs. Then he would refuse to eat. Mom was kind to him and would bring him food. One afternoon, while she was trying to persuade him to eat, and he kept shaking his head, saying, "I am not hungry," Mrs Jivraj walked in. Mrs Jivraj lived two houses down from us, and she always looked pensive. This time she sat Alim on her lap and stroked his hair. "You must eat if you want to grow into a strong young man," she coaxed. Even this treatment did not work. Alim simply shook his head. Then the servant Juma, who had all this while been scrubbing a pot with ashes, suddenly stood up from the chore, a determined look on his face. He took the plate from Mrs Jivraj and disappeared with Alim behind the house. An hour later, they reappeared. Alim looked fed. Slowly, as the days went by, the strained look on his face disappeared. He began to laugh a lot and was his boastful self.

* * *

"Nadiya, go to the market and get a pound of goat meat and some tomatoes." This command came from Mom.

Mom always asked me to run errands for her and Mrs Hasan who lived next door.

"Why can't you send Mina or Nilu to the market?" I protested. Mina and Nilu were my older sisters. Mom replied that they had done their share of running errands to the market when they were six. Now it was my turn. Mina, who was five years older than I, had declared that she would not be seen dead carrying meat or vegetables. Mom told me not to mind her. She was growing up.

On my way to the market I went past six shops, one of which belonged to Mr Yusuf. Mr Yusuf was a Punjabi. It was impossible to avoid his store when I went to the market. The best I could do was to cross the street and walk as fast as I could, hoping that he would not see me. Past encounters had instilled in me a deep fear of him.

Mr Yusuf lived alone, except for a woman servant who cooked his meals and cleaned his house. He was about thirty years old and bald. His eyes were dark and smouldering. "They have venom in them," Mrs Rawji, who lived next door, would say. Most days he spent seated on the front porch watching people go by. It was said that he had a wife and daughter who did not live with him. And that his wife walked with a permanent limp from a beating she had received at his hands. It was only after that beating that her parents had agreed to take her back.

He would shout lewd remarks at African women who passed by his shop, but no one paid any attention. Whenever he saw me passing, he would launch ruthless verbal assaults on my parents and the way they were bringing me up.

"Your father and mother have no shame. Look at the way they let you run around in short skirts," he would yell, eyes burning and voice hateful.

Mom said to ignore him. "He is probably lonely from living in that house all by himself. You have to understand why people behave the way they do." However, she warned me never to step inside that store.

Alim declared that Mr Yusuf's house was probably full of ghosts who fought with him all night long. "That is why he is so bad tempered."

For a while Alim and I took to running past his house. This made things only worse. Mr Yusuf would rise from his chair and in a high voice condemn us to eternal damnation.

"You will burn in Janam, you and your precious family," he would scream. The whole neighbourhood heard him but no one dared say anything for fear of making things worse.

One day I was walking past his house on the way to the market, holding Alim's hand. Mr Yusuf was stationed on the porch. Expecting the usual abuse, I told Alim to hurry up. But Mr Yusuf was quiet. Hurrying past, I stole a look up. Mr Yusuf was getting up from his chair, his face contorted in wrath.

"You Khoja!" he hissed.

We were nearly past his house. "You Punjabi," I muttered back.

For one awful moment there was dead silence.

I looked down the street. It was deserted. I heard running footsteps and saw Mr Yusuf behind us, swinging a baton in one hand.

"I will teach you a lesson," he thundered. I shrieked and ran into Mr Rawji's house, dragging Alim behind me.

The Rawjis were Hindus. Mr Rawji was a quiet man who never raised his voice.

"What a fine gentleman he is. A better neighbour one could not ask for," Mom said of him. He always stopped at our store whenever he passed it. He would formally fold his hands in greeting.

37

Mrs Rawji, on the other hand, was his exact opposite. She talked in a loud, unrestrained voice. She always wore a thin sari that exaggerated her heavy figure. She wore a red mark on her forehead that she called "bindi." Once I asked her if it was permanently etched on her forehead. "Doesn't it come off when you bathe?"

"Of course it comes off when I bathe. But the first thing I do after bathing is put it back on again. Don't I have a husband and isn't he alive and well?"

"If he were not alive, would you not wear a bindi?" I ventured.

"Child," she replied, "a woman is nothing without a husband. It is only women who are sinful whose husbands die before them. It is their evil ways that kill their husbands."

I was stunned. I wondered what evil Aunt Fatma had committed to be left without a husband.

"Come here, child," Mrs Rawji would often call me on my way to the market. "Bring me some green chillies and some dhaniya." She would hold out a shilling.

"How many chillies?" I asked her.

"Get me a small mound of chillies and a bundle of dhaniya and don't be putting my chillies and stuff in the same bag as your meat."

As I was pushing green chillies and dhaniya into a bag, Mrs Nathu walked up to us. She was dressed expensively as usual and smelled of roses. Alim ran a hand across his nose as if the smell was too strong for him.

"So you are finally getting settled down in your new situation?" She said to Alim. Alim nodded without a word.

The Nathus lived in a new building for the wealthy that had been raised in the middle of the town. It was said that all the apartments in it had wall-to-wall carpeting and showers.

The Nathus bought a new car every year and flew to London for shopping trips. Whenever Mrs Nathu found herself in a room with other women, she talked endlessly about her new clothes and her new cars. The other women would nod politely without comments.

One day at a wedding I noticed Mrs Nathu holding out her hand to Aunt Fatma and displaying her diamond rings. Aunt Fatma was politely listening and nodding. I noticed that she had lost that haunted look she had on her face when she first arrived.

"Why does she cry so much?" I asked Mom when Aunt Fatma had just come.

"She misses Uncle. Let her be. She is young. She will regain her spirit yet," Mom said.

She was right. Aunt Fatma established herself in our household and became part of it. Sometimes we came home from school and found her peeling potatoes for the evening meal.

"Change your clothes and come here," she would beckon. We struggled out of our uniforms and ran into the kitchen to await a treat. She would bend down and bring out hot, steaming potatoes from the clay stove. We poured melted butter over them and devoured them.

"How do you like your potato, Food Inspector?" she teased Alim.

Alim had acquired that name because of his uncanny ability to notice even the slightest reduction of food in the pantry. He knew exactly how many marshmellows were left in their box after each of us had been given one. Sometimes in the middle of the afternoon when the rest of the family was napping, one of us would sneak out and eat a marshmellow. Alim noticed at once the ensuing depletion. Even the slightest reduction in the quantity of peanuts did not go unnoticed. He loudly announced it, cajoled, threatened or even pleaded for the culprit to own up. We maintained that Alim walked in his sleep and took stock of the food, committing it to memory. And so he was treated as an expert on anything remotely connected with food.

One evening I walked into the kitchen and saw Alim gingerly pocketing a handful of peanuts. His side pockets were bulging with what I suspected were marshmellows, because the pink was showing in one pocket.

"Caught you!" I said triumphantly. He showed complete surprise at first. Then the expression on his face changed as his mind raced to hatch a story.

"Er . . . There is a sick dog out there." He pointed uncertainly. "I was going to feed it."

"Oh yes?" I said angrily. "And does the dog have black hair and lie a lot?" I attacked him. "I will tell everyone," I shouted, breathlessly, "the Food Inspector's been stealing the food . . . no wonder—"

"Beat a drum and tell the world ! Go to the market and announce ! See if I care!" Alim panted, trying to push me off.

We were scuffling, when Aunt Fatma walked in and separated us.

* * *

39

One day, after she had been with us for a year, I noticed a change in Aunt Fatma. She seemed sad and agitated. Her eyes looked moist and she would rub them impatiently. Alim, sensing his mother's sadness, was despondent. He would cling to her all the time.

Mom also was curt with everyone. I could not understand why almost every one in the household seemed so tense. Even Dad. It was as if they were waiting for something to happen. Something terrible.

Then one hot afternoon I came inside for a drink of water and found Aunt Fatma cooking the evening meal. Mom was kneading flour to make chappatis. Wet hair clung to her face as she punched and pushed the dough. The two women did not see me.

Aunt Fatma was at the other end of the kitchen, bent over a charcoal stove, blowing over the coals to set them ablaze. Beads of perspiration stood on her white forehead and her eyes were red from the smoke. Chicken curry simmered on another stove, sending forth rich aromas, white rice lay uncooked in another pot.

"He seems a kind man," Mom was saying. "So what if he is a little deformed? The important thing is he will provide for you."

Who was deformed? Who were they talking about? My heart hammered in my chest.

"Whatever he lacks, he does not lack in money or kindness," Mom continued. "He is so gentle with children."

Aunt Fatma did not reply. She seemed not to have heard. She went on fanning the fire vigorously. Sparks shot up in the air from the blazing coals.

Suddenly she looked up.

"I will lose my child if I marry him," she said. Her voice trembled.

"Yes, I know," Mom replied harshly. "But if you can think of a better solution, let me know. I can't keep you here any longer. We can hardly feed ourselves."

* * *

"Don't grieve," the women told Aunt Fatma. "You will make yourself ill, and to what purpose?"

They had all come, one by one, all the women in the neighbourhood. They sat in the living room, on the floor, surrounding my aunt. I crouched on a mat in one corner, listening. Across, stood a bewildered Alim.

"The children do not belong to a woman. They belong to the man," Mrs

Nathu said, making gestures with her bejewelled hand. "A woman only carries them in her womb. She should know that the moment she conceives a child." There was no sympathy in her voice.

Mrs Nathu had three sons. Her youngest, Nasir, was as old as I and maddeningly superior. He was dropped off to school in a car. He boasted his family never had to walk anywhere. Once I complained to Mom about him, and she muttered, "He is his mother's son alright."

"You are marrying a rich man now," Mrs Nathu was speaking again. "What more do you want? You will live in a large house, have your own car. You will soon forget about your child once you taste the sweetness of riches."

Her words appalled Mrs Hasan, for she half raised a hand to check Mrs Nathu, then let it drop on her lap.

"Anar is right," Mrs Hasan said, fast, breathless, as if to prevent Mrs Nathu from saying anything else. "The children we bear are not ours. They belong to the husband and his family. It is a woman's lot . . . ." Her voice trailed away as she saw the expression on Aunt Fatma's face.

"Inshallah, you will have more children," Mrs Jivraj spoke suddenly. Her voice was soft.

All at once, I recalled what Mrs Rawji had said to me one time about Mrs Jivraj.

"She is a failure," Mrs Rawji had pronounced scornfully. "She is a barren woman. After ten years of marriage, she still has not been able to bear a child. She has even consulted Dr Fakir. And," she went on relentlessly, "last month she even went to see Old Mother Sakina."

Old Mother Sakina was eighty years old. She lived by herself in a rented room and practised traditional medicine.

I was puzzled by Mrs Rawji's words. When Mrs Hasan had a baby, Mom told me it was God who gave her a child. Yet Mrs Jivraj had been asking people to help her.

Sitting here in the living room and watching Mrs Jivraj's anguished face as she tried to comfort Aunt Fatma, I felt more confused than ever. The hushed silence in the living room weighed heavily. Each woman seemed afraid to break it.

"Whatever happens, one must accept it as the will of God," Mom finally spoke, eyeing Mrs Jivraj with sympathy.

"That's so, that's so," Mrs Hasan agreed, nodding.

Finally, when dusk fell, the women stood up to leave.

I watched in silence as they filed past. Alim was huddled against the wall now, staring at the women and his mother. There was a lost look on his face. Mrs Jivraj fondly stroked his head as she went past him.

Mom walked the women out. Aunt Fatma remained sitting where the women had left her. It was quiet in the room. I could hear Mr Yusuf shouting obscenities to someone outside on the street.

I tiptoed to Alim and asked him to play hide-and-seek. He shook his head.

Mom came back and turned the light on. ''Why do you sit there as if there was a death in the family?'' she scolded Aunt Fatma.

Aunt Fatma jerked her head. ''What do you expect me to do? Cook biriyani while my lap is being emptied?''

''Hush,'' Mom pleaded. ''Look to your child. He is frightened.''

At Alim's mention, Aunt Fatma got angry.

''He is not my child.'' Her voice was cold like metal. ''Remember, a child does not belong to a woman.''

Mom told Alim and me to go out and play. She then shut the door.

But Alim stood outside, ears glued to the door. I tried to pull him away, but he pushed me off.

''What befalls you, you must bear. A mortal does not fight with fate. You must accept this gracefully.''

''How can I accept this—gracefully or no?'' Aunt Fatma's trembling voice came through the door. ''He has suckled at my breasts. How can I let him go without a protest?'' She was shouting now.

Alim softly opened the door an inch and peered inside. Aunt Fatma was holding her face in her hands. Tears seeped between her fingers, gushed forth abundantly from her eyes. All anger was gone.

''He will never turn to me in the middle of the night to ask for milk. He will never run to me when he is frightened of lightning . . .'' she sobbed.

''Hush,'' Mom whispered. ''God will give you strength.''

''Let her be,'' Dad said, having come in from the store. ''It is better if she cries. Crying will soothe her soul.''

The next morning, at breakfast, Mom announced that Alim was going to live with his Aunt Mehrun in Nyanza.

''Who is Aunt Mehrun?'' I asked.

''She is Uncle Moez's sister,'' Mom replied. She turned to Alim. ''You will be travelling by bus. Won't you like that?'' Alim did not answer. He did not finish his breakfast either.

The day after, Aunt Fatma bathed and dressed Alim with special care. She filled two buckets with water and carried them to the bathroom where Alim waited. She even opened a fresh bar of soap and brought a new scrubbing brush.

I stood outside the bathroom door listening to the scrubbing and splashing in the otherwise soundless bathroom.

When she was done, Alim looked well-scrubbed and smelt fresh. He even had on new clothes. A blue shirt, a pair of grey shorts, grey socks, and black shoes.

During the noon meal, everyone paid special attention to him. Mina produced a bar of chocolate for him. I gave him a white handkerchief as a token of remembrance. He took it and silently stuffed it inside his pocket.

Afterwards we all gathered in the living room. All of Alim's clothes had been packed in a suitcase. A sudden hush descended on the household.

"Let's play outside," I said to him.

"No," Mom intervened. "Aunt Mehrun will soon be here."

Again the hush descended over the room. There was a soft knock on the door. It was Mrs Jivraj. She greeted Mom and Aunt Fatma and sat down on the sofa quietly.

The silence continued. I watched a lizard crawl across the ceiling. Suddenly there was a loud knock.

"She is here," Mom said, getting up to answer the door.

She returned, followed by a woman of about thirty. Mom introduced her.

"This is Alim's Aunt Mehrun," she said. Aunt Mehrun greeted us with a nod and kissed the hand Aunt Fatma offered. Aunt Fatma returned the courtesy quietly.

"Come, sit down awhile, Mehrun," Mom said. "You must be tired. You have travelled a long way. Have a cup of tea."

"No," Aunt Mehrun shook her head. "I will rest at my sister's. I am staying there for the night." She spoke stiffly.

She turned to Alim. "It is time for us to go."

Alim looked at his mother. "Are you coming too?" His lips were quivering.

"No," his mother replied. "You are going by yourself. You will be alright," she said, her face blotched by tears.

"I don't want to go without you," Alim replied in a trembling voice. His chin was quivering now.

His mother was speechless, crushed.

"Aunt Mehrun will give you chocolates," Mom said to Alim.

"I don't want chocolates," Alim replied. "I don't want to go."

With determination, Aunt Mehrun picked Alim up. She carried him outside, followed by the servant Juma carrying Alim's suitcase.

Alim was wailing now, calling his mother and kicking his legs.

"May God keep you, may you prosper," Aunt Fatma was whispering, to no one in particular.

Finally, when Alim's cries died out, Aunt Fatma started wailing. No one had words to comfort her.

Bad Luck Woman

CHITRA DIVAKARUNI

"Unlucky. I tell you, that woman's plain unlucky, and she'll bring bad luck to anyone that comes near her." Aunt Seema's loud whisper carried across the dining room and ricocheted off the peeling walls of the Nataraj Hotel of Pahalgaon, where they had arrived just an hour ago.

"Aunt Seema, please!" Lila hissed.

"Yes, yes, I know, you modern girls don't believe in these things, especially you, living in America for ten years now and working in that science laboratory cutting up rats and what-not, but I tell you, it's true! Something evil is bound to happen to us all because of her if we aren't careful. You just watch and see!"

"Aunt Seema!" Lila's face burned with embarrassment. She wished her aunt wouldn't always say exactly what she thought—and so loudly, too. Although she was fond of her aunt and generally tolerant of her ways, today she felt impatient because she was struggling with a secret disappointment of her own.

Aunt Seema and she were part of a pilgrimage group that was now on its way back from Lord Shiva's shrine in Amarnath, in the mountains of Kashmir. It had been a strenuous trip, four days on foot over an icy terrain. When they had finally reached the cave shrine, Lila had waited expectantly. All around her pilgrims were weeping in joy, touching their foreheads to the ground in thanksgiving. Many sang out, their faces bright with ecstasy. Lila waited for something similar to touch her, for grace to pierce her like a ray of light, perhaps, as in old religious movies. Wasn't that the unspoken promise that had sustained all of them through the rigorous climb? But she had felt nothing except a vague awe at the sight of the immense granite cave roof receding into darkness, and she had wondered if she had made a mistake coming all the way from America for this. It was a question that haunted her still as she stared out across the dining room.

The subject of their conversation sat hunched alone at a rickety table, her back towards them. She must have heard what they said. She said nothing, but Lila thought that her shoulders drooped a little more as she drew the edge of her sari tighter around her. Against the dirty white of the hotel wall splotched with garish touristy art, she appeared small, shrunken, childlike. Lila noticed how the bones on the back of her thin neck stuck out like knobs beneath a sparse knot of grey hair, and in spite of her own disappointment, she felt a rush of pity.

Everyone in the Jai Guru Pilgrimage Party, which consisted mostly of middle-aged women, knew about Mrs Ghosh, although most of them had not spoken to her. The woman had truly had the worst luck, not only during the pilgrimage but throughout her life. On the very second day of the trip, the doctor's wife, who always seemed to know these things, had informed all the women who cared to listen that at the age of twenty Mrs Ghosh had lost her husband in an accident. Worse, his property had been seized by his brothers, who declared the marriage—and the children of that marriage—illegitimate.

"Can you imagine that?" The doctor's wife had raised her eyes to the ceiling to indicate the magnitude of the calamity. "She went to court, of course, but her lawyer was no good. Or maybe her brothers-in-law bribed him. She lost everything. Everything! That's when her hair turned white. She had to go to work as a clerk in some office, unfortunate soul, and struggle for years to bring up her two sons. And then, just last year, when she finally quit her job, hoping her sons would take care of her, the older one, an air force pilot, was killed in a crash. Burnt to death. Nothing left of his body. Nothing at all."

A chorus of groans had come from the listeners, but the doctor's wife had not finished yet.

"So now she's forced to live with her youngest, whose wife treats her no better than a maid. I've heard she makes her cook and clean the house. Even the bathrooms!"

As another chorus of exclamations rose, Lila couldn't stand it any more. She had to leave the room. She hated all this gossip, this mindless superstition. She remembered watching these women at Parvati's temple only the day before, offering coconuts to the goddess, praying fervently. How she had admired them. "This is the kind of thing I miss in the US," she had said to Aunt Seema a bit enviously as she saw them devoutly placing flowers at the deity's feet, "this sense of spiritual community that all of you share." Yet now those same women were like vultures, delighting in picking poor Mrs Ghosh's private life apart. And the worst thing was that they had no sense of wrongdoing. Is this what my culture really is? thought Lila. This cruel ignorance, instead of the rich fullness I had hoped to discover on this journey? As though in answer she heard a voice behind her, suspiciously like her aunt's exclaiming, "She was surely born under an unlucky star, that one!"

But as she walked away, Lila could not deny to herself that Mrs Ghosh *had* experienced an amazing number of difficulties. On the train to Kashmir, she had developed a bad case of heat rash which, together with motion sickness, had confined her to her bunk all through the scenic ride. At Pahalgaon, the dandi bearers engaged to carry her up to the shrine had not shown up, and the inexperienced substitutes had slipped on the ice, dropping the dandi so that she had fallen and injured her back. Of all the bedrolls, hers alone had been lost during the trek. If a couple of pilgrims had not lent her blankets, she couldn't have managed through the freezing nights. Finally, the dandi bearers had refused to carry her up the last stretch of stairs to the shrine until she promised them her gold ring, her one piece of jewelry. On the way back, the trauma of the last few days had caught up with her, and she had been sick with fever. Only this day was she sufficiently recovered to come downstairs for a meal.

Could all this really be coincidence? a small insidious voice had asked inside Lila's head, but she had pushed the thought quickly away.

Now, sitting with Aunt Seema, Lila watched the lone figure picking at her food in silence. No one was sitting at Mrs Ghosh's table, although space was scarce in the cramped dining area and the other tables were overcrowded. What idiocy, thought Lila in sudden anger. Perhaps a bit of the anger was directed at the small voice which had appeared from a place within her that she hadn't known about.

"These people are treating the poor woman like a leper just because of some unfortunate occurrences. Much good going on a pilgrimage has done to them!"she said to herself. "My friends in America would be amazed if I told them about this." She tried to picture the expression on the face of her lab mates, Ron and Carolina, when they heard her story. But to her consternation she found that she couldn't recall their features. The crisp white rustle of their lab coats seemed to come from very far away, from a receding world. She fought against a sudden panic, a sense of being dragged headlong into mysteries she couldn't fathom.

"I don't care what these women think," she told herself defiantly. "I'm going to be as kind as I possibly can to Mrs Ghosh as soon as I get an opportunity."

Lila's chance arrived sooner than she had anticipated. She and her aunt had just settled down, with much complaining on Aunt Seema's part, in the dilapidated three-cot room they had been assigned on the top storey of the hotel when there was a hesitant knock at the door. Opening it, Lila came face to face with Mrs Ghosh.

"I've been assigned the same room as you. I hope you don't mind," she said, breathless and apologetic.

Lila noticed that the woman had a raised mole, very dark, to the left side of her upper lip. A couple of hairs sprouted from it, and it moved as though alive when she talked. It gave Lila an unpleasant sensation and for a moment she couldn't respond. Then she moved to screen Mrs Ghosh from the look that she knew must be on Aunt Seema's face and gave her the best smile she could summon.

"Of course not. We'll be most happy to have you with us. Here, let me help you."

Mrs Ghosh looked astonished and then pathetically gratified at this unexpected kindness. Together, she and Lila moved her bags and bedding to the cot on the far side of the room, while Aunt Seema watched with growing displeasure.

"No good will come of this, I can tell you that," she finally burst out. "Heaven only knows what's going to happen to us now, stuck in the same room with her!"

Lila felt a moment of fear. Aunt sounded so certain. Then she looked at Mrs Ghosh, who was fiddling with the catch on her bag, her face turned away, her head bowed. The cheap white fabric of her widow's sari accentuated the grey in her hair. She looked so helpless, so accepting of Aunt Seema's outburst, that Lila's throat tightened in sympathy.

"Aunt Seema, that's a wicked, wicked thing to say! I'm so embarrassed. How can you be so cruel to someone, and right after a pilgrimage trip, too? Don't you remember how, when I was growing up, you always told me to treat others like I wanted them to treat me?"

Aunt Seema shook her head. "You don't understand. She isn't like other people,'' she said, stubbornly. ''Can't you see, she's touched by Alakshmi, the deity of misfortune.''

Lila walked over to her aunt and brought her face close to hers. Her voice had an angry tremor in it. ''That's sheer nonsense, all this talk about Alakshmi. If you keep behaving like this, I don't think I want to come visit you again, and I certainly don't want to go with you on that trip you are planning to Rameshwar next month. In fact, I think I'll cut my stay short and return to the US as soon as we get back to Calcutta.''

''You're asking for trouble, being friendly with that one,'' Aunt Seema muttered, turning away. But she didn't say any more. Instead, she spent the rest of the afternoon on the far cot, her face turned to the wall, covers pulled up to her ears.

To counter her aunt's attitude, Lila made a special effort to be friendly with Mrs Ghosh, and the woman responded to it so thirstily that Lila guessed she must not have many friends. Before Lila knew it, Mrs Ghosh was telling her the story of her life, which was much as the doctor's wife had described it. When Mrs Ghosh spoke, though, her intensity weighted the events with an added tragedy, the sense of a menacing universe. The words welled from her with a desperation that made the young woman uncomfortable. But she didn't know how to stop her without hurting her feelings. So she listened as Mrs Ghosh talked about her sense of guilt at her son's death, the mole near her mouth trembling with agitation.

''Sometimes I really do wonder whether I was born unlucky, whether I'm fated to harm all those I come in contact with, all my loved ones.''

''Nonsense!'' Lila said, and she was, perhaps, speaking as much to herself as to the other woman. ''You mustn't let other people's superstitions affect you. There's no such thing as being lucky or unlucky.''

Mrs Ghosh mulled over this for a while, looking doubtful. ''You really think so?''

''If you look back on your life carefully, for instance,'' Lila said, ''you're sure to find lots of positive things there as well.''

''Maybe you're right.''

''Of course I am!'' Lila's voice sounded adequately convincing, even to her own ears. ''Now, how would you like to go shopping with me? I've heard that the Kashmiri shawls here are the best.''

The outing did Mrs Ghosh a great deal of good. Her face lost some of its pinched look as she bargained spiritedly and finally purchased a beautiful rug embroidered with bright blue peacocks at half its original price. When it started raining and they had to ride back in an old horse carriage that lurched all over the road, she seemed to think it was quite an adventure. She laughed at every one of Lila's stories, even those that weren't particularly funny, and attempted a few weak jokes of her own.

When they reached the hotel, she grasped Lila's hand tightly as the young woman helped her down from the carriage. "You're like the daughter I never had," she said. But even as Lila smiled her thanks, she noticed how Mrs Ghosh's fingers felt dry and raspy, almost like a bird's claw on her arm, and she had to make an effort not to pull away.

At dinner Mrs Ghosh seemed to take it for granted that they would sit together. She talked animatedly to Lila throughout the meal, and it seemed that for once she didn't care about the pointed looks of disapproval that they were getting from the others. But Lila, catching Aunt Seema's unhappy expression, felt a pang of guilt, as though she had betrayed her aunt.

As they walked up the stairs together after the meal, Mrs Ghosh grew hesitant again. "I saw how they were looking at you because you sat with me at dinner. Maybe you shouldn't do it any more. I don't want them treating you badly just because . . . "

"Nonsense!" interrupted Lila, embarrassed because she had been thinking somewhat the same thoughts. "As though I care what they think! Besides, I like you. You're much nicer than most of them, and more intelligent, too!"

"Me? Intelligent? Why, no one's called me that!" said Mrs Ghosh, and her face glowed. She looked so happy that Lila felt a sudden lightness in her own heart. It was almost a physical sensation, and it made her dizzy for a moment. She felt as though she had been given a glimpse into the nature of goodness. This must be what grace is, she thought, and she did not let the glistening mole on Mrs Ghosh's face bother her as the woman leaned forward to give her a kiss.

This new sense of well-being buoyed Lila up through the rest of the evening, making her behave with extra sweetness to Mrs Ghosh. It was still raining, heavier now, the air getting colder. She sat curled up in a blanket on Mrs Ghosh's bed, sharing with her the spicy cashew nuts that she'd bought from a street vendor and telling her about life in the United States. Only once in a while, as Mrs Ghosh exclaimed in amazement over roads so wide that eight cars could travel on them side by side, or shop doors so intelligent that they knew to open when a customer came, did she let her eyes stray to Aunt Seema, who was lying on her cot in disapproving silence, her prayer beads clasped in one hand.

Just before they went to bed Mrs Ghosh handed her the peacock rug.

"I want you to have it."

"No, no, I couldn't do that! That's such an expensive rug," said Lila, embarrassed.

"I want you to have it, so when you look at it you'll think of me."

Before Lila could respond, Aunt Seema cried from the other end of the room, "No! Don't take it! You mustn't take anything from her!"

Lila looked up, a little frightened by the urgency in her aunt's voice. Outside, a gust of wind shook the windows, menacing, sudden. Startled, she dropped the rug. It fell from her hand to the floor, unrolling, it seemed to Lila, in slow motion. The peacocks' eyes, embroidered in thread red as blood, gleamed in the dim light like a warning.

"I'm telling you," Aunt Seema continued, her voice high with agitation, "it'll bring you bad luck. Anything of hers will bring you bad luck."

Mrs Ghosh gathered up the rug and tried to fold it. Lila noticed that the mole on her lip was trembling, like something small and alive and trapped. Had she seen the brief moment of fear in Lila's eyes, guessed the small voice which had returned, whispering that perhaps her aunt was right? Shame made her voice harsh, louder than usual.

"Aunt Seema, that's enough! I *told* you I don't believe in all this nonsense. And I don't want to hear about it again."

Lila turned to Mrs Ghosh, who had retreated into the corner by her bed. Fear is the enemy of goodness, she said to herself, and took the clumsily folded rug from Mrs Ghosh's hands. "Thank you so much. I'll put it in my living room back in San Francisco, and every time I look at it I'll think of you."

Mrs Ghosh's face lighted up, and Lila could see the shimmer of tears in her eyes. The brightness that had left her heart returned with a rush. The air was intoxicating. Like sweet wine, she thought, pulling up the simile from a past that seemed too remote to belong to her.

When she fell asleep that night, listening to the rain, Lila still had a smile on her lips.

She was sinking, sinking into the glacier. There was no trail, only slush, because of the rain. She could feel her feet slipping. Nothing to hold on to. Blackness everywhere and the numbing weight of ice pressed against her chest. She opened her mouth to cry out for help, but her mouth, too, filled with ice. Ahead, there was a face, huge and pale, hanging in the darkness.

It reminded her of someone, but who? Then she knew. It was Alakshmi, goddess of ill luck. We warned you, said the face, opening its cavernous mouth, we warned you. The mole on its upper lip trembled. Behind her, she heard the mountain break open with a thunderous crack, but her feet were too heavy to carry her to safety. And all around her, ceaselessly, the rain kept falling, falling . . .

Lila bolted upright in the dark, her heart pounding so loudly that she was amazed the others were not awakened by it. What a horrible, horrible dream! And so real! She could still hear the angry drumming of the rain, still feel the clammy moisture enveloping her like a shroud. Then with another start she realized it was no dream. She was weighed down by wet bedclothes, and the dripping sound which had now increased to the gurgling rush of a mountain stream was very real.

She jumped out of bed, calling her aunt and groping for the light, and found herself ankle-deep in freezing water. Bewildered, she clicked on the switch and looked around as the bulb swung crazily on its wire, barely missing her head. Part of the ceiling, rotted from lack of repair, had collapsed near the foot of her cot onto their suitcases, bringing with it a torrent of water. The floor was already covered, and more water kept pouring down the walls. Several other parts of the ceiling looked as though they could collapse at any moment.

Lila pushed her way through the debris to Aunt Seema, who slept on, covers drawn over her head, totally exhausted by the rigours of the last few days. She shook her as hard as she could.

"Aunt, wake up! Wake up! Come with me! Hurry, for God's sake!"

As the ceiling creaked ominously, she pushed her half-awake aunt to the door and jerked it open, loosening more plaster in the process. At that moment, her eyes fell on Mrs Ghosh, whom she had forgotten in the turmoil. She was sitting up, bedclothes bunched around her, eyes wide with shock, incapable of movement.

"Get out of the room! Fast!" Lila screamed, and as the ceiling began to crumble, she dashed in and grabbed the dazed woman's arms, and partly dragged her out through the wreckage. She had almost got them both through the door when something hit her head.

When Lila regained consciousness, she was lying on a bed in one of the other rooms in the hotel. Several women were gathered around her, and the doctor was bandaging her head, which ached dully and felt impossibly heavy.

"You cut your head open on a piece of falling sheetrock, young lady," he said in response to her questioning look. "Could have been worse. The bleeding's stopped, and you don't seem to have a concussion. I've put in a couple of stitches and given you a tetanus shot, just to be on the safe side."

He turned briskly to Aunt Seema, who was clutching at Lila's arm and weeping hysterically. "Now, stop that and get her out of these wet clothes fast, before she catches pneumonia. And try not to jerk the head."

Someone brought a towel, someone else donated a sari and a blouse, and Lila was made as comfortable as possible. But Aunt Seema kept on weeping, great gulping sobs shaking her frame.

"It's all her fault, that evil unlucky woman! You didn't know any better, how could you, but *I* should have been more careful. I shouldn't have let you get so friendly with her. I saw it, how she was casting a spell on you, turning you against all of us. Oh, how stupid I was not to insist on another room right away. Look at your poor dear head now! What am I going to tell your mother!"

"Aunt, do stop," Lila whispered tiredly, closing her eyes. Every little sound seemed to pierce her skull. But even through the pain, she could feel her aunt's anxiety, and she tried to make her voice gentle. "I'll be all right, but your crying makes my head ache."

There was relative silence around them, now that Aunt Seema had quietened down. The disturbing noise of gushing water was less, too, so it seemed to have stopped raining. Lila could hear the servants clearing away the debris upstairs. Had the doctor given her a painkiller? Was that why she was having trouble focusing on her thoughts? They flashed through her head in a series of blinding, disconnected images: glaciers, Shiva's shrine, her living room in the US, cashews, a pale, huge face, a rug from which blue peacocks stared out with blood-red eyes.

There seemed to be some kind of commotion outside the room. It shattered the images like bright glass against her eyelids.

"I must go inside! I must! I must see her!"

The voice boomed into Lila's head, almost recognized, but her brain refused to place it.

"No, you can't," the doctor said, "no excitement. She must rest."

Who was the doctor's wife talking to?

"Go away! Haven't you done us enough harm already? Haven't you brought us enough bad luck? Or won't you be satisfied until you've killed her?''

That was Aunt Seema at the door, her voice breaking as it rose hysterically.

"Please! Please! I won't harm her in any way. I won't even talk to her or touch her," the half-known voice pleaded. "I just want to see for myself that she's all right."

"No thanks to you if she is!" Aunt Seema lashed out. "Over my dead body you'll come into this room!" She turned to the bed. "Lila, tell her! Tell her yourself!"

Reluctantly, Lila forced her eyes open, struggling against the weights that pinned them down. How the voices made her head ache! If only they would let her be! Against the harsh rectangle of light from the door, she saw Mrs Ghosh, a gash on her cheek intensifying her lack of colour, desperately trying to push her way past Aunt Seema and the doctor's wife. Her face, with the mole blooming on it like a black, blemished flower—it was the pale one of Lila's dream.

A dark coil of fear that had been waiting inside Lila came to life suddenly, twisting and growing until it filled her throbbing head. Aunt Seema was right. It *was* her fault! All her fault! She *was* touched by misfortune. She was misfortune itself. Lila could see it clearly now, in the pain that burned through her head like a hot red light. Everything had been fine until she had joined them. Until she had enmeshed them in her bad luck. And who knew what else she might do if she remained?

"You heard Aunt." Her voice came out thin and wavery, and she took a deep breath to strengthen it. "Go away. Leave me alone. Leave me alone, bad luck woman!" Exhausted, she pulled the cover over her head, turning from the figure who stood at the door, suddenly very still.

In a few days Lila had recovered enough to join the group on its tour of Srinagar. "Lucky you're so healthy and strong, young lady," the doctor had said as he removed the bandage to check on the wound. "It's healing very nicely." She photographed the prize-winning roses at the historic Mughal gardens, offered milk at the shrine of Bhavani, according to tradition, and rode in a silk-lined shikara on the picturesque Dal lake. She graciously accepted all the attention her fellow travellers showered on her, the little gifts they brought.

Today, the last day of the trip, she sat in the most coveted seat on the bus, the one with the best view, right in front of the big double windows. The scar on her forehead was already beginning to fade to an interesting pink, and the doctor promised that it would be just about gone in a month. Meanwhile, it was certain to afford her special treatment at home. So there was no reason, surely, for this tight feeling in her chest, this heaviness that pushed out from inside and made breathing difficult.

"By the way, Aunt, whatever happened to Mrs Ghosh?" Lila made her voice sound very, very casual.

"Oh, *her*! Who knows? She disappeared that same day. The tour manager asked all the servants, but no one had seen her leave."

Lila felt a cold queasiness deep in the pit of her stomach. She didn't want to hear any more.

"Are you talking about that unlucky woman?" The doctor's wife leaned forward from the seat behind Seema. "Strange, wasn't it, how she went off all of a sudden, without even taking her luggage? The manager had to pay the sweeper to take away her bags. Anyway, good riddance is what I say!"

Lila remembered the brief happy look on Mrs Ghosh's face the evening of the accident and a pang went through her.

Aunt Seema and the doctor's wife were discussing the possible evil effects of having had Mrs Ghosh in their pilgrimage party. "I would do a special puja for purification, if I were you, as soon as I got home," said the doctor's wife, "seeing what-all happened to your niece," and Aunt Seema nodded agreement.

Stop, Lila wanted to shout. Don't talk like that. But she couldn't say a word. I don't have the right, she thought. She reached inside to touch that special lightness, like a folded wing, and wasn't surprised to find it gone.

"Yes, best not to think about people like that," Aunt Seema was saying now. "Lila dear, how about trying some of these delicious grapes? What? Not feeling so good? It's probably car sickness. All these winding roads, they'd make anyone ill. Here, have a lemon drop."

Outside, the green and gold of trees and sunlight merged into a flashing kaleidoscope as the bus picked up speed. The peaks of the Himalayas shone calm and silver against a brilliant postcard-blue sky. But Lila, staring at the suddenly blurry windowpane through wet eyelashes, didn't see any of it.

A New Reading of "Wasteland"

ARUN PRABHA MUKHERJEE

I really don't care much for teaching "Wasteland," and I really avoid the ordeal as much as I can. But there are times in the life of a sessional when you've got to do it, I mean teach all sorts of stuff you neither like nor know very well. What other alternative is there? I mean, I would rather be a sessional—even though at age forty-three I don't have very high hopes of getting into what they call the tenure stream—than go on welfare or some back-breaking health-damaging job.

So what the heck. The tenure streams usually don't like teaching in the summer, unless they are paying for a mortgage or a new car, and so I usually have plenty of work during the summer. That's the time they go off to New York or London or Paris to charge their cultural batteries on the new and old art exhibitions, concerts, plays, operas, and whatnot. I can't stand their just-before-they-go-away talk about "astounding performance," and "blue-tinted purples," and "solidity of form," etc., but I nod and play along anyway. For one because I really need that summer job, for another because I know that the lounge will be blissfully empty of talk like that the whole summer.

So I am submitting myself to the boredom of teaching this perennial classic again. But did I have to get this super serious class of worshipful maidens? It was much more fun teaching David Stratton and his group, mostly from Moose Jaw, Medicine Hat, and other rural communities around Regina. It was David who really made me see how inflated the critical writing about Yeats's "Among School Children" was, when he burst out laughing at "Ledayan body." "You call that poetry," he managed to spit out during his roar of laughter. "Sounds like a body of lead to me."

He had suddenly stripped me free of my adulation of the great, and I had joined in his laughter, forgetting all the critical opinions I had read that morning in my *Twentieth Century Views.*

But this class frightens me. They are all women. And they are all white. And they are all middle-class. And they insisted that we recite the whole bloody poem.

So not only am I teaching it, I have to go through the excruciating pain of listening to their worshipful intonations. They remind me of Brinda Chachi's face during her morning puja, supplicating Lord Krishna. She sat there with the flaming diya in the puja dish, her eyes riveted on Krishna's image, her hair freshly washed and spread on her back. My students' recitations of "The Wasteland" somehow have the same holy quality to them as Brinda Chachi's prayer songs in praise of Krishna.

But I must confess, teaching this class wouldn't have been so excruciatingly, exasperatingly awful, if I didn't have these skeletons in my closet coming out to haunt me, triggered by Eliot's sonority. My dreams have been awful this summer. I guess I must bear with them for a while, now that "The Wasteland" has stirred the waters again.

You see, the first time I read "The Wasteland" was during a hot Indian summer in a small university town in India, with the arm of a rather unattractive and overweight and middle-aged and married professor around me.

I know you are getting curious as to how an intelligent woman would allow herself to get into such a scrape. I have often wondered myself. And I still haven't figured out my behaviour.

For I wasn't really looking for an A, or a job. I already had an A. Some of my friends on the campus were letting their middle-aged supervisors feel their bodies (generally, that is how far things were allowed to go on that campus) for getting fellowships and jobs. But I already had a fellowship. And this guy wasn't really too important in the departmental hierarchy at the time.

So why would I let him put his flabby arm around me? It sounds stupid now, but perhaps there was an inevitability to it, given my place and my time.

He had just come back from, as we said, almost in whispers, "The States." He had come back with something that really set him apart from those who had never been out of the country. As my son would say, we really found him ''cool.'' It seemed to us that he just knew so-o-o much. And we heard in the corridors of the Department that he had studied with the greats such as Harry Levine, Cleanth Brookes, and Paul Elmore More. Okay, maybe they aren't such hot shots today, but boy, in that little Indian university town, they were as glamorous and as distant as the Greek gods. No, no, not Indian gods, because we really couldn't care less for them. They were too familiar and unexciting.

Most of my friends really felt we were in a purgatory. There were no Western movies in this shitty town, no Western-style discotheques as in Delhi. It was a real wasteland we felt. There were a very few lucky ones among us who would go away on an occasional visit to Delhi and come back with tales about American movies, dancing in discotheques, and the latest American tunes.

I felt so starved for culture, I often felt like committing suicide. The sun setting in the hills would make me tremendously melancholic. I would often sit on the steps outside the residences with my collection of *Romantic Poetry* in my lap at such times and recite longingly from Keats and Coleridge. And I really got a charge out of people walking by and looking at me and my book, their awe and admiration so evident.

I and my few friends were really special. We were the only ones in our class who had a convent accent and didn't call ''school'' ''iscool,'' as the local Bundelkhandies did, and ''vision'' ''bhijon,'' as the Bengalis did. Naturally, we inspired awe and jealousy.

So you can see why I and my friends felt so drawn to this ''foreign-returned'' prof of ours. We forgave him his girth and his not-so-hip appearance. He had been to ''The States,'' and that was really all that mattered.

Imagine my surprise when this great personage stopped on the street to ''talk'' to me, let alone nod. Yes, he had been honouring me with his nods every now and then, which alone was enough to make lots of people on that campus jealous of me. For him to stop, just for me, and to ''talk!''

I barely heard what he had to say, so excited I was. It was only later that I realized that he had honoured me with an invitation to come see his library since he had heard about my great love for the Romantics.

And I realized, thank God, that I had the presence of mind to say the right words: ''Thank you, you are so kind!'' You may think they are easy to say. But we Indians often forget to say ''Thank you.'' I still forget it, even though my sophisticated Delhi-returned friends often pointed it out to me, not to chide me but to civilize me. I guess it is hard to develop habits after childhood. And my parents never taught me to say thank you. Nor do I remember them thanking anybody. As a matter of fact, nobody in the small town I come from ever used such words.

"What are you doing this evening?" he said. "This town is so dull, I don't think it has too many things to occupy a pretty woman like you."

I had almost died at his audacity and his sophistication. For no live male had said such words to me, although I had fantasized about both Hollywood and Bombay male stars saying these exact same words to me. Although we had male class fellows, they never dared talk to us though at times they would make these awful faces or even whistle when no teachers were looking.

"Come in, come in," he said as I rang his bell that evening.

"Where is Mrs Srivastav," I said, a little apprehensive, as I didn't hear either children's noises or any activity in the kitchen.

"Oh, Sunanda is gone with the kids to visit her family in Lucknow. We have been away so long, you see," he said. "I hope you are not one of those prudes who can't be alone with a married male in case they become impure." He said that in such a funny way that I again admired his cosmopolitan sophistication.

"We are so repressed in this country that a man and a woman can never hope to be just friends," he went on, with such sadness in his voice that I really felt like touching him and comforting him.

"You don't know how I have longed to be friends with you. To read poetry with you. I am so hungry for intellectual companionship, and there is nobody in this stupid town I can even share a joke with, let alone poetry. You know, the day I saw you, I knew you were the person who would really understand my hunger for beauty, for great poetry, for great literature. You will not disappoint me, will you, Garima?"

I wasn't really ready for this kind of intimacy so fast, but, on the other hand, I didn't want to be judged "prudish" by him, of all persons. And I really was proud that he had known my special worth. I too had hungered for the things he had just mentioned.

"Oh, how silly of me to treat my guest so rudely. Come, let me make some coffee for you," he said, and he led me into the kitchen where he made a great show of finding the necessary ingredients.

I don't think I spoke at all except to say "yes" and "no" a few times, so unsure I was of my footing. I did agree with him that men and women should be able to become friends. I did want male friends and had none, because the moment a man and a woman were seen talking together on that campus, people began to talk about their "affair."

"Come, let me show you my library. And I want you to borrow freely," I heard him say and we went to his study.

I had never known anybody with so many books. Here were all the great names of English literature and American literature. And books so new our library wouldn't get them for another ten years.

"Don't be shy. Take as many as you can read in a week. For you must come again next week," he had his hand on my shoulder now and I didn't know how to respond. Would it be prudish to get out of there? Would it be denying the knock of genuine friendship to remove his hand and walk out of the door?

He seemed an expert at reading my face. "Oh, Garima, just because I have my hand on your shoulder, you are scared I am going to rape you. Right? You Indian girls are such shrinking violets. The American girls are so frank, so open. They don't think anything about kissing their friends."

I didn't want to be prudish, I decided on the spur of the moment. He was older and so well read and so civilized. If he didn't think there was anything wrong with putting his hand on my shoulder, then there wasn't. I relaxed and began to look at the titles.

His kiss on the nape of my neck came so suddenly, I was absolutely stunned. Before I could think or say anything, he was asking me: "Do you think what I did just now is wrong?"

He was testing me, I knew. And I didn't know what to answer. If American girls didn't mind kissing their friends, then it must be alright in the larger scheme of things, wrong as it was in the prudish culture in which I had grown up.

"Answer me, Garima, what do you think of my impulsive act?" There wasn't much time for me to think and I decided to step out of my prudish acculturation, to behave like the free American women he had just told me about and whom I had seen in the rare American movies I had managed to see so far.

I said, "You did nothing wrong because we are friends." I felt I was entering into unchartered waters, waters that no magazine, no movie, no gossip had prepared me for. They had only talked of romantic love and affairs, not friendship. And if I wanted the secret gates of life to open, I must take the risk.

"Bravo, my girl. That is the friend I was looking for. You are a liberated person, not bound by the taboos of your culture. Don't worry, I will not molest you. Although I believe in free sex between friends, I will only go as far as you allow me to go. Fair?''

"Fair," I said, confident that I would not allow him to take "liberties" with me. It was exciting to be called pretty and brave and liberated by such a learned person. I guess it was exciting to play the sexual game without knowing that that is what I was doing. Or maybe I knew but just didn't want to admit it.

We had a most weird summer together. I would go to his house as often as I could, coming and going loaded with books so that my warden, every time she saw me, praised Dr Srivastav for helping one of the brightest students of the university. I liked the game that was played at each of these visits: Dr Srivastav begging me to shed my prudishness completely and go to bed with him and I letting him go only so far as to sit with me with his arm around my shoulder. He tried a couple of times to feel my breasts or plant an occasional kiss but I forbade him, pleading difficulty with my cultural taboos. He would protest about the prudishness of Indian women's upbringing but kept to his promise of not molesting me.

Most of the time we would just talk "literature." Or rather he talked and I listened. He would take out a book from the shelf, say "Listen to this," and would read in, to me then, a terribly impressive way. "Marvellous," he would say. "Did you get it? For the beauties of style can't be taught, really. You either have it in your soul to appreciate literature or you don't."

Sometimes he would serve me tea or juice with a great to-do, bending like a perfect gentleman. And then we would go back to appreciating the beauties of style of a Lawrence Durrell or a Faulkner. I can't remember how many books we appreciated that summer, but I remember reading the whole *Alexandria Quartet* without understanding it at all. I didn't have the guts to admit my ignorance to him.

It was on one of these summer afternoons that he brought out "The Wasteland," and told me that it was the greatest poem ever written in the world's annals. One day we read the first twenty-five lines at least ten times, without my understanding a single word.

"You don't have to understand poetry to appreciate it," he said, his lips lightly brushing my cheeks. "Just let go. Feel the rhythm. Feel the music. Poetry is not for making literal sense. Just feel the sadness. Just flow with the lamenting voice of loss." So I listened and tried to work myself into the proper mood.

I remember that those several days I just felt so sad. The scorched summer landscape around me seemed like a wasteland. The small town with no English movies, discotheques, no nothing, seemed like a wasteland that would destroy me with ennui.

And I didn't know what to make of my "friendship" with Dr Srivastav. At times I felt really excited and euphoric and a "liberated citizen of the world," as he called me. At other times I felt awfully guilty and wondered if I felt guilty because I was doing something wrong or because of my prudish hang-ups.

It was all resolved for me, in a rather rude way, at the tail end of summer. The last time I visited his home, with my pile of books that I carried as a shield against the wagging tongues of the world, his eldest son opened the door. He led me to his dad's study where Dr Srivastav sat preoccupied on his armchair, reading a Lawrence Durell.

"Oh, you have come to return the books. Put them on the desk," he said without looking up from the book he was reading. There were no usual greetings, no jokes, nothing. He just sat there reading.

I stood for a full five minutes. Then I said, "I am going now."

"Okay, will be seeing you some time," he said, still without looking up from his book.

As I left, I could hear the rattle of utensils in the kitchen. Mrs Srivastav was cooking dinner, obviously. She didn't come out and I left, without anybody coming to the door to say 'bye.

"The hypocrite bastard," I screamed inside my head. "He is just another chicken. And I fell for him. Him and his bloody 'friendship.'"

"The Wasteland" has never been the same for me since then. Every time I teach it, I remember Dr Srivastav in his foreign-returned glory and his flabby arm invading my body.

American Date

NAZNEEN SHEIKH

Young ladies should not have their bottoms moving about, says my Texan mother, holding out a girdle. I look at it thinking this must be an American custom like coke floats and charm bracelets. I am seventeen and a foreign exchange student from Pakistan in Texas. When the fluttering silks of my national dress and the soft-spun muslins encase my body it is hard to know where the skin starts and the fabric takes over. My body undulates in a joyous freedom, nothing chafes or restricts. The first kashmiri silk brushing the mounds of my breasts and my inner thighs was a kiss of honey. It fluttered with airy ripples, touched my body and then drew away like the laughter of a butterfly's wings. I wanted to wear it to bed and imagine a phantom lover spin it off my body, spiral by spiral. What he did after that was a blank because I have not even been kissed by a boy as yet.

Blond Burt with eyes the colour of aquamarine is taking me out on a double date. His lower lip is salmon-coloured and puffy. When I first saw him I wanted to take it between my teeth and bite down hard. I was convinced it would burst like an apricot and the hot sweet juice would flood my mouth. But I do not even glance at Burt when he arrives in his father's car to pick me up. I am too busy trying to find the lower half of my body in the linen sheath dress covering it. I am wearing the American girdle, because I just love being American. The girdle is like a massive elastic bandage, the sort you had wrapped around your finger as a child. The one that made your finger numb and a sickly mottled white. That is precisely what the girdle with its garter buttons is doing to me. And in some empathetic rebellion even my nipples have ceased to prickle or stiffen. My American mother has neutered me just the way you would a cat.

Blond Burt has eyelashes made of gold, the sort you want to rub with the tips of your fingers and see if gold dust will stain them. When he looks at me he says why didn't you wear your beautiful Pakistani dress . . . I reply in my new American way, to a football game? The girdle rises between us as a barrier. I can tell when the little feelers attached to my skin are being blanketed, muffled by something. All my life these feelers have teased me into a state of delirium, and always, these feelings are to do with the skin, moisture and pressure. When I had seen Burt's eyes before this is what happened. The aquamarine became a pool of silky water and I bathed in it, all that blue green water entered through my nostrils, ears, mouth and most of all my vagina. Sometimes it just brushed or slid but then it even scratched, probed and thrust itself. It made me breathless. I could not tell, not then, whether it was done to me or I had done it myself.

Everything is wrong about the American date. I am sitting in the back seat, with Kay who has red curls and freckles. She laughs too much and her breasts wobble beneath her angora sweater. She is not interested in her date, she's had so many, she tells me, she cannot even keep a count. I can't understand anything about the football game. Burt puts his hand on my knee just where the hem of the sheath stopped. He keeps it there throughout the entire game. But I am not responding to the warm cup of flesh settled over it. The girdle has taken care of all that. Even the down of golden hair leaves me untouched. When I had seen it first I had wanted to lick his arm and separate the hair with my tongue. Little swirls back and forth. I had read Colette, Nin and Miller and knew these people had done all these things. I could do them, here in America. Far away from all the legions of fathers and brothers. The grim custodians of Eastern chastity. But something has gone terribly wrong. I can tell you why. When I get excited a little spill of fluid seeps out and rolls down my thighs. I usually rub my legs together hard so it doesn't travel further. It's my private game, and I have played it often since I came to America. The boys are different here in America. When you meet them, after a little while they tell you how much they want to touch you and kiss you. When they say these things they stare straight into your eyes. The boys I grew up with in Pakistan kept their eyes downward and some of them even blushed. When Burt's shoulders move beneath his shirt as he steers the car I know I am excited but I can't feel myself getting wet and I imagine that the girdle has cut off my circulation and dried up this little silky pool which lies between my legs. I want to cry like a baby. I also want to elbow laughing Kay right out of the back seat because she is nibbling her date's earlobe from behind.

I am sitting on the edge of my seat as well, but I am not doing anything. "Watch out when he takes you home . . . alone," Kay of the freckles whispers in my ear. They are getting dropped off first and then I get to move up to the front seat. I give her a cool smile and then in a flash I make a decision. I ease back into the seat and pull the hem of the sheath back over my thighs. The garter buttons have left little indentations on my thighs. I pop open the front one and then raise myself to reach the back ones. Kay looks at me sideways and her eyes bulge. She watches me silently, as I slide the sheath right up to my waist. That is the moment Kay becomes my friend for the rest of the year. She breaks out into a sudden patter of conversation with both the boys. Leaning forward she practically hangs forward in the middle of the front seat and stretches out both her arms. She is making sure that nobody turns back suddenly to see what I am doing in the back. I am working silently and fast because we are approaching the canyon road where Kay lives. I hook both my thumbs into the waistband of the girdle and pull it down and my flesh begins to spill out inch by inch. I can tell you how it feels when my crotch is free because all of a sudden feeling returns. The cool leather of the car seat is ridged, and when I ease the girdle down over my knees and ankles and settle back I am sitting on the ridge. I instinctively contract my vaginal lips and know that I am alive and America is still quite wonderful.

Kay looks at me once quickly, the car is entering her driveway and there is a tangle of girdle and stockings lying at my feet. She swoops the tangle into her shoulder bag as her date opens the back door. My handbag is a hand-sized linen clutch. Kay jiggles her breasts and pulls me along out of the backseat. Blond Burt gets out of the car and Kay gives me a slow wink and drags her date up to her front door. I stand by the front of the passenger door, and press my thighs together tight. You know why I am doing that, don't you? I am playing my favourite private game. Beautiful Burt blond and American is opening the door so I can sit in the front with him. I am so excited I scrape my knee painfully against the open ashtray. Two angry lines appear on my knee and then a bit of blood seeps out. I bend forward and raise my knee up and lick it. Burt is in the car now and watching me. He says, you're a little savage aren't you, all the way from Pakistan. Yes, I reply, with the salt of blood on my tongue, we roast people like you alive in the mountains. I can play the game as well. Burt starts the car and we are going somewhere. I know he is not taking me home right away. I'm taking you to the old lookout. That's where everyone in this town goes to neck. I smooth my sheath over my thighs and say innocently, where's that? He just smiles. After a while he says, the view is spectacular, didn't you know?

Blond Burt is also the captain of the football team at Sunset High but he is also very smart. His father is the principal of a neighbouring high school and told him that he must read up about Pakistan before he takes me out on a date. The first time Burt saw me at school in my flowing shalwaar-kameez and my gauzy dupatta, he said, wow you are like something out of Arabian nights. That was when I had decided that I had to play Sherezade right out of *A Thousand and One Nights*. I was going to spin out story after story to stun the American boys because that is all they wanted. But then I had suddenly been ensnared myself by a ridiculous American undergarment that made me feel like the ordinary girls. The ones with flouncy skirts, angora sweaters and penny loafers. Now I hate the linen sheath I am wearing. This pale green bleached-out colour. Blonde Burt hasn't kissed me as yet. He is busy finding the look-out. I don't think he knows where it is. We are taking turns on many roads and then heading back. All of a sudden he says, I've got to take you home. My dad will kill me if I am not home by eleven, it's a school night. Your mom too, he says to me. I want to go to the look-out, I say to him. I wiggle in my seat. I even pout a little, just the way my younger sister does at home when she wants her way. Why can't you tell him that I got sick, you know, like motion sickness, and you had to stop the car for a little while or I would have thrown up. Burt smiles at me in the dark. His teeth shine and his hair is like moonlight, only it is golden. All of a sudden I wish we were in Shish-Mahal where the entire ceiling is embedded with tiny mirrors. It's a particular room in the Lahore Fort built by the Mughals. Then I reach up and start removing the long hairpins holding up my hair, which is tightly twisted into a French roll. I hate these things, they hurt my head, I say, collecting hairpins in my mouth. You are driving all the boys at school crazy, says Burt, parking the car just behind a street lamp. I close my eyes and wait for something to happen. Burt doesn't kiss me, instead he says, I really like boys but I asked you for a date just to look good. Then he says, but you are good at making up stories, aren't you? I am too busy to reply. I'm stuffing hairpins in my head and not feeling at all like Sherezade.

The next morning, my American mother says to me as she packs our lunch for school, I don't think you should accept another date with Burt, he is quite irresponsible. I look at her just the way Sherezade must have when she finished one story and the king was ready to have her beheaded. It was Kay's boyfriend who got lost after the game. It was all his fault.

Free and Equal

LALITA GANDBHIR

Ramesh carefully studied his reflection in the hallway mirror. His hair, shirt, tie, suit, nothing escaped his scrutiny. His tie seemed a little crooked, so he undid it and fixed it with slow, deliberate movements. Then he reexamined the tie. A conservative shade of maroon, not too narrow, just right for the occasion, for the image he wanted to project.

Suddenly he was aware of two eyes staring at him. He turned to Jay, his little son. Jay sat on the steps leading to the second floor, his eyes focused on his father.

"Why are you staring at me?" Ramesh inquired.

"Going to work now?" Jay asked.

Ramesh understood the reason behind Jay's confusion. He used to go out to work dressed this way in the mornings. Jay had not seen him dressed up in a suit in the evening.

For a moment Ramesh was proud of his son. "What a keen observer Jay is!" he thought to himself. "For six months I have not worked, yet he noticed a change in my old routine."

However, the implications behind the question bothered Ramesh.

"I am going to a job fair," he said irritably and again attempted to focus his attention on his tie.

"Can I come?" Jay promptly hurled the question in Ramesh's direction. To him a fair was a fun event. He had been to fairs with his mother before and did not wish to miss this one.

"Jay, this is not the kind of fair you are thinking of. This is a job fair."

"Do they sell jobs at a job fair?"

"Yes." Jay's question struck a sensitive spot. "No, they don't sell jobs. They are buyers. They shop for skills. Unfortunately, it's a buyer's market."

The question had stimulated Ramesh's chain of thought. "Is my skill for sale?" he wondered. "If that is true, then why did I dress so carefully? Why did I rehearse answers to imaginary questions from interviewers?"

"No, this job-hunting is no longer a simple straightforward business transaction like it used to be when engineers were in demand. I am desperate. I am selling my soul. The job market is no longer a two-way street. I have no negotiating power. I just have to accept what I can get."

Ramesh pulled on his socks mechanically and longingly thought of the good old days like a sick old man thinking of his healthy youth.

Just ten years ago he had hopped from job to job at will. Money, interesting work, more responsibility, benefits—any reason that appealed to him, and he would switch jobs. Responding to advertisements was his hobby. Head hunters called him offering better and better situations. He went to job fairs casually dressed and never gave a second thought to his attire.

He had job offers, not one or two, but six or seven. The industry needed him then. It was so nice to be coveted!

Ramesh wiped his polished, spotless shoes with a soft cloth.

How carefree he used to be! He dressed like this every morning in five minutes and, yes, Jay remembered that.

He never polished his shoes then. His hand wiping his shoes with a cloth stood still for a moment. Yes, Rani, his wife, did it for him. Nowadays she seemed to do less and less for him. Why?

Rani had found a part-time job on her own when companies in the area had started to lay off engineers. She had not bothered to discuss the matter with him, just informed him of her decision. In a year she had been promoted, and she was recently offered another promotion if she would accept a full-time slot. "How did she manage to receive promotions so soon?" Ramesh wondered.

Rani still ran the home and cared for their young children. Ramesh had seen her busy at all kinds of tasks from early morning until late at night.

Over the last three months she did less and less for Ramesh. She no longer did his laundry or ironing. She had stopped polishing his shoes and did not wait up for him when he returned late from job fairs.

"She is often tired," Ramesh tried to understand, but he felt that she had let him down, wronged him just when his spirits were sinking and he needed her most.

"She could have made an effort for the sake of appearance. It is her duty towards a jobless, incomeless husband."

He pushed all thoughts out of his mind.

He tied his polished shoes, dragged his heavy winter coat out of the closet and picked up his keys.

"Tell your ma that I have left," he ordered Jay and closed the door without saying goodbye to Rani.

In the car, thoughts flooded his mind again.

Perhaps he had made a mistake in coming to study abroad for his masters in engineering. No! That was not the error. He should not have stayed on after he had received his masters. He should have returned home as he had originally planned.

He had intended to return, but unfortunately he attended a job fair after graduation just for fun and ended up accepting a job offer. A high salary in dollars, equal to a small fortune in rupees, proved impossible to resist. He always converted dollars into rupees then, before buying or selling. He offered himself the excuse of short-term American experience and stayed on. The company that hired him sponsored him for a Green Card.

He had still wanted to return home, for good, but he postponed that and went for a visit instead and picked Rani from several prospective brides, married her and returned to the United States.

The trip left bitter memories, especially for Rani. He could not talk his mother out of accepting a dowry.

"Mother, Rani will earn the entire sum of a dowry in a month in the USA. A dowry is a hardship for her middle-class family. Let us not insist on it. Just accept what her family offers."

But mother, with father's tacit support, insisted. "You are my only son. I have waited for this occasion all my life. I want a proper wedding, the kind of wedding our friends and relatives will remember forever."

Ramesh gave in to her wishes and had a wedding with pomp and special traditional honours for his family. His mother was only partially gratified because she felt that their family did not get what was due to them with her foreign-returned son! The dowry, however, succeeded in upsetting Rani, who looked miserable throughout the ceremony.

"We will refund all the money once you come to the United States," Ramesh promised her. "It's a minor sum when dollars are converted to rupees."

Instead of talking in the same conciliatory tone, Rani demanded, too harshly for a bride, "If it is a minor sum, why did you let your family insist on a dowry? You know my parents' savings are wiped out."

Later he found out that Rani had wanted to back out of the match because of the dowry, but her family would not let her.

Over a few years, they refunded the money, but Rani's wounds never healed and during fights she would refer spitefully to the dowry.

Her caustic remarks had not bothered Ramesh before, but now with her income supporting the family, they were beginning to hurt. "Write your mother that your wife works and makes up for part of the dowry her father failed to provide!" she had remarked once.

"Don't women ever forgive?" he had wondered.

"I am being extra sensitive," he thought and shrugged off the pain that Rani's words caused.

The job fair was at a big hotel. He followed the directions and turned into a packed parking lot. As he pulled into the tight space close to the exit, he looked towards the hotel. Through the glass exterior wall, he could see a huge crowd milling in the lobby, under a brightly lit chandelier.

Panic struck him. He was late. So many people had made it there ahead of him. All applicants with his experience and background might be turned away.

Another car approached and pulled into the last parking space in the lot. The engine noise died and a man roughly his height and build stepped out.

"Hello, how are you?"

Ramesh looked up.

In the fluorescent lights his eyes met friendly blue eyes. He noticed a slightly wrinkled forehead and a receding hairline, like his own.

"Hello," he responded.

The stranger smiled. "Sometimes I wonder why I come to these fairs. In the last six months I must have been to at least ten."

"Really? So have I!" He must have been laid off at the same time, Ramesh thought.

"We must have attended the same ones. I don't remember seeing you," the newcomer said.

"Too many engineers looking for a job—you know," Ramesh offered an explanation.

The pair had approached the revolving lobby doors. Ramesh had a strong urge to turn back and return home.

"Come on, we must try." The newcomer apparently had sensed the urge. "My name is Bruce. Would you like to meet me at the door in an hour? We will have a drink before we go home. It will—kind of lift our spirits."

"All right," Ramesh agreed without thinking and added, "I am Ramesh."

Bruce waited for Ramesh to step into the revolving door.

Ramesh mechanically pushed into the lobby. His heart sagged even further. "With persons like Bruce looking for a job, who will hire a foreigner like me?" he wondered. He looked around. Bruce had vanished into the crowd.

Ramesh looked at a row of booths set up by the side wall. He approached one looking for engineers with his qualifications. A few Americans had already lined up to talk to the woman screening the applicants.

She looked at him and repeated the same questions she had asked applicants before him. "Your name, sir?"

He had to spell it. She made a mistake in noting it down. He had to correct her.

"Please fill out this application." He sensed a slight irritation in her voice.

"Thank you," he said. His accent seemed to have intensified. He took the application and retreated to a long table.

He visited six or seven booths of companies who might need—directly, indirectly or remotely—someone of his experience and education; challenge, benefit package, location, salary, nothing mattered to him any more. He had to find a job.

An hour and a half later, as he approached the revolving door, he noticed Bruce waiting for him.

During the discussion over drinks, he discovered that Bruce had the same qualifications as himself. However, Bruce had spent several years wandering around the world, so he had only four years of experience. Ramesh had guessed right. Bruce had been laid off the same time as he.

"It's been very hard," Bruce said. "What little savings we had are wiped out and my wife is fed up with me. She thinks I don't try hard. This role reversal is not good for a man's ego."

"Yes," Ramesh agreed.

"We may have to move but my wife doesn't want to. Her family is here."

"I understand."

"I figure you can't have that problem."

"No. You must have guessed I'm from India."

After a couple of drinks they walked out into an empty lobby and the empty parking lot.

Two days later Bruce called. "Want to go to a job fair? It's in Woodland, two hundred miles from here. I hate to drive out alone." Ramesh agreed.

"Who will hire me when Americans are available?" he complained to Rani afterward.

"You must not think like that. You are as good as any of them," Rani snapped. "Remember what Alexander said."

Ramesh remembered. Alexander was a crazy history student with whom he had shared an apartment once. Rani always referred to Alexander's message.

Ramesh had responded to an advertisement on his university's bulletin board and Alexander had answered the phone.

"You have to be crazy to share an apartment with me. My last roommate left because he could not live with me."

"What did you do? I mean, why did he leave?" Ramesh asked.

"I like to talk. You see, I wake up people and tell them about my ideas at night. They call me Crazy Alexander . . ."

"I will get back to you." Ramesh put the receiver down and talked to the student who had moved out.

"You see, Alexander's a nut. He sleeps during the day and studies at night. He's a history buff. He studies revolutions. He wakes up people just to talk to them, about theories, others' and his own! He will offer a discount on the rent if you will put up with him."

Short of funds, Ramesh moved in with Alexander.

Much of Alexander's oratory bounced off Ramesh's half-asleep brain, but off and on a few sentences made an impression and stuck in his memory.

"You must first view yourself as free and equal," Alexander said.

"Equal to who?"

"To those around you who consider you less than equal . . ."

"Me? Less than equal?"

"No! Not you stupid. The oppressed person. Oppression could be social, religious, foreign, traditional."

"Who oppressed me?"

"No! No! Not you! An imaginary oppressed person must first see himself as the equal to his oppressors. The idea of equality will ultimately sow seeds of freedom and revolution in his mind. That idea is the first step. You see. . . stop snoring . . . That's the first step toward liberation."

After his marriage Ramesh told Rani of his conversations with Alexander.

"Makes sense," she said, looking very earnest.

"Really! You mean you understand?" Rani's reaction amazed Ramesh.

"Yes, I do. I am an oppressed person, socially and traditionally. That's why my parents had to come up with a dowry."

A month went by and Ramesh was called for an interview.

Bruce telephoned the same night. He and some other engineers he knew had also been called. Had Ramesh received a call, too?

Ramesh swallowed hard. "No, I didn't." He felt guilty and ashamed for lying to Bruce, who was so open, friendly and supportive, despite his own difficulties.

Ramesh's ego had already suffered a major trauma. He was convinced he would never get a job if Americans were available and he did not wish to admit to Bruce later on, "I had an interview, but they didn't hire me." It was easier to lie now.

The interview over, Ramesh decided to put the job out of his mind. His confidence at a low ebb, he dared not hope.

Three weeks went by and he received a phone call from the company that interviewed him. He had the job.

"They must have hired several engineers," Ramesh thought, elated.

Bruce called again. "I didn't get the job. The other guys I know have also received negative replies."

The news stunned Ramesh. He could not believe that he had got the job and the others had not. As he pondered this, he realized he owed an embarrassing explanation to Bruce. How was he going to tell him that he had the job?

As Bruce jabbered on about something, Ramesh gathered up his courage.

"I have an offer from them," he stated in a flat tone and strained his ear for a response.

After a few unbearable seconds of silence, Bruce exclaimed, "Congratulations! At least one of us made it. Now we can all hope. I know you have better qualifications."

Ramesh knew that the voice was sincere, without a touch of the envy he had anticipated.

They agreed to meet Saturday, for a drink, a small celebration, as Bruce suggested.

"Rani, I got the job. The others didn't." Ramesh hung up the receiver and bounded up to Rani.

"I told you you are as good as any of them," Rani responded nonchalantly and continued to fold the laundry.

"Maybe . . . possibly . . . they needed a minority candidate," Ramesh muttered.

Rani stopped folding. "Ramesh," she said as her eyes scanned Ramesh's face, "you may have the job and the knowledge and the qualifications, but you are not free and equal."

"What do you mean?" Ramesh asked.

AIDSwallah

FEROZA JUSSAWALLA

In Los Angeles

"Rohinton! Excuse me, I'm calling for Rohinton? Ronnie—this is your cousin Farida."

"Fadirah? Who Fadirah? Who is this?"

"Farida, remember? They used to call me Fanny? From the university—we were in graduate school together . . . I'm going home . . . to India . . . do you want me to tell your family anything?"

"Well, I'm very sick, very sick you know — I'm HIV Positive — but don't tell them that. Mummy doesn't want me to tell anyone that. Mummy wants me to get married. They want to arrange a marriage. Mummy thinks I'll be better when I'm married —you know—but Aunty knows. I'm living with her friend Trent Sarris. Trent has been very sick too. He is so much older. He needs care. I care for him. We have a Christian Science practitioner coming. But who are you? I can't remember . . . I'm tired . . . I want to go to India too. Mummy can take care of me. The servants can . . . Will you take me?"

At the Agiary

The agiary is a stark white colonnade, pillared and arched in the front and walled in with solid marble on the back and the sides. It is believed that the architectural design was adopted long ago and far away in ancient Persia when the Zoroastrians were first persecuted by the Muslims. The three walled sides of the square building had no windows through which the Muslim bigots could peep in or spit on and defile the fires that had been kept sacred through the millenia since Zoroaster. But the front was made to look normal, and could even be gay and welcoming, festooned with strings of fragrant jasmines over the arched doorways. On the outside, the front presented to the world, the Zoroastrians didn't want to appear paranoid. They wanted to open their hearts to the people who had welcomed them in this foreign land, India. There were Muslims in India. But it was the Hindus who had welcomed them thirteen hundred years ago. The Parsis, or the people from Persia, as they are now called, are still afraid. Afraid of outside influences! Afraid of who will say what about them. Afraid that their religious practices will be mocked and ridiculed. So although the front of the agiary is normal and gay and welcoming, and the stairs up to the arched doorways are decorated with designs in white chalk that spell out welcomes, it is well known that the Parsis will not let anyone but Parsis into their temples and most discreetly keep the others out.

I am home after twenty-five years. I was raised a Parsi and I keep the faith though I did not marry a Parsi. According to custom, those who cohabit or marry outside the faith are automatically disowned and ostracized and seen as betrayers of the secrets—the practices that are to be maintained in silence. But much has changed over time, the priest told me. Children of men who have married outside the faith are now welcomed. And "women, yes women, if they keep the faith, are welcomed in. But not their children or their spouses. Last year, there was a big fuss, yes—a very big fuss. Katy (Ketayun) who had married a Swiss tried to bring her children to the fire temple. That is not permitted. She even wrote a letter to the newspaper complaining that the practice was outdated and citing figures to show that consequently the community was dwindling in size."

But I am alone and I will go in. After all, I have kept the faith for all these years in an even more foreign and distant land. At the bottom of the stairs, I hesitate, afraid to defile the fires kept sacred since Zoroaster, brought on a boat from Persia to the small town of Sanjan on the west coast of India and distributed from there to the various sites where temples were established. But the fragrance of jasmines wafts over me, cleansing and purifying any sense of defilement. At the top of the stairs I wash myself with the holy water from the large silver tubs with their tiny taps along the bottom—solid sterling versions of the plastic purified water jugs we see today. I untie the knots on my long woolen string, the kusti around my waist, murmuring my prayers as I retie it to step inside.

A long hall separates the sanctum sanctorum from the festooned front. The hall is used for miscellaneous prayers, meetings and gatherings. On the floor is spread a white sheet. Sandlewood sticks crackle in a large silver incense burner as a white-robed priest sings out verses composed by Zoroaster. His face is covered with a white muslin mask so that his breath may not defile the sacred flames. Trays of fruit and flowers to placate the dead are all around. Across from him sits a pale woman in a white muslin sari. As soon as she sees me, she jumps up. "You have come from America—you bring me news of my son—how is he? You know he has been very ill. He first fell ill in Germany. I don't know what happened to him in Germany. I brought him home and made him well. Fed him milk and ghee and made him healthy and strong. I should've got him married and made him stay here. So many nice young girls. So many virgins whose love and health are only to blossom. But he wouldn't marry. Said he couldn't marry. Why couldn't he marry? Such beautiful girls I presented him with—complexions like rose petals floating in milk. But he wanted to go back to 'Kangal' America—Oh wretched country! Every time he goes back he gets ill—I have remedies for him to make him strong—but he goes back—who is it there? What is it there? Tell me you have seen him! He is better?"

I assure her I have talked to him. "He sounded fine," I say. "He is going to New York in April to see some plays," I say. "He sounds healthy."

"I want you to see the girls I have picked for him," she continues. "I want you to tell him we have picked one when you go back. Ronnie is so handsome I wanted to pick a good-looking one and one with a good dowry. When he marries, he will be well." I flush at the thought, unable to lie any more, I push past to the sanctum sanctorum.

A room inside a room holds the sacred fire in a large silver urn. A bell hangs above the urn to be struck at nine a.m., twelve noon, three p.m. and six p.m. to drive the evil spirits out. The priest circles the fire on my behalf as I genuflect outside the door, and rubs ash on my forehead. I am tapped on the shoulder. It is Dolly Aunty. "You shouldn't be here—you are married to an American. You shouldn't be here." She calls to the priest, "Rustomji, her name cannot be taken in the prayers. She is married to an American. She is a traitor!" Then she turns to me: "I am president of the Anjuman—you did not take my permission to come here. You disgrace us all. One of our family—married to an American when there are so many nice young men in our family—your own cousin Ronnie! And you in America with him—you filthy traitor. And how many half-breed children have you begotten—Out! Out! Out!"

On Exhibition

Ronnie was much depleted in size but remained considerably handsome. He used to be about six feet tall and weighed two hundred and twenty-five pounds. He had retained his cherubic dimpled face with the round eyes and winning smile. He was sitting in his traditional clothes—boosted up by a brief period of remission and some treatments of AZT. He had always been willing to smile and be friendly. It was this all-encompassing warmth and friendliness that had started everything anyway. But he kept on smiling—never unhappy, never begrudging. "A bit of a buffoon," people thought. "A little soft in the head," the cousins thought. After all, his parents were first cousins—isn't there something about all this incestuous intermarriage. But there he was—always smiling.

"How delicious he was when he was little," thought the bachelor uncle: "Plump, juicy, always smiling, never one to make a noise when he was fondled. And I gave him his taste for life. There, there . . . he isn't going to marry is he? But so what? The little wretch will keep him here. Sick, like he's been. But what does it matter—I can always have him when I want now—though he won't let me touch him—keeps muttering the name Trent. Must be some American sahib he's got himself!"

Ronnie looked especially handsome. He wore a black paghri on his head, ironed to a shiny starched smoothness. A black sharkskin Nehru jacket had been especially tailored to fit his now almost winsome frame together with the white raw silk pants. His uncle had plucked for him a prize budding rose to wear in his buttonhole. The budding rose was meant to signify the reopening of their relationship. The fragrance wafted him back in time. It wasn't his uncle who had introduced him to the joys of anal sex.

The local rajah, Suraj Prasad, was a great friend of the family and particularly his uncle. Bachelor friends have always been held in great esteem among the aristocracy in India, having supposedly foregone the pleasures of marriage for celibacy. Their every whim is everyone's wish. Ronnie was always taught to respect and obey the respectable bachelors in the family and he had grown particularly fond of the uncle who grew roses and tended to the roses for three to four hours every day. As a child, Ronnie ran around among the potted tea roses, named after prime minister Nehru, Eleanor Roosevelt, etc. Whenever Ronnie bent over to tend to something, his uncle poked him in the bottom with his big toe and peals of laughter came from the rose garden. Ronnie in turn picked up his uncle's violin bow and poked uncle in the behind. One day when Uncle was having a party, Rajaji took him aside in the rose garden to play the game. But it felt so good Rajaji poking and pulling inside his pants. He liked this poking and pulling and tried to explore it with his friends, who spat on him and ran away from him and called him "Chamcha! Chamcha! Chamcha!" One day an Anglo-Indian boy stuck him in the behind with a spoon and called him "Homo! Homo! Homo!" Ronnie felt lonely and sad. But there was always Uncle or Rajaji to turn to. And Rajaji always rewarded him with strings of pearls—pearls which he said were the purest real pearls—satladas—seven strands—panchladas—five strands—teenladas—three strands.

Bapsy

Nubile, sixteen-year-old Bapsy sat with her bridegroom-to-be. Her heavy silver-threaded sari had slipped off her shoulders, revealing her plump arms and the grey silver tanchoi-silk sleeveless blouse. Posies of jasmines circled her thick dark hair. She should pull the sari pallau over her head, she should look modest, she thought. Her bridegroom would like her modesty. He was handsome, with a winsome smile and deep dimples on either side of his mouth and on his chin. "Dimple on the chin, devil within," she thought. The paghri enhanced his head. The dark dagla-sherwani framed his face. It seemed, however, to pick up the dark circles around his eyes. "I wonder why his eyes seem so darkly circled," she thought. "Perhaps he's studied too much; you know in America they work so hard. His cheeks are pretty hollow too and his bones seem to jut out of his skin."

There was a hullabaloo all around them. Because this was an old Parsi family that had served the aristocratic Nizams, a shehnai had been sent for. This was not even the engagement day but nuptial music was playing. Shrill old aunts came in and out bearing garlands of roses.

"Look at him! What a prize he has won!"

"After all these years of saying that he would never marry."

"My, my and he used to say he was never interested in girls."

"Janum you have won the fleshiest little prize," they said to Bapsy. "England-returned, America-returned."

"Yes, yes the boy is America-returned—so he is commanding big dowry."

"The bride's parents are giving a red BMW and its trunk is full of cash!"

The headiness of the shehnai, the laughter, the voices, the fragrance were all making Bapsy feel very languid and sexy. Doe-eyed, she looked at her husband-to-be, but he kept turning his face away from her. He was sitting between his uncle and Rajaji with a faraway look in his eyes.

"Come on, come on children, the car has been brought around. Ronnie take Bapsy for a ride. How else can you get to know each other. Go children, get to know each other." Dolly Aunty was always organizing something.

Ronnie was feeling weak and dizzy. But he was shoved into the driver's seat and Bapsy delicately got into the car next to him. Ronnie drove through the portico into the dark winding lanes towards the bazaar.

"No, no, let's find a quiet spot to talk," Bapsy urged. She had come to the conclusion that her groom-to-be was shy and weak from the Indian heat. She was alone with a man for the first time in her life and feeling sexy. But Ronnie's illness was catching up on him. Abruptly, he stopped the car to step out and vomit. With all her tenderness and passion, Bapsy reached out to wipe his mouth. "I will make you well," she said as she reached out and firmly planted a kiss on his mouth swallowing the last bits of his vomit. "Come hold me, let me give myself to you." Ronnie hadn't felt such tenderness and caring in a long, long time. He let himself fall limp on her shoulder. "You are to be my husband, don't you want to feel my body—" "No! No! I can't do this—I've never done this with a woman—leave me alone!" "I will do whatever you want to make you happy and like me," she said. "I'm so proud that you've never had a woman before . . . boys in India are getting so fast . . . touch me," she pleaded not knowing what made him turn revoltingly from her. She knew her plump sexiness had attracted men before. She was not going to let him defeat her. Sick and weak but longing for what he knew was one last encounter, Ronnie turned her over, loosened her sari from behind and let himself reach between the plump buttocks. Bapsy knew something was strange but wrote it off to the strange ways of America-returned men.

Ground Pearls

That night a fever ravaged Ronnie's body, causing him to be delirious. Sweat poured from his brow and his armpits. The pillow was soaked as were his bedclothes. His mother sat on his bed fanning him with a dried grass fan soaked in water. "Khas-khas ki tatti," he thought as he smelled the fragrance of this dried grass. It took him back to his early childhood when children loved to pour water on the drapes made of this grass. It kept the rooms cooled and shaded—an early version of the gulmarg air conditioner now humming away. "Air conditioners," he thought. "Air conditioners—it is the same problem everywhere—never cool enough on a hot muggy night." And he thought of his roommate Trent in Los Angeles. And he called his name. And his mother couldn't understand who and what he was calling for.

"Doctor ko bulow, Doctor ko bulow," she called. Ronnie's father dialed and dialed. The old butler Joseph was dispatched on the bicycle and he pedalled as fast as he could.

Treatment

"Aré baba nahi jao—nahi jao," Imtiaz Bibi, the doctor's wife, implored. "Everybody says he has AIDS, he vomits, he bleeds! If anything happens to you, who will take care of us?" she pleaded, half awake on her charpoy. "Babamma—Joseph ko bolo nahin até." Joseph wouldn't be daunted. "The doctor cannot come—why did he become a doctor if he cannot come. He must come when the sick need him. I'm not going till he comes." And Joseph leaned on his bicycle and started ringing his bell, rousing the whole neighbourhood. "He will not come, he will not come," the little urchins had already relayed the message.

In the meantime, Josephine Ayah had run to the ayurved. "You must come, the baba is dying, someone must come." The old brahmin washed his mouth out with neem leaves as an antiseptic and fastening his dhoti, adjusting the holy string diagonally around his chest, proceeded in his fastest bow-legged walk. He looked to the sky to see what star dominated. It was Uranus. It is the star of astrologers. "These people need an astrologer, not me," he thought but stepped across their threshold. "Madam, your son needs pearls, ground pearls. He has a watery moon and his disposition is watery. Look at all the water flowing from his body."

"I need AZT . . . I don't need this fool . . . I need to get to LA," Ronnie thought.

"The pearls have to be real, Madam. They cannot be cultured. They cannot be baroque. They must be circles as perfect as the full moon and luminous pearly grey and white."

"I will get my satlada. The pearls were given from the Nizam to my father," Ronnie's mother said as she turned to her safe. Josephine was already waiting with the mortar and pestle and the rhythmic grinding began. The pearls were ground smaller and smaller as each of the seven strands turned to finest dust.

"Mix it with a little honey."

"Give it to him with honey."

"No. No. I need AZT."

"AZT? AZT kya bolta hai? What is he saying?"

"Aré bichara bimar hay. He is sick! He is sick!"

No one could understand Ronnie. But Imtiaz Bibi had won the day at the doctor's. The ayurvedic brahmin, unafraid, was fulfilling his karma. He could see that the young man was near death. "Ram, Ram, Ram, Ram," the words poured from his mouth as he urged Josephine to pour the ground pearls into the patient's mouth. But a trickle of spit with pearl dust leaked from the side of Ronnie's mouth, his eyes rolled back, his body became limp.

The Rumours

Joseph remained firmly planted by the doctor's compound gate ready to accost him when he emerged for his early morning rounds. The grey light was piercing the dark pink of the sky around the yellow bungalow. The plaster was peeling on the verandah around which hung huge smoky cobwebs. On the portico arch hung honeysuckle. The driver cranked the Ambassador—once, twice, thrice, and it started. Spitting out his bidi, he said to Joseph, "Aré jao yar—go home—the baba is already dead!" "But why didn't doctor come?" Joseph demanded. "AIDS" hissed the driver. "Don't they tell you anything? Ask the American doctors in the mobile van. It is bad, yaar, nobody wants to catch it. You have been serving the baba. You probably have it—mopping up that vomit day in and day out. Dactar Sahib knows—it is AIDS."

"AIDS?" Joseph said, "AIDS, what is this bimari—never heard of it—"

"Hijrahs—hijrahs get it . . ."

"Baba is no hijrah."

"Might as well be, yaar."

Shuffling his feet in the sand, head bowed low, Joseph stopped at the paanwallah for tea. "Aids," he asked paanwallah, "what is this, yaar—"

Paanwallah jumped from his flat wooden stool, shut the slats that made up the blue doors of his paan stand in Joseph's face and yelled, "Get out! Get out! Get out! No one with AIDS come near my stand—you have it, you have it, you served him, you have it. Get out! Get out!"

Newspaperwallah, hearing the commotion started to chase Joseph. "Leper, AIDSwallah, jao, jao!"

He has been serving the boy with AIDS!

He has been serving the boy with AIDS!

He has been serving the boy with AIDS!

The cry rang through the bazaar. Up past the Gandhi statue. Up to the compounder who still doled out red medicine, a special compound, to sick children. Up to the Parsi temple.

The Messengers

At the Soonimai Taraporewala Agiary, the call had come already. Ronnie had passed away. The priests were needed. The specially designated pallbearers were needed to wash and clean the body. Otherwise, it could not be carried to the Towers of Silence. The soul could not make it past Chintonmoy, the mythical bridge, if the pallbearers' dog did not view the body. Like a St Bernard, this dog was supposed to take the soul to the otherside. But the bazaar whispers had already come through.

There was a terror of AIDS. The American doctors in the mobile vans, handing out those little plastic circles—condoms they called them—French letters the British used to call them—had terrified the people. AIDS could kill you. There is no cure. The women beat their breasts, "Aré baap baap." "These American diseases." "The Americans brought them." "Our America-returned children brought them." "Aré! Aré! Why do we go to America?" "No, no, you couldn't touch their things. You would catch it." "Everything must be burned! Everything must be burned!"

"Madam, the body must be cremated!" the brahmin said. "Madam, we must not contaminate the soil of our Mother India. Madam, Madam, please listen to me, Madam. Mother India will not forgive you."

"What does he know! This fellow doesn't know anything," Ronnie's mother said. "He killed my son with his pearls recipe and the doctor wouldn't even come. Contaminate the soil of Mother India! What nonsense—he needs a proper Parsi burial."

The Riots

Short, squat, dark and square Alamai, who normally called people "My kidneys," "My livers," "My darlings," wouldn't budge. She sat on the outside bench of the Agiary refusing to budge.

"We will not come. What is this? America? We have no insurance? What if we get sick? We don't know what the boy died of? We will not come. They must handle the body themselves, the Parsis in the family—the servants cannot do it. Then the priests will come to say the prayers."

Meanwhile the brahmin made his bow-legged progress towards the Moosi river rubbing himself with neem paste, chewing on neem leaves, disinfecting himself inside and out. The priest of the Hindu temple emerged: "Vedacharya," he called. "You have done your duty. What do they do now?"

"They are taking the body to the Towers of Silence," the ayurved said. "Those birds will bite into it and then come bite our cattle and our children. The terrible disease will become a plague. The memsahib must be stopped."

Round, chubby, well-oiled Ramarajya, the priest, tied up his hair in a knot, adjusted his string, pulled the dhoti between his legs, and proceeded to the home of the Parsis. "Madam, it cannot be done! The body must be cremated. This is a bad illness, Madam. The birds will spread it."

But Aunty Dolly was now in charge, waving her hands on the doorstep. "Go away, get out! What is this nonsense? Of course we will follow our rites—who are these people anyway—no, no—boy didn't have AIDS, no AIDS! Leukemia! Leukemia! That is what Ronnie died of."

"Lay him out here! Come on! Bring the body! Here in the living room."

The priests came in their white muslins—white muslin turbans and flowing gowns, their muslin masks around their mouths. The chanting had begun.

The chanting had begun outside too:

Burn him
Burn him
Burn his things
Burn his family
Burn everything that had contact with him.

But the family was determined. They would go up to the Towers of Silence. On a makeshift stretcher they carried the body towards the towers.

Ramarajya mustered his forces at the temple, calling all the young men.

"See, this will happen to you too."

"You will all catch it! Yes, you will."

"It spreads with bites! The birds will bite the body, then come down here and s-w-o-o-p down on the children with the guavas. And the children will get AIDS. Yes! Ask the doctors in the mobile van!"

"Saar," one fellow ventured. "When the body is dead, the germs are dead!"

"No! No! Not this disease!"

"These Parsis! They will ruin us by their ways."

The solemn procession kept on moving. Side by side the chanting continued—the prayers and the call for cremation. But all were afraid to go near the body. Some boys began to pick up a few sticks, some a few rocks, some a few branches. Then one threw a rock. And soon the shower began thick and fast—small rocks, big rocks, yellow rocks, brown rocks, sandstone rocks. Some started charging with the branches. Others ran home to get lathis. The Muslims began to join in, their nunchunk-like martyrdom balls and chains brought out for the attack. Shouting, screaming, all surrounded the procession. A small Molotov cocktail was thrown at the body. It ignited with sparks flying everywhere. "Burn the Parsis! Burn the Parsis!" Running, shouting, screaming. Alamai began to bar the temple doors, tying her scarf around her head as she went towards the sanctum sanctorum. "And all because of that boy!" She shook her head. "Again, our fire will be defiled."

Crossing the Threshold

SURJEET KALSEY

The bitter experiences of her married life sometimes drove Chetna towards the edges of that existence, to strike against the bounds. Each time, though, she felt her courage crushed by the shut doors of the house. She couldn't cross the threshold, she couldn't break the barriers. This was her husband's house where she came as a bride clad in gold and silk and would leave only when her body died. She had become accustomed to all the pain and suffering she was forced to bear during the long period she had spent with her husband, his parents and his relatives. It did not seem to matter then in what manner the twenty-two years of her marriage had passed.

Their daughter was twenty-one and got married last year. Their son who had turned twenty went to live in the university residence. The nest was empty except for her husband Chandra, his very old mother and herself. They did not have anything in common to talk about. The mother and son were the ones who made all the decisions and Chetna was required to carry them out.

Emptiness was even more obviously felt in their huge house, which Chandra had built a few years before when the land was a little cheaper. Their children never wanted to live in Surrey, no matter how much larger the house was that they were going to move into. So there had always been disagreement between the children and the parents. The children were especially resentful against their father, whose word was always final. Chandra was the one who had a strong desire to own a huge house and a luxury car. Furthermore, father and son had always fought over the car, because the son wanted a sports car.

Anyhow, these everyday fights and noises ceased when the children

85

moved out. Now the three people living in the house hardly spoke, except for Chandra, whose loud heavy voice would penetrate the silence whenever he couldn't find his things or thought Chetna had not performed her wifely duties.

They were living like robots performing their programmed chores. This hollowness of the relationship had been somewhat hidden before, with the noise and quarrels of the children. Now the hollowness was more notice-able, emptier.

Early one morning, at about six, when Chandra was getting ready to go to work, the phone suddenly rang. It rang and rang, until he shouted from the shower, "Can't you hear the phone ringing, you deaf?" Chetna, who had been sleeping, awoke with a jolt when she heard the shout. The phone was still ringing, and she hurriedly grabbed the receiver and hoarsely said, "Hello!"

A male voice at the other end was trying to make a connection with her, saying, "I have been in Canada for the last two months and have been trying like crazy to find your phone number in this vast country. Finally, I hear your voice." Chetna was not sure who the person was. She asked, "Who would you like to talk to?"

The gentle male voice on the other end sent a shiver through Chetna, she had never heard such a gentle male voice during her twenty-two years in Canada. Who could it be?

The voice spoke again, "I know it is you, Chetna, how could I forget your voice? I haven't been able to forget your wet eyelashes from our very last meeting at Hissar College. Remember now, who I am? Sagar. Used to teach literature, remember?" The receiver fell from her hand when she saw her husband storming out of the washroom.

She did not know how to handle the situation, she became nervous, and stammered, "Wrong number."

Chandra looked at her piercingly. "Huh. Wrong number? Then why did the person keep on ringing?" He was getting angry. Chetna noticed that his behaviour and actions were the symptoms that he was about to blow up at her. The first thing he would do, to intimidate Chetna, would be to give her the silent treatment. But he was in a hurry, and he left, without waiting for breakfast, slamming the front door behind him. So he's gone for the day, Chetna thought, and she heaved a sigh of relief.

The telephone conversation kept echoing in her mind: "Sagar. Used to teach literature . . . how can I forget your voice, I haven't been able to forget your wet eyelashes from our very last meeting . . ." Chetna felt she was losing touch with reality. The distance between those days twenty-two years ago and now had suddenly disappeared.

She went to the washroom, looked at herself carefully in the mirror. Her face was wrinkled and sagged somewhat with age. Her eyes had lost sparkle but the long eyelashes flickered . . . Her husband had never paid her any compliments about her eyes. She needed the compliments today, to sail out of her drowning life . . .

No, it couldn't be true, it must have been an illusion or simply a crank call. She wanted to deny the reality, that a man from her past had called and complimented her, a married woman for the last twenty-two years. Throughout all those dark times, her heart and mind had always remained unmarried, waiting for someone to come and help her break the chains of tradition. She longed for someone to take her by the hand and lead her out of the threshold of this house, which had given her only despair and pain, loneliness and a sense of worthlessness.

She felt as if for the first time someone was trying to drill a hole through the thick walls of tradition which held her against her will. For the first time she wanted to get free. She desired for the phone to ring again. She wanted to let someone console the scars of her soul caused by the everyday shouting, yelling, fighting, which had demeaned her and crushed her self-worth and confidence. That was why she hadn't been able to leave the relationship.

She stood in front of the mirror for a long time, perhaps the first time she had done so in years. She felt guilty about ignoring and neglecting herself. She was still at the mirror when the phone rang again. Her body trembled with anxiety. She felt an electric current go up her spine. She wiped her tears as she picked up the receiver.

Even before she said hello, she heard her husband's angry voice, "Where were you? Were you sleeping again? Why did you let the phone ring so many times? Why didn't you pick it up quickly?"

He showered all possible questions at her so that Chetna could not even begin to answer. His voice felt like hot lead in her ears.

She hurriedly said, "What's the matter, I am here."

"I forgot my bag this morning in my hurry, look for it and I'll be over soon to get it. OK." And he put the receiver down.

Chetna looked everywhere but she couldn't find his bag. Then she recalled the moment when he was leaving, when she had run a few steps after him to ask him about breakfast, and he had stormed out and slammed the door. Chetna recalled that he had been holding his bag in his hand at the time. So how would she find his bag? She became panicky. What if this was just an excuse for beating her up?

What if? What if he had left his handbag at Rajo's house? Rajo met him when he came to Canada and got him his immigration papers. He had once been married to Rajo, though his relatives called her his adopted sister. But people talked about Rajo's only son as if he was also Chandra's son.

Chetna knew that whenever her husband was upset he stopped by Rajo's house and told her from A to Z the full story of the quarrel. Chetna felt exposed by this. Rajo felt empowered by him and expressed her concern and grief over Chandra's bad marriage. Rajo had even suggested that Chandra divorce Chetna and marry another woman.

Chetna was terrified. She could already imagine her husband's temper when he came.

The phone rang again and after three rings she picked it up saying, "Hello!"

It was Sagar, the same gentle voice. His words fell like cool dewdrops on her frightened heart. She began fantasizing having had him in her life all those twenty-two years. But she couldn't say a word, just asked if she could have his number. She wanted to see him but could not say so. He said he was going back to India tonight, and had wanted to say hello to his student whom once he had admired a lot, and he could not forget their last conversation. She had gone to him to beg him to save her from the claws of an arranged marriage with a stranger. Chetna did not want to marry a stranger, nor did she want to leave her country, where she had her friends, parents, school and above all Sagar.

The Indian tradition was so strong that no Sagar could save a girl's life from ruination in the sacred vows of marriage with a stranger.

The front door opened. Chandra entered with fire in his eyes, as if he had known all along that Chetna would be unable to find his bag. He knew that he had not left his bag here, he had left it either at Rajo's house or somewhere else, perhaps at work. This was simply an excuse to take out his anger on Chetna.

The atmosphere became tense, Chetna's tongue stuck to her palate and she could not utter a word. There was a dreadful tension, of the kind as when a wild tomcat is about to jump over his prey.

With his heavy, grim and loud voice, Chandra asked, "Did you find my handbag?''

"No," Chetna answered quietly.

"Why? Didn't you hear what I said on the phone?" His eyes were red.

Chetna felt like a criminal being interrogated by a prosecutor who had to be always right.

"Yes, but you took your bag with you," she said, gathering up her courage a bit.

"Liar, you filthy hog, you are blaming me? How dare you? Get out of my sight, or I'll kill you," he shouted with his utmost strength.

Chetna was terrified. She knew from a developed sixth sense that he would attack her. She quickly ran into the bedroom and locked the door from inside.

Chandra ran after her. Failing to intercept her he began banging at the closed door with his broad fists, swearing and yelling uncontrollably, and kicking at the door.

Tears rolled down Chetna's eyes, she was trembling like a leaf, her whole body was shaking. She tried to calm herself down. In spite of her fear, she felt a new energy within her, which boosted her confidence. She felt she was not worthless, and would no longer be his punching bag.

She made a decision. For the first time in her life, she felt she was in control. She pulled a suitcase from the closet and put some necessary clothes in it. She looked at herself in the mirror once, then she was ready to go.

She did not know where.

She was afraid he would attack her when she opened the door. So she decided not to open the door. She would wait a little while. Then an idea struck her: she could jump from the bedroom balcony. She opened the sliding door towards the balcony and considered the height.

In the driveway, her husband's royal blue Cadillac was parked, its engine still running. Either he had simply forgotten, or he had planned to return soon after taking out his anger on Chetna. But this gave Chetna her chance to escape. She forgot about the height of the balcony. She threw the suitcase on to the driveway. Hearing the sound, Chandra opened the front door to look. Apparently he saw nothing, the suitcase had fallen on the other side of the car. Quickly, Chetna jumped and landed next to the driver's side of the car, she rushed to open the car door and got in quickly. Once inside the car, she backed it out into the road before Chandra could get to her, and with a sense of great relief she drove off.

Freeze Frame

UMA PARAMESWARAN

Maru switched off the radio so she could concentrate. Now, where was Glendown Bay? She would recognize Purna's house if she saw it, with its cathedral roof trimmed brown and its florist showcase windows of fresh flowers right through the winter that was no doubt the envy and apprecia- tion of the whole bay which is why Purna had it; but with Chancellor Road running through Waverly Heights in three different directions, it was rather chancy that she would get it right the first time. No matter. One couldn't possibly get lost in South Winnipeg. Maru did not believe in looking at maps, though she faithfully carried two to three copies of city maps of all her usual haunts—Winnipeg, Regina, Calgary and Vancouver—and all the highways maps from coast to coast. If one cruised along on memory routes, one eventually found one's destination and often many new places en route. Provided one had time, and that she had always had. She had figured out the slave master Time a long time ago; nothing made him run with tail between his legs as a person who couldn't care two hoots about him. She could now go to bed telling herself she had to wake up at a certain time, and she did; nothing of that restless tossing and turning at the knowledge that the alarm would, or should, ring in a few minutes. It was not quite easy to figure out how she allowed herself exactly enough time to make all the wrong turns in the road and yet reach on the dot of whatever the time she was supposed to be wherever. But why waste time trying to figure out such oddities, there just was too much living, one's own and others', to be done.

Eureka. She had made the right turn after all, for Anne's station wagon was just ahead, with its tacky Anne H license plate. Maru followed the station wagon. Anne parked in Mala's driveway, behind Purna's red Saab that stood next to Sohan's grey Saab in the open double garage. Good. Maru could park behind her in the driveway and so leave whenever she felt like it since there would be no room for any other car behind hers. People who came to parties had a habit of parking bumper to bumper, and though Maru would never admit it, she was not at all that comfortable with getting her van in or out of parallel parking spots, bumper to bumper or not. As Maru got out of her car, Meera came up behind her, with a Bay bag in one hand and a bouquet of carnations showing through transparent plastic in the other. What was in the Bay bag? Was today's do a potluck? She had never thought to ask. But even at potlucks no one expected her to bring anything for where would she cook in her van? But potluck or no, Maru always arrived with chocolates or chocolate-covered liqueurs. Like an alcoholic who must resist drinking alone, Maru kept her addiction under control by eating chocolates only in company. There were far too many hostesses nowadays who stashed away the box instead of opening it during the party, and so Maru had learnt to hang on to the box until she herself could open it at some suitable moment and make sure she got to eat some of her own chocolates. Oh the little tricks one had to think up to get one's fair share.

Meera and Maru waved to each other. Maru wondered to herself how Meera was getting on with that recluse of a husband, and how she would react to Purna's party and Purna's usual crowd of with-it feminists.

The showcase window that had an efflorescence of flowering plants all winter was now framed at the bottom with tulips and irises. The long slender leaves of the irises hid the buds that were just beginning to open. Just as she joined Meera, Bhupi drove up and parked her car alongside Barb's, behind Sohan's Saab, quite unmindful of the courtesy of keeping a lane clear for him. He was probably trying to swallow a quick lunch and get away before the party started, as he and all the other husbands always did. Probably wishing too that women invited for one o'clock would arrive only at one and not a minute early. Sure enough, Sohan came out of the house, jacket in hand and shoelaces undone. Bhupi tossed her permanent-black permed curls and waited, making no move to get into her car and reverse. Maru and Meera greeted each other and waited for Bhupi to turn towards them. Saira who had walked down from her house across the street took Maru's elbow. "Come on Maru, you know her. With ohs and ahs and her come-on looks she has to flirt with Sohan for a few minutes." "Oh, don't be mean," Meera said, "she is always so sweet."

They went in, ringing the doorbell more to alert Purna than to wait for her permission to enter the door which they knew would be unlocked.

Purna's voice floated from the kitchen. "Hello people, it is a basement party today; go down and make yourselves at home. You know what is where." They could hear Vimmy's voice as well, and could smell garnishing oil and hear the exhaust fan on full blast. They walked down the stairs. "New panelling! and what a lovely painting—not Amrita Sher-Gill is it?" Maru peered appreciatively at the print on the wall at the bottom of the stairs. Saira said, "The art piece is new, Vimmy bought it for her from Delhi last month. But the decor is at least eight months old. Where've you been? Of course, I forgot, you nomad."

"I am usually here mid-April to end of June, you know. Don't ask me why I come to this freezer in April and never in August but that's the way it has been ever since we moved West. Probably some unconscious assertion that my heart is Manitoban, no matter where I live, and like a homing pigeon I have to return to the familiarity of the freezer."

"I see you have a new van," Saira smiled.

"As a matter of fact, yes it is new, but as Henry Ford used to say, I don't care what colour my car is as long as it is black."

"This is a dark blue, I would say?"

"Meera, don't be moronic, Maru means it is always a van, not always black. It's got to be a van because she lives in it half the time."

"I've always meant to ask you," Meera said, "do you really live in it?"

"Well, I don't quite live in it but I do travel a bit. It has a bed and a kitchen counter except that it's got to be one or the other any given time, and it is insulated."

"Really! how do you get all that in a van? I mean, do they come that way?"

"Nowadays they do, but mine is ancient, like everything else I have it is from our first years in this country; long before your time. I had the modules made to fit an old milk van from the early sixties, and I take them apart and put them together each time I buy a new van. The windows are adjustable just right and so they always fit any new van. I'd give you a conducted tour if you didn't have those perishables in hand. It's got to be a Dodge every time though. The way Vidya's is always a Volvo."

"Wow, Aunty Maru," Meera said shyly, "you are quite something."

"So are you Meera, so are you."

They were in the basement bedroom by now, their coats on the bed, comb or brush or lipstick in hand.

"So tell us, Maru, what is the party for?"

"I thought you would know, Saira."

"Out with it Maru, Mala is always into this surprise thing, but not with you, though I sure don't know why everyone tells you everything." Maru decided not to hear a trace of jealousy behind Saira's words. She stuck in a pin that was sticking out from her coiled-up hair. "Somerset Maugham's characters are forever baring their souls to strangers."

"You are not a stranger," Meera said, "every time you come, all of us seem to see each other more often than through the rest of the year."

Before anyone could put Meera down on her reading illiteracy, Maru said, "This party isn't for me."

Zarina, Sally and Chitra came in, followed by Savitri, Veejala and Jane. After the exchange of all-round greetings, and spilling over into the rec room, someone asked the same question. What or whom was the party for?

Purna and her surprises. Why on Saturday? When were they to do their grocery shopping?

Wasn't it crazy the way they dropped everything on their agenda and rushed at short notice any time Purna left one of her peremptory messages on their answering machines?

Why not? No one ever regretted dropping everything, did they? That's the solidarity network, always being there for one another.

"Exactly. You know how great Kiran looks nowadays, thanks to that party last November where they made her cut out all that crap about blaming herself for that jerk's alcohol abuse."

"How's he now?"

"Who cares? The point is Kiran has put her life together."

"So, Maru, be a sport, what's all this about? Who is in trouble?"

"Look, I don't want to take the wind out of Purna's sails. She said it was a celebration. Sally would know more, I'm sure, since they drive together everyday. Car pools have that about them."

"She didn't tell me it was a celebration. But she did hint it was for Sunda, and I came fearing the worst. You know the shameful furor Sunda and her nag of a partner had at Zarina's wedding reception, I mean Fatim's. How is Fatim doing?"

"Why are women seen as the proverbial nags? I think men nag a lot more than women do."

"Fatim's fine, thanks. I missed it totally, being the mother of the bride means you are too busy picking up after people to notice what's happening right under your nose. Of course I heard about it later," Zarina said.

"As did the whole world, I guess. But they've been snapping at each other for years. So it doesn't mean a thing. It is a celebration for something else, I suppose."

"Maybe Sunda has got her promotion."

"I am not surprised, the way she's been apple polishing everyone in her department, minister all the way down to her mcp section head."

"Oh don't be mean, she deserves that promotion. She would have got it two years ago if she were even half white. Oh, I shouldn't've said that?" Meera looked apologetically at Sally and Jane.

Sally laughed her loud raspy happy laugh. "I agree one hundred percent, Meera, this is a goddamn racist, sexist, homophobic society. You are wrong though, in thinking that being half white will take you anywhere. Every other person among us is half white, and where has that gotten us?"

"I'd never have guessed you were Native, Aboriginal, First Nations I mean." Meera was trying to be politically correct. "I mean your name . . ."

"I got the McGuire from my father who was first generation Irish and was a schoolteacher on the reserve. But when he disappeared into the wide blue yonder, Mom came to the city. Yeah, this is for Sunda, that's for sure."

"Sunda deserves it all right; let her be happy at least in her job is what I say."

Purna came down with Vimmy, carrying samosas and chutney. Everyone turned expectantly towards them. Purna was even more adept at dramatic flattery than she was at making others work. She complimented Sally on her colour coordination, and Saira on her hairdo; she thanked Meera for the flowers and got a vase, which she handed to Saira to get some water. She asked Anne as the tallest to get the punch cups down from the top shelf of the china cabinet, and Chitra to get the wine glasses and corningware dishes from the lower shelves. And then she raised her hand.

"Hey people, thanks for coming. This is really Vimmy's idea. So let her tell you."

Vimmy smiled. As always she looked chic, this time in an embroidered Kashmiri kaftan that was the latest craze in Delhi. "Ta Purni. Here's what. When I was in Delhi last month I got a real high. You won't believe this. Remember why I came to Canada at all when my marriage broke down? Twenty years ago I felt there was no go for a single woman in India, certainly not for a divorcee. And so I came. And sure as hell I don't regret it. But you should see Delhi now. Everyone living with everyone else and calling it off whenever they wish.''

''Among the artsy-fartsy circle only, right?''

''I like your phrase, Anne, but I couldn't say it seeing as I myself come from that kind of artsy background. And then one day Dipti, that's my cousin in Delhi, calls me over for a surprise party. And what do you know? It was a separation party! No kidding. The sisterhood get together any time there is a separation. Makes perfect sense, if you know what I mean. All very well to sing and laugh together, at weddings when one is happy anyhow and a new beginning and all that, but to be there to laugh and sing when the relationship ends, way to go. And so when Purna told me Sunda and Mahesh have just split, I said Hey let's have a party. Isn't that a great idea? You should see Delhi and Bombay now, way to go. And so when Sunda comes, we greet her with this song, sung this way (how'd you like my translation?) to the tune of 'Jeeyo hazaaron saal':

Way to go Sunda way to go,
Congrats on your new lease
May such occasions increase
'mong all our friends and so
We toast your health Sunda
Way to go.

It sounds much better in Hindi but will do as long as you sing with your soul.''

''Maybe we could then move the party upstairs, from the basement to the sun and sky,'' Maru said.

Purna twirled gracefully and clapped her hands as she sang, until others joined. Meera stopped. ''Oh why am I clapping? This is terrible news.'' She turned to Maru, next to her. Maru shrugged and pointed to the two punch cups she was holding that prevented her from clapping. ''Herd reflex. Besides that's what we are here for, remember? Solidarity.''

''Please don't joke, this is terrible. I've known Sunda all my life.''

''That's why you are here, Meera. Else you don't really belong with us,'' Chitra said, making no secret of her dismissal of the young woman.

''To our generation, she means. All of us grew up on Maugham and Hardy, for instance, and they were before your time so to say.''

Vimmy clapped for their attention. ''Feel free to start on the samosas and punch. Don't wait for Sunda. We've asked her to come at two to give us some time to get the situation sorted out so we don't do a Kammy.''

''Oh don't be mean. Kamal is a sweet person, really.''

''Foot in her mouth, more often than not. And we don't mean it maliciously; Kammy is a sport. We know that. Too bad she has to work today.''

''I have something to tell about a recent touchy topic we should avoid. But Meera is there anything about her childhood we should know so we don't dredge up something unawares and upset Sunda?'' All eyes turned on Meera. ''Just say the first thing you can think of, don't be shy.''

Meera spoke hesitantly and then with ease.

''She was my oldest sister's classmate. They were such live wires, we used to have so much fun listening to them every evening. The two shared a rickshaw to school and back and the rickshawallah was quite deaf, as I recall.''

Chitra gestured Go on with her hand. Sally said, ''Recall something pertinent please, unless she ran away with the rickshawpuller.''

''I remember one Diwali. We usually had the fireworks on our terrace rather than anyone else's because we had the biggest house in the neigh-boorhood. My maansi's family would come too, from Thana. And Grandpa always sat in his easy chair—you remember those cane woven long chairs with curved wooden frames? Only the boys were allowed to light the real crackers—Vishnu Chakras that spiral up and the thunder top and all the fun ones—while we girls got only sparklers and chitchitis. Sunda thought it was most unfair of Grandpa to have this rule, and I remember this one time when she set off a whole strip of chitchitis under his chair. Chitpit chitpit it went on and on and it isn't easy to get out in a hurry from one of those easy chairs you know.'' Meera couldn't contain her laughter at the memory.

''Seems true to form for Sunda. She won't take no shit from nobody.''

''But shit is all we seem to get, it pisses me off honest the way men think they can get away with murder. So she was spirited as a kid, hunh? More power is what I say.''

''She told me the other day, You know what kills me, she said, not his refusal to share housework, not his potato-couch TV-watching but that he has twisted my spirit so much, I used to be so independent, so confident before he took over my life and now I have no identity; no spirit; I hate myself for what I have allowed him to do to me. That's what she said. So sad.''

''Men, who needs them? Okay people, let's get some food and start the party rolling. The samosas are crisp enough, I hope. I'm famished. There's lot's more food in the kitchen but we'll wait for Sunda before we bring it down here.''

While some helped themselves to plates and samosas, Maru helped

Barb as she handed more cups from the cabinet and set them on the table. Meera set about arranging in a vase the carnations she had brought. "I can't believe this," she said, almost crying, as she stripped unaware a carnation of its petals one by one. "Sunda, not Sunda, this is terrible." Maru came to her side. "So, how are the kids? Do they like their new school?"

"Yeah, they're okay, Seema was lonesome for some time but this is a really nice neighbourhood, and she's found friends. I love the house and the lake. Helps that there are so many of our people here too."

"Just how far are you from here?"

"It is walking distance, really. Come and visit us, please do, I am home in the mornings."

"Oh, have you taken up a job or something afternoons?"

"No, not yet, maybe when Suraj starts school. No, most afternoons there is some class or the other to which I have to drive the children. Suraj loves his swimming lessons and so we've been enrolling him every session. And now Margaret Grant Pool isn't as close as it was from the apartment. Maybe he'll be with the Marlins soon and that means driving him to Pan-Am pool at six in the morning."

"And how is your husband?"

"Aunty Maru, you've forgotten his name!" Meera laughed, in a soft sing-song way that matched her voice, "Even I know that no one ever says 'husband' any more, not in Purna's house."

Maru looked at Meera's round face that had no cheekbones, her skin as soft and clear as a child's, and her eyes too, the white of them almost blue. But there was no doubt that she was tactfully evading the question.

Meera was now on stripping her second flower. "I don't believe this," she said mournfully, "not Sunda and Mahesh. I remember the time at Didi's engagement." Hearing Meera, others came closer. "Sunda had been married six months, and she and Mahesh drove down from Gwalior two days before the engagement ceremony. That afternoon Sunda and Didi and I came back from some last-minute shopping, and she ran up to our guest room upstairs and I followed instead of going to the drawing room as Didi had. And there they were, she with her hennaed hands around his neck, her saree pallav off her shoulder, and he burying his face in her jasmine hair. It was so romantic. I knew then that everything I'd read was true, Darcy and Rodya, Heathcliff and Mr Rochester, yes they were real, and one day it would be our turn . . ." Meera's eyes were closed as she listened to some distant music from another space. And when she spoke again, she was crying. "How could anyone who's had that moment ever do this, I don't believe this. How can they?"

"Wake up and smell the coffee, Meera."

"Welcome to the real world."

"E M Forster has a scene like that in one of his novels, where what's-his-name sees Gerald Dawes and Miss Someone in just that freeze frame and carries it in his mind bank forever."

"Oh come on, Maru, you and your literary garbage. Everyone goes through that mush-mush moonstruck phase, it's no big deal. You don't have to bring in Forster, that overrated faggot."

"But if you've ever had that moment with someone you have to stay true to it, stay loyal to that spark, to the divinity that raises us out and beyond our self."

"Maru!" Vimmy waved an admonishing finger at her, "Are you on our side or aren't you?"

Maru shrugged. "I am just paraphrasing what Meera wants to say. It is a beautiful thought, you must admit."

"Oh shit. I can't believe I'm hearing this in my own house. In every group of women there is someone who stands up for men and gives us that claptrap about these jerks being nice guys or insecure or as much a victim as women blah blah, but I didn't expect it from you, Maru. Oh Judas shit. Let's get a drink, people, let's start the party." Purna opened a bottle of wine with an experienced hand and shoved away the corkscrew. "Judas shit, we've got to devise a bottle opener and a name that aren't such damned p-words."

Because I Could Not Stop for Death

RAMABAI ESPINET

Because I could not stop for Death
He kindly stopped for me
The Carriage held but just Ourselves
And Immortality.
                    —EMILY DICKINSON

When he stopped I did not recognize him. I was told afterwards that is the
only way—you wouldn't have stopped if you had known, they said. And I
stayed with him for a long, long time. My best friend Shalimar called him
Svengali and said to me over and over, "You can't see it, but you have
changed, you have changed. He's chipping you up into small pieces and
eating you. He's a dark—he's feeding off your life supply—soon all your
energy will be depleted. And when he's finished you'll be like what a spider
hangs at the end of his web—a dried-up old skeleton. No one else will want
you, but what's worse, you won't want yourself."

I never listened—or I heard but the words made very little impact. Death
was very demanding: as a person, as a lover, as a thinker, as a companion,
as a dependent. I lived on the edge and one false move would mean that I
would go over forever. I knew that, and I knew too that it would be me who
would take myself over. That's how Death works. He never pushes you.
You have to reach the point where within your deepest self you contain
your own readiness for death; then you do yourself in. Death means that
the body kills itself, plain and simple. Suicide means that the self kills the
body before it has arrived at the point of readiness for death. All this he
taught me while he stayed awake at night and slept through the day so as to
sustain his own readiness for the depletion of my storehouse of life.

Why did I stay? The moons were white and splendid, the nights velvety and long, the dawns new as only one who has been condemned, about to face the hangman's noose, can experience them. I stayed because I had to. Why else? He never beat me, but his abuses were unspeakable ravages of the soul. I did not merely endure them, I entered into them fully because they spoke a ghastly truth. Even their lies spoke a truth about fear and cowardice and the imploding nature of existence.

And Death was totally dependent. He had no means of living in the world of light and life and of human beings. He was forever imprisoned in a dark space where existence is an unthinkable torture and where one can only look on from the outside while human beings enter fully into living. The only experience he had of this living was through other people: through experiences of joy and pain, ecstasy and fear, of other people. Not his own. Never his own. Death was envious—of this and a lot more. Envious and sad.

Soon after we met he found it impossible to be away from my side for any time at all. And once after we had spent only a few weeks together he awoke in the night crying and calling my name. I had left the bed and had gone into the kitchen for a drink. An ordinary domestic occurrence. But for Death nothing was ordinary or domestic. Everything was possessed of apocalyptic significance. He was so afraid of being utterly destroyed, by what forces he alone knew. He knew death so intimately, he was it, after all, that he could not bear to contemplate losing even that small fraction of what he dared to call life.

What pleased him most was miniature life of all kinds. You could control it so effortlessly. One spring I planted some seeds in a box in preparation for my summer balcony garden. When the tiny plants came up, a thickly treed little forest, he laughed like a child and cut out dozens of tiny paper horses and unicorns to send them galumphing through the seedling forest. And once, in a more tropical climate, there was a flood in the rainy season and the rivers overflowed. We heard that all the river creatures had been washed out of their habitats and that in the middle of the island, right there on the roads surrounding the largest river, baby alligators were running wild. He could hardly contain himself. We got into the old car and tore off for the country. It was a magical day—wet and absolutely new after the flood. The Death I knew worshipped new beginnings.

By the time I met him, Death was utterly helpless. I was to be his sole means of existence while he took me at accelerated speed into the plains of nothingness. But he didn't look helpless to me—just temporarily disabled. I thought he needed only to regain his strength and that I could quickly spend a little time doing that for the sake of art and all the rest.

For Death was also an artist. He had savvy and more clarity than anyone else. He was never guilty of crooked thinking in matters of the world— always pure like a mountain spring. How could he fail to be? The world was outside him, he was never one of us. But he was impelled to confront his soul's deep eye again and again. It was an irresistible flirtation. He looked often, and couldn't help showing me too, a lagoon of such indescribable murkiness that I have often doubted since that one being could contain all of it. Even he, dark messenger, could not stand its depths.

Shalimar began to see physical changes in me. "You're not so old, and look at what is happening. Your mouth is drooping, your face is strained all the time and your neck is creased. And you're tired. When was the last time you got a whole night's sleep? You're driving yourself to death. And for what?"

For Death, that's what. I didn't think I was driving myself anywhere. I only knew that there wasn't enough time for anything anymore. I was always on the go—doing all kinds of jobs, studying, cooking, cleaning, fetching and carrying from the beer and liquor stores, from the pharmacy, accompanying him to the hospital by day and also in the dead of night, having a few drinks with him in the evening and talking normally together and then falling asleep sitting upright in the middle of the conversation. He was deadly then: "Women have no stamina, they sleep as soon as you start to discuss something serious. They can't drink, they can't talk, they can't stay up with a man." Or he would try to hypnotize me, especially when I was in this twilight state. "Say my name, say it," I would often hear as I slowly swam out of a tiredness so great that I would sooner have sunk there forever than made the effort it cost to swim.

One night Death stalked me. His intention to kill me was very clear and it was only because he was overpowered by that murky lagoon of his own mind that he was unable to do it. And what that did was to free me forever from the fear of death. I had never been particularly afraid of death, accepting it at a distance as part of life's cycle and knowing that when it fastened itself upon me—I would have to go. But not now, not soon.

On the night of his stalking, Death did not come to bed with me, but waited up alone for hours as he often did. I became aware of his presence in the room in an unfamiliar way because he was scrabbling at the door, trying to lock it. And our doors are tropical—we never lock ourselves away at night. In my sleep I was alerted to strangeness. And then he sat at the edge of the bed as he often did for hours while he talked at me and I only answered sleepily. And in the middle of the incoherent ramble I heard something like, "I thought I could go alone but I have to take you with me." It had a familiar clichéd resonance, but where had I heard it before and what did it mean? I couldn't tell right away and my mind groped towards finding the meaning. My hands groped too, under the pillows, and closed around a long thin kitchen knife. It was my sharpest kitchen knife, used mostly for transforming cheap blade roasts into sandwich steaks. In the bed? My body froze into alertness. This calls for everything I have. I hid the knife on my side of the bed, and I talked and talked and talked and carressed him until he was the one being talked at and sleepily answering. But not before he had noticed the loss of the knife and had tried to pry it away from me. Because he was drugged and murky he couldn't cut a straight path through to my centre. Death lost. The knife under the pillow pried me away from his embrace.

But it wasn't easy to leave him. His carriage had stopped for me, after all. And there was every reason for him to continue to be with me. Shalimar said: "You have to be ruthless. I always knew he reminded me of a vampire. He's a dark, I tell you, he sucks the light. Use your wits, you're still alive and somehow you must get out of this one. Otherwise you're dead."

This time I knew it was true. I didn't know how to do it though, and I had to learn everything from scratch like a very small child. But I knew it was either him or me.

When I was gone Death tried to die. But he couldn't. He had no means of reaching the state of readiness for dying because he was Death, you see. So he thought that the only way out was suicide and he tried that too. But always the promise of radiant dawns which he could never enter except through a joyous woman, kept him chained to life. Like a panting vampyr, he would watch the new day being born and only then ebb slowly into sleep.

Then he tried to kill his body from inside—he curled up and got very small. He didn't eat, and only drank. He collapsed in the street and awoke in a hospital bed, his arm twisted, his eyesight half gone. But alive. The nights are dark and fearsome, and for one who embodies the shadows, there is no tree, no rock, no shelter.

Chance brought him to something more in his line. Someone else stalked

Death. She hunted him down and waited until he was laid utterly low. It was when, in the tropical heat of the day, the frenzy was the most intense. It was the Spirit of Carnival who killed him. Her real name was Juniper. The spirit of Carnival was tall and slim and she wore dark clothing and a high headdress. She carried a green medicine bag. Her face was masked by Carnival make-up and barely recognizable. But Death knew her well. They were familiars and had had numerous old battles between them.

The Spirit did it painlessly by persuading Death to ingest a substance. And as they sat together in his narrow room, Death wept and wept for life. He wept as only the demonic, consigned forever to the carnal sensuality of flesh, forever shut out of human joy, as only they can weep. As only they can long for and envy. The Spirit was patient. She waited. And as Death's speech grew slower and his eyes more languid, the Spirit laid him gently on his narrow bed. And, moving like a cat, delicately sealed every crack of the cell. Then she vanished, locking and bolting the door from outside.

In the end neither suicide nor forced implosion could do it. It had to be murder. The Spirit of Carnival murdered Death. And her tall headdress never lost Death's last smell of fear. I didn't know what to feel when it happened. It was numbing and new to me, this vague sense of an absence. I had a strange feeling inside me now that he was no longer around in the world. And one night I had a dream. It was like in the early days when we had so much to say that we would spend the nights just talking. I was never tired then. I talked and talked in the dream and it was so close and exciting, like in the beginning. And then I became aware, slowly, that I was talking on the telephone and then, even more slowly, that the telephone jack was unplugged.

Love in an Election Year

TAHIRA NAQVI

I

Benazir Bhutto has a notion she will win. The mullahs, their hands raised in ominous fatwa, their eyes glinting passionately, are up in arms because, as they see it, a woman cannot, and if they can help it, will not, hold executive office. Pictures appear in every newspaper. Pronouncements are inked everywhere. But the gaunt-looking young woman with large piercing eyes and dark sweeping eyebrows, seems determined to become our next prime minister. She reminds me of another woman who had, in a similarly brazen move, wished to be the president of the country her brother had helped found. That was many years ago. I was only fifteen that winter and the mullahs hadn't been given a voice as yet.

Winter in Lahore was one's reward for having suffered through summer and come out unscathed. Friendly sunshine offering a warm, tantalizing embrace, a furtive chill in the evening, lurking in the darkness, but never threatening; and plump, tangy tangerines that looked like balls of pure gold; afternoons of storytelling in the verandah where the bricks on the floor lit up with terra-cotta lights when the sharp, bright sun filtered through the holes in the latticed balcony. And there was Baji Sughra.

That winter, Baji Sughra was in love and I was her confidante and ally. She was twenty-one and I only fifteen, so I had to call her Baji, but the years between us were a mere technicality; we were friends. And it wasn't that we had become friends overnight. We had always been compatriots, the way most cousins are; even when she and her family left for Multan and were gone for three years, we knew that as soon as we met again it would

104

be as if we had not been away from each other. That's how it was with cousins—they were always there.

Within an hour of her arrival from Multan we were chattering away like two myna birds. Uncle Amin, her father, had been transferred to Lahore again, and until their bungalow in Mayo Gardens was ready Baji was to stay with us. Although I tried not to show it, I was amazed, no, overwhelmed, at the change I saw in her. As if by magic, by some process I had no wit to fathom, she was suddenly so beautiful. Like a sultry actress in an Indian film, like a model in a magazine ad for Pond's cold cream. Her hair, which used to hang limply on either side of her face in thick disheveled plaits, was now neatly pulled back and knotted with a colourful paranda into a long braid down her back, leaving little wisps to dance on her wide, shiny forehead like errant question marks. She smiled constantly, as if there was something making her happy all the time, something only she knew about. Her lips were fuller and I could have sworn she was wearing pink lipstick, except that Auntie Kubra, her mother, would have killed her if she had. Lipstick was for secret dramas enacted in your rooms when the adults were having their conferences, or for when you were married. I think there was something the matter with her eyes as well. They twinkled and glimmered as if there were secret lights in them. As for the lashes, they were thicker and sootier than I remembered, and her eyebrows, without a doubt, were longer and darker. Later that day, when I found myself alone for a while in the bedroom I usually shared with my younger sister but now with Baji Sughra, I examined my own face closely in the dressing-table mirror: the front, the sides, then at three-quarter angles. Nothing had changed.

At first Baji and I cleared dust from old business. Cousin Hashim had run away from home twice, Aunt S was pregnant with her first baby, Meena was to become engaged to Hashim's older brother who was in medical school, Aunt A's cold-blooded, unrelenting mother-in-law was a crone whom we would have all liked to see tortured if not killed, I had seen *Awara*, the latest Nargis-Raj Kapoor film, and we, at our house, were all rooting for Fatima Jinnah, who was running against President Ayub Khan in the 1964 elections. As for Multan, Baji Sughra said it was dusty and hot as always, but she had made new friends in school, the mangoes in summer were sweeter and plumper than anywhere else, and yes, she too was rooting for Fatima Jinnah.

"A woman president for Pakistan. Can you believe it Shabo? And she's running against a general too. But she's so like her brother Jinnah, how can anyone not vote for her! She'll win.'' Baji Sughra looked even more beautiful when she was excited. I wanted to ask her why she was surprised we might have a woman president; sometimes the finer points of politics eluded me. But I knew she had something important to tell me, so I let the query pass.

And finally, when the sun had settled beyond the verandah wall, and we had been talking for nearly an hour, she broke the news to me. She was in love. With Javed Bhai, another cousin, a Multan cousin. If I had done my calculations correctly, he was three years older than she was, twenty-three. He was in his second year at the Engineering University in Lahore. He and Baji Sughra had met while he was on a visit to his parents' house in Multan. It was at one of those family gatherings when the adults are too absorbed in conversation to keep an eye on what the children are doing, or even know where they are. Suddenly Baji and Javed, who weren't strangers and had known each other since childhood, felt they were more than just cousins. This rather overpowering revelation led to secret trysts on the roof of Baji Sughra's house while everyone was taking afternoon naps. Promises were extracted and plans made. Later, after he returned to Lahore, Baji wrote to him, but he couldn't write back for obvious reasons, she said to me. I didn't ask her to elaborate; if the reasons were so obvious they would reveal themselves to me sooner or later.

"We'll be married when Javed gets his degree," Baji Sughra informed me with her dimpled smile. "In two years."

I knew Javed Bhai. He came to our house frequently as did other cousins, especially when they were visiting Lahore from elsewhere, or were students away from home, as Javed Bhai was. He was good-looking, tall, and fair-skinned, with an ever-tousled mop of hair. A thick, black moustache jealously hugged his lips so you didn't see much of them ever. And what a voice he had! He sang film songs in a way that made you feel nervous and mysteriously elated all at the same time. He sang willingly, so we didn't have to beg and beg as we had to do with some of our coy female cousins with good voices, like Meena, for instance.

There was no reason to be amazed at what had happened. Baji Sughra and Javed were like Nargis and Raj Kapoor, like Madhubala and Dilip Kumar. They belonged together. I began to envision Baji Sughra as a bashful bride, weighted down with heavy gold jewelry, swathed and veiled in lustrous red brocade and garlands of roses and cambeli.

"He'll come to see me Shabo, so you have to help." Baji Sughra held both my hands in hers.

"What can I do?" I said, the excitement at the thought of secretly helping lovers forming a knot in my throat. "How can I help?" I repeated hoarsely.

"We'll be in your room upstairs, you just keep watch, make sure no one comes up while we're there."

"But what if someone does come, what will I say, and . . ." I couldn't continue because all of a sudden I realized this wasn't going to be easy. I had to think. Baji Sughra and I had to make plans.

"Shabo, you have to promise you won't tell anyone about this, not even Meena, not even Roohi, promise." Baji Sughra looked at me as if she were a wounded animal, and I a hunter poised with an arrow to pierce her throat. Her eyes filled with tears. I put my arms around her.

"I promise I won't, I won't tell, Baji, please believe me, I won't." I hugged her, feeling older than my fifteen years, filled with a sense of importance I had never experienced before. Perhaps that is how Fatima Jinnah feels, I told myself, empowered and bold, ready to take on not only a general but the whole world.

The rendezvous went smoothly. After lunch my parents, Auntie Kubra, and Baji's father Uncle Amin, left to go to our grandparents' room for their usual talks. I could never understand how their store of topics for discussion was never depleted. There was so much to say all the time. Politics, family quibbles, who was being absolutely, ruthlessly mean to whom, and who should marry whom and when. Well, finding ourselves alone, Javed Bhai and Salim (another cousin who had come with him that day, as advisor and helpmate, no doubt), Baji Sughra, Roohi, and I, all took up Javed's suggestion that we play carom.

Four people can play at one time, so we selected partners and found we had one person left over—Roohi. She was the youngest in our group and hadn't quite grasped the intricacies of carom strategy as yet.

"No, no, Roohi can play," Baji hastily intervened when I tried to coax Roohi into observing first and playing later. "She can be your partner, Shabo. I'm going up to finish putting the lace on my dupatta. I'll be back soon and then Roohi can be my partner and Salim can watch." Baji had instructed me that I was not to act surprised; assuming a rather nonchalant tone I was to say, "All right, but hurry up," which I did.

"I only have one side of the dupatta to do," she said and quickly left.

The remaining four of us sat down at the carom table, which always remained in the same place in the verandah, right across from the windy gully separating the verandah's east and west sections. Even now, when it was cold, we kept the table there, because that was also the sunniest spot in the verandah. What was a little gust of bone-chilling wind every now and then when the sun was bright and warm on our faces?

Within minutes we had formed pairs. Quickly and expertly, Javed Bhai sprinkled some talcum powder on the board to make it slippery and slick, and Salim arranged the black and white disks in a circle, placing the large red disk, called the "Queen," snugly in the centre.

I had the first turn, and taking the posture I had seen Javed and the other boys use, eyes narrowed, I aimed and hit the striker towards the pieces in the centre. All the disks darted frantically across the wooden board and soon they were falling into the snug, red nets at the corners of the board. Finally Roohi was given the opportunity to "push" the queen into the net.

The first game was over so quickly I began to get nervous. How many games could we play? As Salim rearranged the disks, Javed said, "I'm going to run down for a pack of cigarettes. You people go ahead without me. I'll be back soon."

Of course he was gone a long time. Roohi began to show impatience and said the game was no fun with only three players. She was learning fast. Salim said, "I think this is better, you can have more disks to hit. Javed was taking them all away from us." Roohi gave him the look children reserve for adults when they think they're being duped. But, finding him placing the disks together with a solemn air, she turned to give me a stare, and seeing me gazing intently at the carom board, gave up.

"All right, but where's Baji Sughra?" she muttered.

"She's in her room, where else? Now come on, pay attention." I was getting irritated with her. If we had been in a mystery novel, she'd be the unwanted and unexpected interloper, and would have been knocked down senseless by now.

After a second game in which Roohi won because we more or less forced her to, I asked Salim if he would sing for us. He too, like Javed Bhai, had a strong voice and the uncanny ability to imitate Mukesh, who was my favorite singer. He put on his Dev Anand smile and nodded.

"*Awara hun*," he began. Then, pausing solemnly for a few seconds with his eyes closed, his head tilted to one side, before I knew it, he was keeping beat with his long fingers and the heels of his hands on the carom board as if it were a tabla. Roohi sat back slumped and sullen; she wasn't into film songs as yet. She was getting more and more restless and I thought very soon would offer to go and bring Sughra Baji down from her room.

But at that moment we heard Baji Sughra's voice. "Well, what's going on here?" She had silently made an appearance from the back of the gully. I was engrossed in Salim's singing. "And where's Javed?" she asked boldly, raising her eyebrows inquiringly without looking at any one directly.

"He went to get cigarettes," Roohi said petulantly, "and we can't play any more with only three people. Why did you take so long?"

Roohi was still grumbling when Javed Bhai reappeared. Within minutes we were embroiled in another game of carom. Roohi won again. After two more games we decided to stop playing; the sun had wandered off somewhere and it was getting chilly. I noticed Sughra Baji was flushed, and couldn't stop smiling, while Javed Bhai hummed and hummed. What was that song? They never once glanced at each other, except in the most indifferent, casual manner. Such subterfuge! I was impressed.

II

We were making streamers with flags and string to decorate the front door and the balconies. Aunt A, who was visiting, had cooked flour paste for us to use for the gluing. Cousin Hashim had been entrusted with obtaining twelve dozen, tissue-thin paper flags from a stationery shop at the corner of Allama Iqbal and Davis Roads. He had had another quarrel with his father about his academic shortcomings and was staying with us for a few days. We were working feverishly so we could have the streamers ready that afternoon. One more day would be needed for everything to dry, and the elections were only two days away.

Our work wasn't going too well, and we were slow. This was our first time at making streamers. The idea was simple; apply the glue to the narrow white strip of the flag (which represented the minorities in Pakistan), attach it to the string, overlap part of the white strip over the string so it came over and deftly press the two edges together. But our hands were sticky, and the tips of our fingers were numb and caky from the starchy globs that had dried on them.

But there was no shortage of help. Aunt S kept the glue coming, and Abba too got his hands dirty stringing up flags after coming back from work in the afternoon. Dadima and Dadajan watched us constantly, she from her place inside the quilt, he from his easy chair, gurgling his massive, copper-based hukkah, occasionally twirling the ends of his large, white moustache between draws. Amma, meanwhile, was concerned with how much mess we were making, and that we would go to supper without washing our hands.

Suddenly, around three o'clock, there was a sound at the front door and I was startled to see Auntie Kubra and her husband walk in with Baji Sughra in tow. They had moved to their bungalow in Mayo Gardens only a week before, so why were they here? Of course it was Sunday, and anyone could be expected to drop in for a visit. I suppose scheming in secret makes you nervous. I was relieved to see Baji Sughra not looking worried at all and smiling. Soon she had joined us on the floor. She told me to hand her the flags one by one, and efficiently slapped the glue on the flags before handing them to Hashim to attach them to the string. We had set up an effective assembly line, and were having so much fun I even forgot Javed Bhai.

Then, just when we had almost ten feet of string ready and there were only ten more to go, Baji's parents, Abba, Amma, and our grandparents trooped out one by one. They were heading for the room we used as dining room and living room, which meant they were going to have tea and a conference. I didn't like the way they all went out together. If it was a dialogue about Fatima Jinnah's future they were planning, they would have stayed in the verandah and conducted the discussion right here, Alla Rakha would have brought tea and samosas on a tray, and he would also have refreshed Dadajan's hukkah with fresh water and more coal. Obviously the elders had in mind some other topic, not suitable for our ears. Once again I was gripped by the same feeling of dread that first assailed me when I saw Sughra Baji's parents walk into the house earlier.

Cousin Hashim, perhaps anxious to run out for a quick cigarette, suggested we take a break. Roohi, her frock front soiled with a combination of glue and dirt, agreed, Sughra Baji said she had a whole batch of the party's pins for us, so we took the unfinished streamer up on the parapet to dry, and washed our hands. The pins were small, but the lantern, Fatima Jinnah's emblem, was clearly visible in all its detail. I had thought it odd that General Ayub's emblem should be the rose. A military dictator had little use for flowers. A sword perhaps, or a canon would have been a more appropriate symbol for his party.

"He's just trying to look benevolent, show people how gentle he is, how harmless, but it's just a front,'' Sughra Baji explained when I took the predicament to her. "But you see why the lantern is important? It's a symbol of light, of enlightenment. Also, the lantern is a poor man's source of light, so there are social implications too." Sometimes Baji Sughra forgot I was so much younger than she and said things I did not grasp easily. But happy in the thought that she trusted my intelligence to address such complex matters to me, I often pretended to comprehend more than I actually did.

The streamer went up the next day with the joint endeavours of Cousin Hashim and Allah Rakha. It looked so short and inadequate at first, especially when you compared it to the rows and rows of ready-made flags, colourful banners and streamers that decorated shop fronts and other buildings up and down our road. But after a while we ignored its length. Filled with the satisfaction of having created it all by ourselves, we congratulated each other on a job well done. Dadajan and Abba went further; they boasted about our endeavours to any one who came to visit. "All done right here, they worked hard,'' Dadajan told uncles and aunts whose visits were increasing as the day of the elections drew close.

Election day came and went. All night, as the votes were being counted, we stayed up. Even Dadima, who couldn't usually keep her eyes open after ten, was awake late into the night, huddled in her quilt, listening to songs, dramas, news bulletins, vote counts. Roohi, stubbornly fighting sleep, was curled up under Dadima's quilt. We gathered around Dadajan's Philip's radio, a small, plain-looking, unpretentious box on the surface, but of such immense import this night, holding so much excitement. Rounds of tea for the grown-ups were followed by milk and Ovaltine for Roohi and myself. Cousin Hashim, in deference to his green stubble I suppose, and because he was a guest, was offered tea also. Aunt A had made thick, granular carrot halwa for the occasion, and there were bags of roasted, unshelled peanuts for everyone.

III

Fatima Jinnah lost the election. The voting was rigged in such clever and inventive ways that no one could prove how it had actually been done. There was a picture of her in the newspaper the next morning in which she looked sadder than any tragic heroine in any movie I had ever seen. She seemed to have aged twenty years. Her face had crumpled in one night, and in her eyes was an empty, faraway look. This is how the Quaid-e-Azam, her brother, must have looked, I thought, as he lay dying from a disease no one could cure.

Celebrations in the streets consisted of cars tooting their horns, tongas hitched with loudspeakers blaring away film songs and war songs, anthems about soldiers surrendering their lives for the motherland, paeans reeking of patriotic fervor. Young men on motorbikes, obviously elated by the victory of the handsome general, raced down the road in front of our house in both directions, recklessly and dangerously weaving in and out of traffic that was frantic enough on ordinary days, and was tumultuous that morning.

A pall hung over our house. Dadajan had begun by cursing heavily, calling Ayub Khan a mother-fucker and a sister-fucker, and then had lapsed into unhappy grunts as he rummaged among the things on his desk and the contents of his drawers as though he had lost something important. Dadima continued to mutter, "She had no chance, the poor woman, no chance to begin with, ahh . . .''

Amma and Abba put up stoical fronts and went about their business with long faces and deep sighs, but no harsh words. As for me, I had a sinking feeling in my stomach, the sort of feeling one experiences after poor marks on a test or a disparaging remark from one's favorite teacher. I also wanted to take a club to General Ayub's head. Our sweeper woman, Jamadarni, proclaimed angrily, waving her straw jharu before her like a baton, "Someone should go and pull his moustache, the dog!" Roohi, a little overwhelmed by the expression of grief she saw around her, burst into tears. Cousin Hashim was restrained with great difficulty by Allah Rakha as he threatened to go out and cuff the man who was attempting to break into two a large, cardboard lantern that had adorned the entrance of the little tea shop next door to us. And so we mourned.

That evening Baji Sughra came to visit with her parents. She wore a sad look, and seeing her face so pale and her eyes wet with unshed tears I thought how beautiful she was when saddened. I also envied her. She was feeling the same emotion I was, I thought, but she could feel more deeply than I and that was why there were tears in her eyes. She wanted to go upstairs, so after the preliminary salaams and what a terrible thing had happened, and may God curse Ayub Khan etc., etc., she and I slipped away, leaving the adults to their intricate philosophical analysis of Fatima Jinnah's crushing defeat.

No sooner had we entered my room than Baji Sughra fell on the bed and began sobbing. I was startled by this unexpected show of emotion and then, because I wasn't altogether stupid, I realized her anguish had its origin in something other than Fatima Jinnah's failure to attain the leadership of our country.

"What's the matter, Baji?" I bent over her prostrate form anxiously. "What's happened?" In my head, like words from a screenplay, a voice whispered warnings about love gone awry, my heart knocked against my ribs as if ready to jump out of there.

"Oh Shabo, my life is finished, I'm going to die," she said brokenly. "Abba and Amma have arranged a match for me, they had been making plans all this time and I didn't know. They don't like Javed, Amma said it would be a long time before he was ready for marriage, ohhh . . . what am I going to do?" She covered her face with her hands, flung her head down on her knees and wept brokenheartedly.

I was stunned. This was just like in the movies. Cruel society and equally cruel fate.

Taqdeer ka shikwah kaun kare
(Who can complain about destiny)
Ro ro ke guzara karte hen
(We spend our life crying)

Lata's soulful voice floated into my head so clearly I could even trace the musical notes. Ahh, poor Baji!

"But did you explain? Did you tell Auntie you love him and you can't marry anyone else?" I shook her arm.

"Yes, yes, but Amma said this was just foolishness, oh Shabo, she doesn't care about my feelings, no one does, and neither Amma nor Abba like Javed . . . I'll kill myself if they force me to marry someone else." Sughra Baji wailed.

"But why don't they like Javed?" How could anyone not like Javed?

"He's too young, he has no means of supporting a wife as yet, such nonsense! And that bastard they've found for me, he's a businessman, he has a big house, he has a car, oh Shabo they think he's perfect. But how can I marry him? What about Javed?" A new wave of anguish swept over her; she smacked her head with her fists.

Frightened by her despair I said, "Maybe we should talk to Dadima, she's the only one who can help, and she'll talk to Dadajan and no one can go against his wishes.'' Suddenly I felt better. Dadima had come to my aid in moments of crisis many a time, and her influence over Dadajan was complete.

''They've already talked, they've discussed everything and Dadajan has given his approval. Oh Shabo, my life is over, I'll kill myself, I'll be a corpse instead of a bride, they'll see.''

''Don't talk like that Baji,'' I said fearfully, visions of her dressed in her bridal garb and laid out like a corpse careening madly in my mind. ''There must be something we could do.''

''What? What can we do?'' she asked, looking at me pleadingly.

''What about Javed Bhai? Why doesn't he come and beg, why doesn't he tell Auntie and Uncle that he loves you and he'll take good care of you and . . .'' I realized how foolish my words sounded. If we were in the movies Baji Sughra would have indeed killed herself by taking poison which someone like myself would have supplied her, or she would have run away at the last minute, just as the maulavi sahib was getting ready in the other room to conduct the nikah. But this wasn't the movies, alas. And I was in no position to supply poison or any other form of assistance. All I could manage was unhappiness and tears. It didn't surprise me that in the space of one day I had experienced the urge to take the club to the heads of two men.

IV

The wedding was grand. No one expected it to be anything less. Auntie Kubra and her husband had a very large circle of Railway friends and our aunts, uncles, cousins, second cousins etc., didn't come in small numbers either. Also, this was the first wedding in Auntie Kubra's family. Baji Sughra's dowry was overwhelming. Thirty suits, nearly all richly filigreed and embroidered with gold, five sets of jewelry, furniture, carpets, cutlery, crockery, a television set—the list was endless.

Baji Sughra cried continuously, but only in front of me and our cousin Meena. She didn't want to distress her parents; they had enough on their hands already, and sending off a daughter is cause enough for sorrow, although joy has its place too on such occasions. Baji Sughra's tears went unnoticed. A sad bride is traditional, so that if anyone saw her in tears the only conclusion drawn was that the poor girl was weeping at the thought of leaving her parents' home. In fact, if you showed too much excitement at your wedding, you'd be accused of immodesty.

One evening, soon after all of Baji's friends and female cousins had finished applying ubtan (that foul-smelling turmeric paste which was supposed to make her skin glow for her husband) to her legs, feet, hands and face, she gestured to me to follow her into the bathroom.

"This is for Javed," she whispered when we were alone, handing me an envelope. "You'll see him in a few days I'm sure, please give it to him. You'll take good care of it, Shabo, won't you? If it falls into the wrong hands, I'll be ruined." She sniffled.

"Of course I'll take good care of it Baji, don't worry." I couldn't bear to see her so sorrowful. My heart was wrenched at the thought of this tragedy. I hated tragedies. When I started reading a new novel, I'd check the ending first just to make sure it wasn't a tragedy. If it was, I wouldn't bother to read it. Why waste your time with dead ends? But this was different, I told myself confidently. There was hope here.

In the days I waited to see Javed Bhai, the letter secure in my possession, I began listening to sad songs on the radiogram. Lata's melancholy melodies and Talat Mehmud's sad laments drenched my spirits until I felt I was a part of Baji Sughra, a small, hidden component of her self. I even dreamt about Javed. In one disturbing dream he clasped me in his arms and together we ran across a heath; there was a mist, and then a storm preceded by dark, billowing clouds and I lost him. He reappeared later, and we sat side by side where we had played carom, on the sunniest spot in the verandah across from the windy gully. He sang. In another dream, even more disturbing than the first, I saw Baji Sughra being laid out for burial. But she wasn't wearing the white kuffan; instead she was dressed in her bridal suit, the gilt-embroidered, heavily filigreed dupatta covering her face, the long strands of the gold kiran dangling limply from the dupatta's edges.

I protected the letter Baji had entrusted to my care with the utmost diligence. Afraid of leaving it in a place where Amma, Roohi or Aunt S or Aunt A might accidentally stumble upon it, I carried it in my bra, which was only a size 28 so that at first I had difficulty straightening out the bulge. Finally I found a corner below my armpit which held the epistle snugly. At night I took it out and slipped it under my pillow.

Javed Bhai was a long time in coming. He didn't show up until the night before the wedding. When he came, he brought with him a large basket of oranges for us, saying these had come from his father's orange groves near

115

Multan. He explained to Dadima that he had been instructed to drop them off right away.

He looked like someone who had been living on the streets. A Majnu, the legendary mad lover. His clothes were wrinkled and shabby, his hair tousled and uncombed, there were gaunt hollows in his cheeks, and his eyes were restless. He smiled when Dadima asked him about his parents, and inquired if they were planning to come to Sughra's wedding, but it was the smile of a ghost not that of a man.

I slipped him the note, which was badly crushed by now and streaked with sweat, while he was talking to Dadima. She had turned to push the heavy hukkah closer to her bed and was briefly engaged in a minor tug with the long pipe which had become tangled, when I swiftly transferred the envelope to Javed's hand. I had read the letter many times. Baji had instructed me to memorize the contents in case I had to destroy the missive and was compelled to give Javed her message verbally. The letter didn't constitute a coherent bit of writing and consisted of phrases like, "Fate has played a cruel trick on us," "Don't forget me," "I was not unfaithful, you'll see," "Remember my love," etc. Certainly I would have worded it differently, especially when I knew it was to be a last confession. I would have given it a literary twist, for after all, who knew where it might end up. Javed stayed for a few minutes longer afterwards and then left. I will always remember the haunted look on his face as he walked out the front door.

The next day the nikah ceremony took place around four in the afternoon. The maulavi sahib asked Sughra Baji if she would agree to marry Salman Ali, son of Numan Ali with a mehr of fifty thousand rupees to be paid to her when she requested. You're not supposed to exceed the bounds of modesty and respond enthusiastically with a "Yes" right away; all brides must wait until the query is repeated for the third and last time and then, after a reasonable pause, come out with a demure "Hmm."

I was seized with a horrible thought. Was Baji Sughra planning to say "No" in the presence of the maulavi sahib, the two uncles who were acting as witnesses, and her own father? In one movie at least, I had seen a bride take to such recklessness. The huddled form swaddled in red and yellow dupattas was still. Oh God! What was going to happen now? My heart raced. Maulavi sahib was getting ready to present the question for the third time. The Koranic verses poured effortlessly from his mouth while he stroked his beard. Soon he asked, "Do you, Sughra Bano Rehman, agree to marry Salman Ali, son of Numan Ali, for a mehr of fifty thousand rupees to be paid upon request?''

One of our aunts, Auntie Najma, who was sitting close to Baji Sughra, patted Baji with one massively ringed, chubby hand. Up and down the hand went, slowly, deliberately. ''Come on child, come now, don't be shy, daughter.'' She smiled with lowered eyes as she whispered into the place on the dupatta behind which Baji's ear presumably was. There was a slight tremor in the bundle of dupattas and then we all heard a sound. It could have been a whimper. A sob. Even a whisper of protest.

''Congratulations!'' The maulavi sahib said, turning to the men with him with a self-satisfied smile. Aunt Najma clasped Baji Sughra to her breast and started crying and soon there were cries of ''Congratulations! Congratulations!'' everywhere.

Finally, as every bride and groom must, Baji Sughra and her groom were sitting together on a sofa while everyone watched them. The bridegroom, contrary to my expectations, was neither short, pudgy, nor bald. Most businessmen I knew were. This one, unfortunately, was tall, slim, sported a moustache like Javed Bhai's, and a crop of dark, wavy hair, all of which didn't make it easy for me to hate him. To make matters worse, he kept smiling in a rather delightful way. I felt guilty that I couldn't despise him immediately, and the sense of betrayal grew strong in me as I continued to watch him sitting next to Baji Sughra looking so handsome and elegant in his cream-coloured kemkhab sherwani and white and gold silk turban. Like a prince, I admitted to myself shamelessly.

I forced myself to look away and turned my attention to Baji Sughra. Tears trickled down her smooth, silvery cheeks as if moving along of their own volition. She was so pale and still. Almost as if drained of life. I tried to get close to her, but the crowd of guests, women, young and old, and children, especially girls, jostled and crammed and shoved for a place from which to view the bride and groom clearly. There was such laughter and giggling. So much free-floating gaiety. Everyone could dip into it without reserve.

Someone pushed me and I fell, my dupatta got tangled with a woman's stiletto heel, and before I could get to my feet and steady myself, Baji and Salman had been engulfed by the fervent throng of wedding guests.

V

The valima, the reception at the groom's house after the wedding, is an important event. The bride's parents get an opportunity to see their daughter in her new surroundings, shy and reticent still, but happy. However, happy was not a word that came to mind that evening for me. When we arrived at Salman's house my head buzzed with such horrible visions that I had difficulty concentrating on anything. I forgot to carry in Dadima's Kashmiri shawl from the car, left my own sweater with the mother-of-pearl buttons at home, and dropped an earring somewhere which made Amma lose her temper.

I knew Baji hadn't tried to kill herself, or we would have heard about it already and we wouldn't be coming to attend the valima. But there were other possibilities I had entertained all night. She tells her husband the truth, thereby incurring his wrath; she tells him nothing but remains cold to his affections, thereby incurring his displeasure; she offers him her body but keeps her soul from him and he guesses there's something wrong and turns from her, rejects her in private, maintaining a subterfuge for the world in public.

We arrived to find Baji Sughra sitting on a bright red sofa, surrounded as every bride is fated, by women and girls. She was wearing a pink tissue gharara embroidered heavily with gold thread and sequins. The dupatta, this evening, only partially covered her face, and her hair had been swept back from her forehead, perhaps in a plait braided with a golden paranda and threaded cambeli buds. She looked lovely, like a fairy princess on a throne. I went up to her. At first she didn't see me because her head was lowered. I touched her hand.

"Salamalekum, Baji," I whispered.

She immediately turned to me, and we hugged. I felt a lump in my throat, my eyes misted. As we embraced, the sharp gold edges of her long kundan earrings cut into the side of my cheek. I looked at her face. Her skin was as pink as the pink of her clothes, her eyes were luminous, as if lit from within, her lips opened shyly in a smile.

"Shabo, my dear Shabo, how are you? I've been waiting for you."

"I'm fine," I said. "I gave your letter . . ." I began.

"Shhh . . ." she cut me off urgently, "we'll talk about that later."

"So, are you happy?" I asked, a bitter note creeping into my voice as if she'd wounded my feelings.

"Yes Shabo, I am happy. Salman is such a wonderful man, he's so nice." She spoke coyly.

Nice? What had happened to her? What was she saying? Nice? What about Javed? I wanted to ask her.

"There's something you must do for me," she whispered when we were alone for a few minutes during dinner. "You must get my letter back for me."

"What?" My heart lurched. I felt as if she had slapped me. "But Javed Bhai . . ." I tried to say, my eyes fixed on her face, her beautiful pink face.

"Shhh, please Shabo dearest, just get it back, will you, please?"

"But why? And how . . ."

"Oh, you're such a baby, Shabo, how can I tell you anything, you don't understand, do you? Please, my dear little sister, just do this last favour for me." She held my hands in hers and for a moment I could have sworn I saw tears floating in her eyes. But it might have been an illusion created by the bright overhead lights in the drawing room and the dark kajal she wore in her eyes that evening.

I didn't appreciate being called a baby, and I wasn't keen on bringing the letter back to her. If I had any courage I'd have told her to do it herself. I was no longer her friend and ally, I'd have said. Anyway, even if I tried, I couldn't force Javed to return the letter.

"All right," I said helplessly when she began to sniffle, and patted her small, thin, heavily ringed hand.

Of course, Javed Bhai refused to give the letter back. He cursed the whole world and said unkind things about Baji.

"She's false, inconstant, taken in by the highest bidder, so easily sold." His words sounded like a dialogue from a film. Secretly I agreed with him.

"But Javed Bhai, she couldn't do anything, you know, what could she do?"

"She could have fought, she could have taken a stand, why didn't she?" He stared at me questioningly, but perhaps hit with the realization I was too young to give him a satisfactory answer, he turned away, biting his lips and shaking his head sadly.

"But the letter isn't important any more, why don't you give it back?" I begged. At first he ignored my pleas. Some moments later he took the letter out of his shirt pocket and angrily tore it into a hundred pieces, his face contorted as his hands worked the letter into shreds. Then he flung the pieces over the parapet. Slowly the tiny scraps flew down and away, this way and that, scattered by the wind like eddying autumn leaves.

VI

Time hasn't been very charitable to Baji Sughra. She's fat and dour.

Yesterday, while I sat in the drawing room of her large, spacious bungalow and had tea and crispy, spicy samosas, she went on and on in a sullen, unhappy voice about the shortcomings of her female servant, complaining that it had become tiresome finding suitable help these days. Cutting short her impassioned discourse on the subject of female help, I asked her about Benazir Bhutto. Was she rooting for her?

"She's had plastic surgery, you know," raising a plump, ringed hand, Baji Sughra offered in response to my question. "And she's too much in love with that horrible husband of hers, that playboy. She'll never win."

While Baji poured another cup of tea for herself, I thought about Fatima Jinnah. One could say the country at that time was young. That Fatima Jinnah was old and weary. That she reminded people too much of a past that needed to be put aside so the country could move forward unfettered. That democracy was a word with enormously complicated and rather foreign connotations. And so she didn't win.

"As I see it Shabo, my dear," Baji Sughra continued philosophically, "she just likes to take risks. Why, she's always pregnant. What can she do if she's pregnant?"

"She's not crippled or disabled, Baji, pregnancy is not a debilitating illness." I found myself using a tone of voice I had never used with Baji before.

"Well Shabo, she wants too much. Just think, you can either be a good wife and mother or a good leader. And she wants to be all three. Now, tell me Shabo, is that possible? How is that possible?"

"Do you ever think about Javed Bhai?" I asked.

Crossmatch

FARIDA KARODIA

Sushila Makanji sat on the step of the verandah at her parents' home in Lenasia, an Indian township just outside Johannesburg. On her lap, face down, lay the script for a stage play *Love Under the Banyan Tree.* Sushi found the story fascinating; a tour de force of emotional torment. From the moment she read the script there was a powerful connection with the main character. It was as if the role of the young wife, trapped in a loveless marriage, had been created specifically for her, and she was eager to get back to London to audition for the part. She leaned back against the verandah wall, tilting her face to the sun, imagining what it would be like to be forced into marrying someone she despised.

Through the window, Sushi caught a glimpse of her mother and her sister Indira, who was six months pregnant with her second child. Although Indira was making a valiant effort to disguise it, Sushi had sensed a sadness about her that she had not detected on her previous visit. She had sensed this change in her sister almost immediately, but their mother, around her all the time, seemed to suspect nothing. Indira had always been good at hiding her emotions. They were so different, the two girls, both in looks and in temperament: Indira the pretty child with the endearing shyness; Sushi the wilful one, disconcertingly frank. She had large intelligent eyes and a bold gaze which could fix with such intensity, that it was difficult to be anything but honest with her.

Paradoxically these unsettling traits were what made her such a desirable actress, because in her five years in theatre she'd never once been without work. Her success had not changed her. She was still dogged, intractable and tactless, a born cynic, and her earlier rebelliousness had merely intensified with age.

When her mother asked her why she always went out of her way to be rude to family friends who visited, Sushi said, "I have no time for all this insincerity. I know what they think and say about me."

"They all like you, darling. They think you're fabulous," her mother had said. "You mustn't be rude."

"Bullshit!" said Sushi.

Her mother had gazed at her in astonishment, the language totally unexpected, even from Sushi.

"Those are the people who would chase me home. They thought I was a bad influence on their daughters because I smoked and swore."

"You smoked?" her mother asked, aghast.

"We all smoked, but I was the one who took the rap."

Sushi had an uncanny knack for getting into trouble. Her secrets were always the first ones to be discovered, no matter how hard she tried to conceal them, like the photograph Indira had found the previous night, of her and Kevin in an embrace. Kevin was shirtless, the matted hair of his chest crushed against the spandex of her gym suit, the two of them pressed so close they seemed to be joined at the hips. "Look at it," Indira had said, "You guys are practically doing it for the camera."

"Oh come off it. We're just kissing. Some idiot took the picture."

"Some kiss. There'll be hell to play if Ma or Papa see this." Sushi could imagine the furore. The mere thought of her living with a man, let alone an Englishman, would drive her parents crazy. She took the picture from Indira and tucked it away under the newspaper-lining in the bottom drawer of her bureau, confident it was safely hidden.

"Please don't even mention Kevin or this photograph again. Walls have ears and if Ma ever gets wind of this picture and has the slightest suspicion that something is going on, she won't let go until she drags the truth out of us."

"God, Sushi. . . If they ever find out . . . ."

But Sushi cut her short. "Find out what?" she demanded. "The only way they'll find out anything is if you tell them."

She tried to dismiss the conversation and Indira's warning, but of course her sister was right. It wasn't so much the fear of discovery, which constrained her, but the energy required to deal with the firestorm which would result from such discovery. She was exhausted, emotionally burnt out from her last role. She had reluctantly agreed to visit her parents, in the hope that the time away from her work would restore the passion drained during all those nightly performances. The thought alone of a scene with her mother was exhausting.

She closed her eyes and turned her face to the sun, soaking in the warming rays. She missed London . . . missed Kevin and the comfort of his arms. The ripple of anticipation which accompanied thoughts of him roused her. She opened her eyes, leaned forward and gathered her damp hair, tying it in a knot on the top of her head.

Her mother watched as Sushi tied her hair back. She feared that Sushi had grown apart from them and that it was too late to bridge the gap. Sushi knew that her mother worried about her. She had no idea where her mother got the idea from that everyone in London lived a debauched life-style.

Thoughts of Sushi in London preoccupied Mrs Makanji. Even though she tried not to dwell on it, it crept into her every waking thought. Sometimes, at night, the anxiety awakened her and she would lie in the darkness thinking about it. It was difficult for her to watch her youngest daughter drifting beyond her sphere of influence. Even more difficult was the possibility that Sushi might have abandoned her Hindu traditions.

What to do? she wondered. The question repeated itself over and over again, like a mantra echoing through her thoughts. What to do? What to do?

She turned to Indira. "We should never have let her stay in London. Just look at her. Who dresses like that, eh?" Mrs Makanji inclined her head to where Sushi sat on the verandah.

Sushi, dressed in black leggings and a brief top, was absorbed in thought.

"Slacks are okay. I wear slacks too," Mrs Makanji said. "But what is that she's wearing? Those tight, tight pants? You can see the shape of everything. Has she no shame to be seen in public like that?"

"It's the fashion in London, Ma," Indira said.

"Those people in London are all Mangparas! It would be much better for her to be wearing decent clothes, nice dresses, so she can look decent like a nice Hindu girl should. Why don't you take her to the Sandton Shopping Centre?"

"She doesn't want to go shopping with me," Indira said.

"She'll go. She'll go. Just talk to her. If she doesn't want to buy dresses let her get a couple of salwar-kameez or sari, or dress slacks at the Plaza in Fordsburg. Anything but what she is wearing now," Mrs Makanji said, her lips curling contemptuously. "I'll phone my friend Shantiben. She'll pick out some good stuff for her."

"Forget it, Ma. You're dreaming. Sushi will never do it. Why don't *you* take her?"

Mrs Makanji shook her head. "You know how stubborn she can be with me. Whatever I say, it's the opposite of what she will do."

The expense of such shopping trips was of little concern to Mrs Makanji, who spent quite lavishly. The old argument of Sushi's that she was saving them thousands of rands in wedding costs, just didn't wash with her parents. By local standards her family was well-off. In the days of rampant apartheid, when there had been no choice about where they could live, her parents had built their dream home here in Lenasia. It was at a time when Lenasia was designated a residential area for Indians.

"What do they care?" her father had asked, referring to the Group Areas Board. "They are going to implement their policies of Separate Development whether we like it or not. So why fight it?"

Mr Makanji had grown tired of the uncertainty. He had wanted to provide a decent home for his wife and his family, and so had moved before the evictions began.

"I had to give up the ghost," he explained with a wan smile, when asked why he had been amongst the first to move.

Sushi and her father often discussed the changing face of the country. It was apparent to Sushi that considerable transformation had taken place since her last visit. And in the new liberal atmosphere many people who had made their money quickly had moved out of the townships into affluent white areas. Places like Sandton, Houghton and Rivonia had become neighbourhoods of choice for those non-whites who could afford to live there. Admitted to these hallowed neighbourhoods, the new rich sported all the trappings of their wealth. Electronic gates swung open to admit their brand new Mercedes Benzs and BMWs.

But for the Makanjis this was home. Despite the fact that the crime rate had increased in Lenasia lately, Mr Makanji was quite content to stay where he was. There had been some incidents. Some break-ins. And once a woman had been murdered only a few blocks from where they lived.

Sushi observed her mother from under lowered eyelids. Her mother was still very youthful. She was tall with a good figure and there was a certain elegance about her that Sushi admired. She also admired the way her father lavished attention on her mother. He was thoughtful of her. Whenever he went on his business trips to India and Taiwan, he always brought back exquisite gifts for her, seeking out the finest silk saris money could buy.

Mr Makanji considered himself fortunate to have found a woman like her and hoped that Sushi would turn out to be more like her mother. Sushi was his favourite even though she was stubborn and wilful, and not at all like Indira who had never given them a day's trouble. Sushi was always stirring the trouble-pot.

Now that Sushi was home for a visit, her mother was preoccupied again with finding a good *match* for her. Mr Makanji had reminded his wife that they had not been successful before, but Mrs Makanji was adamant that this time would be different. He was not so sure. They had already arranged three meetings, none of which had turned out well. Sushila had been rude and indifferent towards the boys and their families. It was embarrassing for Mr Makanji, who had known the families of two of the three boys for a long time.

"What kind of parents do you think we'd be, if we made no attempt to find someone for her?" Mrs Makanji demanded, when her husband remarked that Sushi would only frustrate all their attempts. "You have to put your foot down, Arun. You're her father. She has to obey you."

"When has that ever happened?" Mr Makanji asked with a grimace.

"We have lost her, Arun," Mrs Makanji despaired. "We have lost her. I can't bear the thought of her going back to London to work on that stage." She spat out the word *stage* as though it were an obscenity. "What kind of a life is that for an Indian girl from a good home?" she demanded.

Mr Makanji was at a loss and shook his head. It was obviously too late to forbid her from continuing this kind of work. They had made a mistake by giving into her pleas to stay in London after she graduated from college. She was only supposed to stay for a few months, but the few months dragged into years. He was sorry now that they hadn't insisted she come home at once after getting her BA degree.

When she didn't come home right away, and they had heard she was working as an actress, Mr Makanji had gone to London immediately to see what was happening. He was horrified. "A BA degree to do this?" he demanded.

"Papa please, just for a little while?" she pleaded.

At first he was adamant, but she put up a tearful scene and he didn't have the heart to see her so miserable. He returned home without her, and he and his wife worried themselves sick about their youngest daughter.

One day she sent them a copy of a review in the *The Guardian*. Mrs Makanji hid it in a drawer, but couldn't help thinking about the nice things they had said about her daughter. Eventually, after showing it to a few friends and receiving a favourable reaction, she took the review out of the drawer and left it where it could be seen by everyone.

All her gray hair, she often complained, was due to Sushi, and she was as convinced as ever that the only solution to all their problems was to get her married.

Mrs Makanji had heard that Dilip Vasant was in town visiting his family. He was a Chemical Engineer, teaching at Stanford. The boy sounded like an answer to their prayers.

Mr Makanji did not know the Vasants very well but he was acquainted with Mr Vasant whom he had met at a few social gatherings. Now, pressed by his wife, Mr Makanji made enquiries.

Sushi entered the front room, wearing her tights and the scandalous little top, even shorter than the choli blouse worn under a sari. Sushi became aware of her mother's disapproving gaze.

"Are you talking about me again, Ma?" she asked, winking at her sister.

Mrs Makanji threw up her hands and rolled her eyes.

Indira grinned. "Think we have nothing better to do than to sit around gossiping about you?"

"Come sit here," Mrs Makanji said, patting the seat next to her, but Sushi ignored her mother's invitation.

"I see you've hired two more security guards," she said.

"You know your Papa," Mrs Makanji replied.

This was so typical of her father, Sushi thought. Her mother didn't have to do a thing. He took care of everything. Others envied her mother, but it was not a life that Sushi would have wanted for herself. Her mother only had to speak once, to voice a thought, or a desire, and her father would respond. Her mother had a safety-deposit box full of jewellery, diamond rings and gold necklaces to attest to his generosity. She had all that jewellery and couldn't show it off. Even the ring with the enormous diamond had to be locked away. Instead, she wore a piece of coloured glass on her finger—a trinket made in Taiwan.

Mrs Makanji complained bitterly about the exploding crime rate. Nothing was sacred any more, not even the gold chains around your neck. Thugs just walked by and yanked them right off. If they came off easily, you were lucky, otherwise they dragged you by the chain until they broke either the chain, or your neck.

She told Sushi that costume jewellery was preferred. Big pieces, so gaudy that it was obvious to any fool that they were worthless. Women flaunted them, wore them brazenly. No one was interested in stealing the junk. Sushi's father had cashed in on this trend; he'd seen it coming. Now his company sold tons of the junk jewellery, imported from India and Taiwan.

Mrs Makanji sat on the sofa in the living room. The room had all the trappings of wealth. The TV and stereo were concealed behind a secret panel which opened with the flick of a switch. It was one added feature of security.

Since she could not display her wealth on her person, she had lavished it on her home. The furniture was leather; the carpets from Afghanistan and Iran. The pictures on the wall were of Hindu deities; prints of Krishna playing the flute with the gopies dancing around in their colourful skirts, pictures of

Lakshmi and Ganesh—all in the best quality crystal frames which her husband had bought on one of his trips.

Sushi sat on the floor with her legs crossed, still wearing the clothes her mother found so offensive. She was applying the final coat of Scarlet Passion to her toenails, with as much care as an artist putting the finishing touches to a canvas.

Mrs Makanji sat cross-legged on the sofa, her gold bracelets jangling as she gestured with her hands. Sushi surreptitiously watched as her mother's long elegant fingers fluttered and curled, jabbed and sparred in the air as she spoke. Her mother had been a dancer. One could see it in the graceful way she walked and moved.

In the background the sound of music seemed to rise into the dead spaces of the room. Sushi had put on a tape of ghazals by a popular Indian singer. She had brought many of her tapes from London. She was familiar with the words and sang along under her breath. Mrs Makanji, drawn by the plaintive wail of the singer, stopped talking to listen. Better this, she had said to Indira, than the other unbearable loud pop music for which Sushi seemed to have such a passion.

"Sushi, I think you ought to wear a pale-blue sari on Sunday. What do you think, eh Indira?"

"I told you Ma, I'm not going to dress up for anyone. I'm not interested in this idiot from Blythe or wherever it is he comes from," Sushi said without looking up from her toenails.

"He's from California," her mother added.

"Just so you get your story straight, Ma . . . his brother is from Blythe, he's from Stanford," Indira said. "Both places are in California."

"Well, same thing. No difference," Mrs Makanji said, tossing her head.

"Who cares!" Sushi cried, her gaze shifting from her mother to her sister. "How come you suddenly know so much about him, Indira? Have you been in on this, too?"

Indira chose not to respond. Sushi noticed that her sister was more subdued than usual. She had complained about the baby being too active and that she was constantly tired. Sushi had noticed how edgy she was and had assumed that it was because Ravi was away. Sushi finished painting her nails. She screwed the bottle shut, carefully got up and padded into the next room.

Indira exchanged glances with her mother.

"She has turned down every eligible young man. What is wrong with her? One of these days she'll be too old. Then what?" Mrs Makanji asked. "You speak to her, Indira. She'll listen to you. This is a nice boy. He's an engineer, teaching at Stanford. Good-looking, too, or so I've heard. He's just visiting with his parents. He's not going to be around for ever. We have to get the two of them together for an introduction."

"You know you're just wasting your time," Indira said.

Mrs Makanji called out to Sushi in the next room. "He's a nice fellow. You're making a mistake not wanting to meet him. He can have any girl he wants."

Sushi returned. "If he's such hot stuff, why isn't he married yet?"

"Perhaps he's fussy," Indira said.

Sushi went over to the stereo to change the tape. "Or perhaps there's something wrong with him. Have any of you considered that possibility?"

Mrs Makanji threw up her hands in frustration. "Better that I would have had a dozen sons. Boys are much less trouble!"

Sushi laughed. "Ma, you're so quaint!"

"What does that mean?"

Sushi continued to laugh. Indira joined in despite her attempts at self-control.

"What does it mean, this being quaint?" Mrs Makanji's glance darted from Sushi to Indira.

"It means, sweet Ma. Sweet," Indira said.

"A little old-fashioned, too," Sushi added.

Mrs Makanji thought about what her daughters had said. Old-fashioned wasn't exactly the way she perceived herself.

"You should've asked for a snapshot, Ma," Indira said.

"I did. Mrs Lalji, who is his mother's cousin, said she'd send me one. But I never got it."

"Likely story. He probably thought we'd figure out he looks like the rear end of a jackass."

Indira laughed so hard she almost lost control of her bladder. She struggled out of the chair and waddled over to the window, still laughing. She gazed out into the yard as she pressed her hands into her back. She was six months into her pregnancy and enormous. Most of their friends took one look at her shape and promptly declared, "Girl!" It was disconcerting because Ravi had set his heart on a boy. One girl was enough. Now he wanted a son to carry on the family business.

When Sushi left the room Mrs Makanji turned to Indira, patting the seat beside her on the chesterfield. "Sit down, Indira. Are you all right?" she asked, leaning forward and gently lifting a strand of hair out of her daughter's face. "You don't look well."

"I'm fine, Ma."

"Listen, my darling, talk to your sister. One of these days she'll be too old and then no man will want her."

"She doesn't have to worry, Ma. She has a career. . ."

"What career?" Mrs Makanji snorted. "What is acting? That's not a career!" She paused, her glance softening as she gazed at her daughter. "Why can she not be more like you? Look how happy you and Ravi are. We knew the instant we saw Ravi that he was the one for you."

Indira's glance flickered away. She just couldn't bring herself to tell her parents about the problems she and Ravi were having. Her mother gazed at her affectionately.

"And now the baby is coming too," Mrs Makanji added, "Maybe this time it'll be a boy?"

Indira seemed to brace herself against her mother's words, and then slowly raised her head. "Boy or girl, it doesn't matter," she said.

"Of course not. We're so happy for you, Indira. We know how long you've waited for this pregnancy."

Indira nodded and smiled with a touch of wistfulness. "I know you are," she said, patting her mother's hand.

"I just wish you would speak to your sister. She has great affection for you and Ravi." Mrs Makanji's hands fluttered to her lap as gracefully as a butterfly settling on a delicate plant. "Better we talk to her now, than have trouble when Dilip Vasant comes with his family on Sunday. Go please, Indira, my dear. See what you can do, eh?"

With a boost from her mother, Indira got up off the chesterfield, but did not go after her sister. She was in pain and uncomfortable. Her mother, however, didn't seem to notice.

"I don't know what to do with her any more. Stubborn! You will not believe how stubborn that girl is. I don't know where she gets such stubbornness," Mrs Makanji said. "Your Papa is not like that."

Sushi heard this comment as she went upstairs to her room. She needed some quiet space to concentrate on the script, but there was obviously not going to be any peace and quiet until this whole issue of meeting this boy was over.

"God," Sushi muttered as she flung the script onto the bed. "I should've stayed in London."

At breakfast the next morning Sushi listened indifferently to the conversation at the table. Her father had left for his office already and her mother was making plans for Sunday. It was hard to believe that her parents had gone to so much trouble, they had even consulted an astrologer to fix an auspicious date and time for the meeting. But though Sushi might have found the situation amusing, her parents were proceeding in all earnestness.

"I know this time will be different, Sushi," her mother said. "I have a feeling about it."

Sushi exchanged glances with her sister, who smiled encouragingly. She wondered for a brief instant about the "boy," imagining that he was probably being subjected to the same pressures as she.

In the meantime, across town the Vasants had just finished their breakfast. Dilip was seated in an easy chair enjoying his second cup of tea while listening to a CD on the brand-new stereo system. He seemed distracted and drew a hand through his hair in a characteristic gesture of frustration.

Mrs Vasant watched her son. A robust, traditional Indian woman who always wore a sari, she sat cross-legged on the sofa. On her lap was a thali tray, with an assortment of relishes, chutneys and pickles. Mrs Vasant seemed quite unperturbed by the loudness of the modern Indian music as she nimbly picked at the food on the tray.

Her son was thirty-six years old and still unmarried, a fact she feared might raise questions in the minds of others. She had prayed that he would return to stay but he was home only for a short visit. Her sari slipped off her shoulder. As she raised an arm to carry the food to her mouth, she revealed a too-tight bodice which exposed the upper rise of her breasts. Around her midriff, pinched, pale folds of skin were visible. Her hair hung loose to her waist.

Dilip got up and walked over to the stereo. He had the easy fluid grace of a dancer and although his face was pocked with acne scars, there was still something very attractive about him, something in the expressiveness of his eyes. But he was thirty-six and unmarried and try as she might, his mother could not get beyond that fact. She studied him as he leaned over the stereo and for the first time noticed that his hair had receded.

Mr Vasant, seated in an easy chair, seemed preoccupied.

Mrs Vasant paused in her eating to gaze fondly at Dilip. "I have told everyone about our son who is an engineer at Stanford in California, USA. But I wish you could stay here with us and not go back there," she said.

Dilip raised his head and smiled distractedly at his mother.

Mr Vasant seemed to rouse himself from his thoughts. "Arunbhai Makanji has invited us on Sunday. It seems he has expressed great interest in meeting you. He's heard about you."

Dilip glanced up from where he was sorting through the CDs and shook his head. "There's a cricket game on Sunday. I promised some friends I'd go with them." He selected a CD and slid it into the player.

"Your father and I are very proud of you, son. You cannot refuse such an invitation," Mrs Vasant said to Dilip, and turned her eyes on her husband in a mute appeal for help.

Mr Vasant frowned his disapproval. "Forget cricket. On Sunday you will come with us."

Dilip felt his throat tighten. His parents tended to have this effect on him. Sometimes he felt as though he was going to choke, but he suppressed his feelings and turned away from them so they couldn't see his expression. He hated it when they made decisions without consulting him. But, above all, he hated the way they still treated him like a child. His visit had been nothing but an aggravation. First they criticized his taste in music, then it was the earring. To keep the peace he had removed the stud from his ear. Now they were putting the pressure on him to meet this girl. He opened his mouth to protest, but saw the look of eager anticipation on his mother's face and his anger dissipated. He wished that they didn't have so many unreasonable expectations about him, and that his mother didn't always give him this guilt trip. She had actually cried when she discovered he was eating meat. The underlying issue, he realized, was not only marriage, but also their desire to keep him at home.

"I wish you'd drop this idea. I've told you, I'm not interested in finding a bride," Dilip said returning to his chair.

"What makes you think we're finding a match for you?" Mrs Vasant asked coyly.

"Because I know you."

His mother smiled. "I hear their daughter Sushila is very educated and very beautiful. You'll see. You'll change your mind once you meet her," she said.

"I'm not going to change my mind."

"Don't worry about liking her or not liking her, just come along so we can meet the family. If you don't like her it's okay," his mother said.

"Ma, please. . ."

"We will not utter one more word about it, dikra. See my lips are sealed." Mrs Vasant put up her hand to silence any further discussion. Then she laughed and gave her son an affectionate glance. Dilip shook his head in resignation and smiled, tightly.

"Your brother phoned from Blythe this morning. He says you don't visit much anymore," Mr Vasant said.

"I told you that I've been busy. I've had my hands full with my new job," Dilip replied.

"That's why you need a wife . . . to help you," said his mother.

"I don't need a wife. Now will you please drop the subject," Dilip snapped.

Mrs Vasant's startled gaze sought her husband's. She sensed a new element. Something was wrong. "There is someone in your life already?" she said, turning the statement into a question.

Dilip got up abruptly, almost upsetting his cup of tea. He walked to the window and gazed out. He wondered how he could tell them. They would never understand. Never. He had to lie again. His whole life had become a lie. His parents waited. "There is someone at Stanford. . . " he said.

Mr and Mrs Vasant exchanged troubled glances.

"I was going to tell you about it," he muttered.

"Who is she?" Mrs Vasant asked.

"Why have you not mentioned this before?" Mr Vasant demanded, leaving his chair with startling agility.

"Who is she, my darling? What is her name?" his mother asked, her shrewd glance studying her son's face.

Dilip tried to remain calm. He had opened the sluice gates, now he had to control the flow.

"Well," his father said. "Why don't you answer your mother?"

Dilip regretted that he had given them an opening. They were obviously not going to let go of it. His mother was like a dog with a bone.

"Who is she, Dilip?" she asked.

"Where is she from?" his father asked.

Dilip felt the room closing in on him. "It's someone from California," he said, affecting nonchalance. The music ended and he went over to the audio system to change the compact disk, turning up the music a little more, to make conversation awkward.

"What is her family name?" His mother had to speak loud enough to be heard over the music.

Dilip mumbled something.

"Turn the volume down!" his father cried.

Dilip hesitated. He needed time to get his thoughts together. His father glared at him. His mother put her hand to her head.

Dilip turned down the volume. "Sorry," he said, smiling sheepishly. He glanced at his mother. Her arm was poised above the thali tray. He could feel the noose tightening.

"Ma, I'm going to tell you all about it, but not right now. Why don't we meet this lady on Sunday and we'll see. . . ?"

"We'll see what?" his father asked, still perturbed by the way Dilip was avoiding their questions.

For the moment, though, his mother was satisfied.

"Okay," she said. "It's a deal. No problem now, eh? We go to the

Makanjis on Sunday."

Mr Vasant watched his wife eating. "I wish you would stay here instead of going back to the USA. There'll be good prospects here for engineers. It'll be much easier to get a job at the university. They're going to need people and we have a responsibility to this country. We can't just run. We have to give something back to make it work."

"It's ironical, isn't it, Pop, that there was a time when blacks couldn't even enroll in engineering. It was one of the faculties closed to them because the government figured they would never be able to work as engineers in this country. Now here we are. . . " Dilip said with a sardonic shrug.

"So, what do you say? You don't need to rush back to California," Mr Vasant persisted.

"My life is in California, Pop. Not here."

"I was hoping that someday the business could be passed on to my sons," Mr Vasant said. "But now you have your engineering job and your brother has his motel in Blythe. . . " He paused, his expression pained. "Work, work, work, all my life and for what? Who will there be to take over the family business? I fought to stay here . . . I went to jail even," he said, shaking his head at the recollection. "I spent my life building this business, expanding it. . . and for what?" Mr Vasant shook his head. His heart ached with disappointment and a tear gathered in the corner of one eye as he stared at the food tray on his wife's lap. "We'd better get to the shop," he said.

Dilip said he'd join them later. He didn't feel like going with them. He'd never imagined his visit home would be so stressful. It was as though he had been dropped into a fishbowl, everything he said or did was subject to scrutiny by his parents. In a matter of three weeks, his mother had somehow managed to reduce him to a twelve-year-old boy again. Although he hated it, resisted it, he was no match for his mother, who was an expert at manipulation. She'd had years of practice on his father. He was anxious to get back to Stanford and his life there. He had only been home for three weeks, but it already felt like months.

At home in Lenasia Sushi shared these sentiments. She glanced into the mirror and with a start saw her sister. "I didn't hear you come in," she said. She examined her image in the bedroom mirror, turning her head this way and that way, holding her hair up in a knot at the top of her head. "What do you think?" she asked. "You think I should cut it?" She turned to Indira. "I've been thinking of cutting it and maybe getting a perm. I'm so tired of the way I look."

"Don't be silly. You look wonderful. I like your hair the way it is," Indira said.

133

"You're so old-fashioned," Sushi retorted. "You're just like Ma."

Indira groaned. "I don't think so. But never mind me," she said. "What are you going to do when they find out that you're shacked up with an Englishman?"

Sushi shrugged. She gazed into the mirror and caught her sister's eye. "I don't know," she said to her sister's reflection.

"He's cute. I suppose you're being careful?" Indira said, with the same habit as her mother of turning a statement into a question, or vice versa.

"Oh come on, Indira! What do you think? I'm not that stupid!"

Indira grimaced and leaned back against the pillows. "This is the fourth boy they've invited," she said.

"I don't care. It's their problem. Anyway, I'm only humouring them. In another ten days I'll be out of here and all of this will be history." Sushi glanced at her sister who looked so forlorn. "You okay?" she asked, sitting beside her on the bed.

Indira nodded and was silent for a moment. She scowled at Sushi, her expression darkening with pent-up frustration. "Oh damn. . . No! I'm not all right! My back hurts. I'm exhausted. I don't sleep well. I eat like a pig and I throw up like a fucking sick dog!"

Startled, Sushi glanced at her sister—Indira's strongest expletive was usually "Shoot", which under extreme conditions could be translated into "Shit" —then she fell back on the bed, howling with laughter. "If Ma could hear you she'd have a fit!" Sushi said, amidst peals of laughter.

Indira started to laugh, holding onto her belly, shedding tears of mirth and pain. Finally she caught her breath. "God, I hate being like this," she said, dabbing at the tears with a crumpled tissue. "Look at me, only six months and I can't even get my shoes on by myself. I have to ask Ma or Anna. What am I going to be like when I'm eight or nine months?"

Sushi saw the sad look returning to her sister's eyes. "I think Ravi is a jerk. He doesn't know what a wonderful wife he has," she said. "I sure as hell would never put up with his crap. And where is he? . . . He's jetting around while you're struggling to function with this . . . this enormous belly." She put her hand on her sister's stomach and felt the baby move. "Why do you put up with it, Indira?"

Indira's glance slid away. She took a shuddering breath. "Ravi is away on business. It's not like he's deliberately staying away. . . "

"Bullshit! When are you going to stop covering up for him! He took off the moment you started your morning sickness! It's easier to send you gifts and make long-distance phone calls than to be here supporting you through this time. And what about those tests he wanted you to take?"

134

"How. . . ? "

"You wrote to me, remember? I read between the lines. I know you too well, sister."

Indira picked at the edge of the bedspread, twisting and untwisting the cloth around her finger. "I don't care about the sex of the child . . . but Ravi wants a son. When I refused to take the tests he went on a business trip to the UK and India." She paused, glancing away. "I used to go with him all the time you know, but now it's like he's punishing me because I refused to take the tests."

"The bastard. . . " Sushi muttered.

Indira raised her head, her expression disconsolate.

Sushi's glance softened. "Never mind it'll all be over soon and whatever it is, it'll be adored by all. I'm glad you refused to have the tests," she said.

"I almost agreed," Indira confessed. "But I heard him telling his mother that if it was a girl he would try to persuade me to have an abortion in the States."

"Crafty bastard, he knew that if you came to London, he'd have to deal with me. Do Ma and Papa know about this?"

Indira shook her head and shut her eyes, too ashamed to look at her sister sitting cross-legged, looking for all the world like a vengeful Buddha.

"You're too soft. Too easy to manipulate, that's why everyone thinks you're such a good daughter."

Indira was silent, uncomfortable both physically and emotionally. She swung her legs off the bed, looking so miserable, so unhappy, that Sushi could only feel sorry for her. Indira had leaped directly into marriage. She had never had the opportunity to explore her potential; to see what she was capable of, or to determine her own worth.

Sushi got up and returned to the dresser. She caught her sister's eye in the mirror and quickly glanced away.

"Ma and Papa," Indira said, "are wondering why you've been turning all these men away. You should tell them something. . ." She knew her parents would persist. Things might have been different for her if she'd had the strength to stand up to them.

You're right," Sushi said. "I'll talk to them. Isn't it incredible. I'm twenty-eight years old, I've walked in off the street and auditioned stone-cold for major roles, I've played to tough audiences, and yet here I am worrying about telling Ma and Papa that I'm living with a man."

"Yes, but this isn't just any man. It's an Englishman. . ."

Sushi grimaced wryly, picked up the brush and started to brush her hair again.

*

On Sunday Mr and Mrs Vasant and Dilip arrived at the Makanji house in Lenasia. Mrs Vasant gazed around curiously. It was obvious the Makanjis were well-off. This, of course, was no surprise. She and her husband had made discreet enquiries about their hosts. She maintained that it was always good to be prepared, so no time was wasted fumbling around. In this case, everything seemed to indicate a good match.

Mr Makanji and his wife welcomed them. The men shook hands. Mrs Vasant put her hands together. "Namaste," she said. Her glance travelled around surreptitiously before she raised her head. In that brief instant she had made a mental note of the entire entrance hall and the living room.

Nita, dressed prettily in a dress of flounces and bows, shyly joined her grandmother in the entrance hall. Mrs Makanji gently urged her forward to greet the visitors.

"Come inside please," Mrs Makanji said, taking Mrs Vasant's arm and escorting her to the smaller entertainment room, leaving the men in the care of Mr Makanji who led them into the living room.

"You have a lovely home," Mrs Vasant said.

Mrs Makanji beamed. "Thank you," she said. "We'll sit over here and I'll bring my daughters to meet you. Go call your mother and Sushila," she said to Nita.

Nita hesitated, her grandmother waved her on and she hurried away to call her mother and her aunt.

Mrs Vasant sat down. "She is a darling," she said.

"My daughter Indira's little girl," Mrs Makanji replied proudly.

Mrs Vasant smiled, glancing around the room at the pictures on the walls while she and Mrs Makanji made polite conversation. Mrs Vasant sat back in the sofa, but her legs were too short and dangled uncomfortably. She tried sliding forward, perching on the edge of her seat so that her feet touched the floor, but she was still uncomfortable. She would have loved to draw her legs up on the sofa, but she couldn't; it wouldn't be polite. She shimmied back in her seat, and reaching for a pillow, placed it behind her back.

Indira waddled in, looking pained and uncomfortable. She greeted Mrs Vasant and sat down. Sushi sauntered in a few moments later, looking unconcerned. She had resisted the pressure from her mother to wear a sari. "Not on your life, Ma," she had said. "I'm not wearing a sari just to impress anyone. I'll wear one because I want to, and I don't want to wear a sari today."

Mrs Makanji had wrung her hands, had put on a tearful performance, but

Sushi was adamant.

"You're not going to wear any of the stuff you brought along with you. . . Are you?" Mrs Makanji had asked, in a small pained voice.

"I'll wear slacks," Sushi tossed back casually.

Fearing something even more outrageous, Mrs Makanji refrained from critical comment when she saw Sushi's white tight pants and long Nehru-style blouse.

Sushi greeted Mrs Vasant, noting the woman had none of her mother's elegance. Mrs Vasant was fat and squat. From her sister's expression, Indira knew that there was no hope for Dilip Vasant.

The older women took Indira and Sushi into the living room to introduce them to Mr Vasant and Dilip. Sushi was extremely polite and Mrs Makanji could find no fault with her behaviour, except that she was so cold and aloof. It was as though she was deliberately putting the boy off.

What is wrong with this girl? Mrs Makanji asked herself as they sat down with the men. "The servant will bring some refreshments in a moment," she said to the others. Anna came in with a tray laden with cold drinks and snacks. "How's business, Chimanbhai?" Mr Makanji asked Mr Vasant.

"Not bad for me, but many of the shopkeepers in town are complaining. They say that the African vendors are ruining their business. They are opening stands everywhere. If there is a fruit shop, right in front of the fruit shop they will open a fruit stand. If there is a dress shop, right in front of that dress shop they will have a rack of dresses on the pavement, selling much cheaper than the shop because they don't have to pay any rent."

"Some people would admire such entrepreneurial spirit." Dilip said.

Mr Vasant shrugged. "Depends on how you look at it. If you were one of the shopkeepers, you wouldn't be saying that."

"I wouldn't be downtown if you paid me to go there. Too many robberies lately," Mr Makanji said.

Dilip laughed and shook his head. "It's a sign of the economic crisis here and elsewhere. People have to survive somehow. It's the same problem in the States."

"I hear you're an engineer there," Mr Makanji said.

Dilip nodded, his gaze straying to Sushi, who had not as much as given him a second glance. Mr Makanji noticed the glance and was hopeful.

"So you're a university teacher?" Mrs Makanji said, turning the statement into a question.

"Yes. I'm teaching at Stanford."

"Are you thinking of coming back to South Africa?" Mr Makanji asked.

Dilip glanced at his parents and shook his head.

"It was my question to him as well," Mr Vasant said. "Just the other day I was saying, now that things had changed, it might be a good idea to come back home."

Sushi looked across at Dilip. She couldn't help feeling sorry for him as both sets of parents put him through the third-degree. She and Indira excused themselves and went to the kitchen. Neither of them were there when Nita sidled over to her grandmother holding the picture of her and Kevin which she had discovered in Sushi's drawer. Nita, fascinated with everything about her aunt, particularly enjoyed rummaging through her possessions and playing with her make-up. As usual she had been going through Sushi's bureau drawers when she found the photograph.

Nita quietly waited in adult company for the opportunity to show off the picture. She leaned up against her grandmother's lap, photo in her hand, waiting for a break in the conversation knowing her grandmother would be annoyed at her for interrupting.

"Nani, see this picture of Aunty Sushi," she said, the moment her grandmother paused to take a breath.

Distracted, her grandmother took the photograph from her, smiled indulgently and glanced at it. The picture was a blur without her glasses. She still held the picture in her hand as she gestured, while conversing, her gold bracelets clinking with every movement. Dolefully, Nita gazed at the two women, disappointed about being ignored by her grandmother who was merrily laughing at something Mrs Vasant had said. Mrs Vasant paused as she noticed the expression on Nita's face. Mrs Makanji became aware of Nita still waiting beside her chair.

She glanced at the photograph again. "Later, darling. I'll look at the picture later. I don't have my glasses," she said, handing the photograph back to Nita. Sushi entered the room as Nita slipped away feeling slighted. She didn't notice the photograph in Nita's hand, or notice Nita pausing at the sideboard to put it in the drawer.

In the meantime Mrs Vasant had observed the look Sushi had given Dilip as she entered the room and was relieved. The match would be an excellent one. The girl had a nice face and was respectful. She seemed like an obedient daughter, just the kind of girl Mrs Vasant was hoping Dilip would meet. It would have been better, though, if she had worn a sari instead of those pants, she would have preferred a more traditional girl for Dilip, but at this stage she wasn't going to let minor details distract her.

Mrs Makanji thought that everyone was getting along splendidly. Still, she held her breath. Even though Sushi seemed to be on her best behaviour, Mrs Makanji wasn't prepared to trust her luck. Any moment now she expected her happiness-bubble to burst.

After dinner they sat talking again. Sushi had managed throughout dinner to avoid glancing at Mrs Vasant who was eating with such uninhibited relish. Once or twice she had caught her mother's eye and her mother had shaken her head unobtrusively to discourage any comment from Sushi. Dilip had intercepted the exchange. Embarrassed, he had glanced away.

Later, Indira, Sushi and Dilip went out onto the verandah. Dilip and Sushi were a bit awkward with each other at first.

"When is your husband coming back?" Dilip asked Indira.

"In about two weeks," Indira said.

Sushi studied Dilip. He wasn't too bad, she reflected. Of the four men, or "boys" her parents had introduced her to, Dilip was the least offensive, but . . . his mother was definitely a different story.

They spoke for a while. Dilip asked her about her work in London. She asked him about his work at Stanford. He was easy to talk to. She was genuinely beginning to like him and felt relaxed and comfortable in his company. There was something non-threatening about him and she listened with great interest as he described his life in California. Indira, feeling left out of their common experiences and anecdotes, went inside.

"It's crazy isn't it," Dilip said to Sushi. "I'm glad you're not taking any of this seriously."

Sushi grinned. "They're just buzzing with excitement now," she said.

"Each time I come for a visit, we go through the same routine. That's why I don't get back that often," he said.

"I know what you mean," Sushi chuckled, imagining how their parents would probably be interpreting this exchange she was having with Dilip out on the verandah.

They sat outside, perched on the wall, talking as though they had been friends for years. Mrs Makanji smiled, the brilliance of her smile spreading around the room until Mrs Vasant felt it too, and smiled in return. Things were certainly going much better than either of them had hoped for.

Eventually Dilip and his parents left. There was no firm commitment from either family to meet again, but there was hope. Lots of hope. It was there in the smiles as the two families said goodbye to each other; it was in the sparkling air and in Mrs Makanji's laughter which was so rich with undertones.

Mrs Makanji was anxious to find out what Sushi thought about Dilip. *She* thought he was perfect, but knowing her daughter she didn't dare ask, in case Sushi turned him down out of contrariness. So Mrs Makanji went to bed that night, bristling with questions and anxiety. She was so highly strung that Mr

Makanji had to sit up half the night, reassuring her.

"They were talking so much. Didn't you see?" Mr Makanji said.

"But darling, you don't know her as I do," Mrs Makanji said.

"Don't worry. She'll make up her mind."

"But when, Arun? When she's an old woman and no one will want to marry her?"

Mr Makanji laughed.

"If only she would be as easy to please as Indira," Mrs Makanji muttered.

"We have given her an education. We have taught her to think independently. Now we have to trust that she will make a good decision."

"If we had boys we might have had less problems," Mrs Makanji grumbled.

Mr Makanji smiled. He knew not to take her seriously.

"Look at Indira. I can see that something is wrong, but she is not telling me," Mrs Makanji continued.

"She will tell us when she is ready. Only then can we help her," Mr Makanji soothed. "For now we have to be satisfied and be thankful that we all have our good health."

In Sushi's room, Indira and Sushi were up, talking.

"He's not too bad, but I don't think I could take much of his mother!" Sushi said, laughing. "My God!" she cried, giving a mock shudder.

"She wasn't so bad. . . " Indira said.

"What!" Sushi cried. "I'd rather be dead. . . " she threw her hands up into the air with all the drama she could muster. Then she leaped onto the bed and bounced up and down with child-like exuberance.

"I'm surprised you're taking the meeting with Dilip so lightly." Indira was puzzled by her sister's lack of concern. She had expected her to be angry.

Sushi laughed. "He's very sweet and . . . he's also very gay."

"You're joking. Right?" Indira said.

Sushi shook her head. "No, I'm not."

"How do you know?"

"I have lots of gay friends in London."

"I can't believe it. Are you sure?"

"Of course, I'm sure. Why?"

"Well . . . Hindu boys. . . I mean. . . "

"Come off it, Indira. . . Why do you find it so hard to believe that a Hindu boy can be gay?"

"I don't know. I've just never known any."

Sushi smiled and shook her head in gentle reproach. "You're still very naive, you know."

Indira smiled. "I suppose so." She paused and met her sister's glance. "I'm going to miss you when you're gone," she said, suddenly serious again.

"If things here get really rough for you, come and spend some time with me," Sushi said, ". . . And bring Nita. You'll like Kevin. He's a lot of fun. And don't worry. We do have a spare bedroom." She reached for the light. "I'm going to miss you, too. Believe it or not, I'll probably miss Ma and Papa as well, but it's better to keep my distance from them. We get along much better that way."

Indira sighed and lay back. "God, I can't get him out of my mind," she said in the dark, the issue of Dilip and his being gay still troubling her.

"Who?"

"Dilip."

"Why?" Sushi asked.

"I can imagine what's it's going to be like when his parents find out."

Sushi was silent. She too, had been thinking about it.

Mrs Makanji sat up and turned on her light. "I can't sleep Arun. I think I'll go make myself some warm milk." She got up and went to the kitchen.

She warmed some milk in the microwave. She usually kept a small box of sleeping powder in the sideboard drawer. It was an ayurvedic remedy for insomnia and the only things that helped her through those awful nights when she couldn't get to sleep.

Mrs Makanji opened the drawer. Lying right on top was the picture of Sushi and Kevin in passionate embrace. She found her spare glasses in the other sideboard drawer and took the picture into the light. Stunned, she felt her knees weaken. Her hand flailed behind her for a chair and she sat down heavily. She studied the picture and then turned it over. On the back of the picture was the corny message—"To Sushi. My lips, my heart and all those important parts, love you forever! Kevin."

Her face was ashen.

"Sushi. Oh Sushi," she moaned, clasping her chest, writhing. "Such a curse!. . . Oh my God. . . Oh my God," she cried softly.

Sushi lay awake in the darkness, thinking about Dilip. It was going to be a shock to her parents when she told them the truth about him. She knew that somehow she was going to have to tell them about Kevin, too. But she wanted to ease into it, slowly. She wasn't quite sure how, yet. Sushi sighed wearily. She was too tired to deal with it now. There would be time enough tomorrow.

141

No Nation Woman

MEENA ALEXANDER

Why is it so hard to tell my story? Hard to think of the years I have lived as worthy of story. Is it because my life has been so torn up, and when set out in the heart's space makes nothing but bits and pieces? And when I have encountered others who have lived as I, a foolish pity in me, a cover of shyness in the face of the real, a cowardice even, has made me turn away from seeing the true lines of story I might tell. There were times when it seemed to me blameworthy, shameful even, that I made the choice to come here with a man, in the hope of personal happiness.

As for my earliest departure from India there was nothing in it that could make the stuff of epic. After all I did not leave my motherland because of terror, or political repression. I was not torn away from my ancestral home through fear or armed militants from the RSS. I did not come from a shtetl, forced out a worldless child by marauding Cossacks.

On the brink of turning five I left with my mother on a ship, left behind the radiant love of my grandparental home, quite simply because my father got a job he wanted to take, for a few years, far away, in another country. A country in North America across an ocean and a sea.

Over the fault lines of my life I have unfurled a resolute picture, a flag that fluttered into a sheet and grew and grew, a simple shining topography. A large house with a red tiled roof and two courtyards, one in which the passion fruit vine spreads its delicate tentacles by the kitchen window, the other in which the mulberry bush my grandmother planted years before my birth stubbornly thrusts its root into the soil and refuses to die. A house with a garden, a street running by it, a little dusty in the dry season with the water buffaloes, a bridge, a white-painted church.

But that shining picture has tormented me. Faced with it, my real life has dwindled and diminished. And my words have recoiled back into a vacant space in the mind, a place of waste, dingy detritus of a life uncared for, no images to offer it hospitality. And I ask myself, Am I a creature with no home, no nation? And if so, what kind of new genus could I possibly be?

And sometimes I have puzzled it out: if I were a man, I might have turned myself into something large and heroic, a creature of quest and adventure, a visionary with power in his grasp. Instead, as a woman, the best I can be is something small and stubborn, delicate perhaps at the best of times, but irrefutably persistent. After all, when has my life gone according to plan? It seems a poor thing to say, but the best I have learnt has had to do with unlearning the fixed positionings I was taught, trusting my own nose, diving into the waves.

For the houses and places have multiplied under my nose, with dizzying pace, till the possibility of recall has been much like thrusting a hand under the floorboards and discovering a stinking corpse. Something so mutilated that one no longer knows whether it's a beaver or a muskrat or a human creature stumpy and ingrown, dead of its own needs.

Houses shatter and fall in me. Shards of them, bits and pieces of them, a room with wall all askew, a kitchen with the side door blown off so the sun shines in, a bit of a threshold, part of a high latticed window, teak steps as high as a grown man, bits of sand and gravel someone's foot brought in, thumbprints on a table still moist with river water.

When I try to look back at my life, there's no backness to it. It's all around, a moistness like sweet well water, the houses crumbled up inside. How many houses have there been? When I try to count, it sears me: a hot dry wind that destroys generations. Makes history a mad, mad joke. Let me try to count it out in all the languages I know even if I sound like a three-year-old. Numbers tumble in the spray of sound: Aune, runde, mune, nale. Eak, do, theen, char. One, two, three, four. Wahid, ithineen, thalatha, arba. Un, deux, trois, quatre. I have used all my languages, I have only got as far as four. But there were more, many more houses. Were there four times four? More than that too. The forest of numbers makes no sense.

The cloth turns into a great sheet of paper, but the paper is stained, uneven, fit to shred with the pressure exerted on it. The houses grow tipsy.

Why not keep it close to home. Play it close to the chest, lay it out. Can I lay it out? Learn from the housewife who smoothes out the damask cloth, hiding the stain where the fish curry splashed, where turmeric tainted the shining fibres. Quick, set an empty vase over the spot. Move the dishes over a little to the right. Grab the cloth back when a grubby hand from under the table drags it and the plates wobble.

Houses to be born in, houses to die in, houses to make love in, with wet sticky sheets, houses with the pallor of a dove's wings, houses fragrant as cloves and cinnamon ground together. Ah, the thickness of this tongue that will not let me be, will not let me lay it out saying: I was born here, I lived here, I did this, I did that, saying it all out in the way that people do, or like to try. Houses in Allahabad, in Pune, then southwards, through the Nilgiris and the curved rock face of the Palghat Pass, the ancestral houses in Tiruvella and Kozencheri—houses of blood and bone, where I have lived and died in countless lives before mine. In an old steamer painted white, westwards over the Indian Ocean, through Port Sudan with the waters stained maroon by hidden corals, by train through the desert till we reach the houses in Hai-el-Matar in the town of Khartoum.

Off and on I lived there for thirteen years, on and off, by the meeting of waters, the sluggish White Nile swelling the barks of acacia trees, and the fiercer water of the Blue where whirlpools drew in the unsuspecting swimmer. There was gunfire there, and tear gas in the market place. I carried the acid scent with me over the Atlantic. I am eighteen now, shivering in my thin clothes as I glimpse the waters under the airplane etched into steely grey tongues.

I live in a tall house on Oxford Street in the city of Nottingham, Lawrence country. I have a dormer window, I paint, love riotously, write a thesis on memory. It drives me mad writing that thesis, all about reclaiming time and crap like that while the mind cuts loose from the body till it roams, circling empty space. Small spells in Galway, in Amsterdam, in Chinon where the Loire pours through rocks. At Oxford Circus, in Nottingham, I lean out of the window. Where is the blood hidden here? In the cherry trees, in the dark leaves that hide the clusters of fruit, in the bronze air above the coal pits.

I am I, I cry, returning through the Palghat Pass again not far from the Kerala coast, the rock face harder now, echoes my cries. I become mute. I roll myself in reams of paper and wait in the dry houses of Pune and Delhi and Hyderabad.

I am all shit and paper now. I have no eyes, no face. There, there. I stop myself. I can't stand it. This housekeeping exercise isn't getting anywhere. What to do with the rest of life? With the houses in America, the rooms, the parquet floors, the fireplaces in Minneapolis, the little rush basket for wastepaper I set on fire with a smouldering cigarette? What to do with the trucks that rumbled by under the windows at 242nd Street and Broadway in the great city of Manhattan, where the air is never clean? Trucks rolling by Poe Cottage in the Bronx where old Edgar Poe moved into the Bronx for the cleaner air. Now the air is filthier than where he was, the bars burnt out, the streets covered with potholes. They managed to set his little cottage on a piece of parkland, put chain fences around it, and install a poor lecturer from City College who gives visitors a little speech on electricity, how Poe was struck, what lightning did to him.

But what is Poe to me? I have not been to his tombeau. What do I know of ravens and women called Annabelle Lee? What does he know of me, I might ask? My house is split through, a fault in the ground where it stands. They're auctioning my soul where they auction the fish, catfish, swordfish scooped from the Arabian sea, ten thousand miles from Poe's cottage, by the old wharf, by the paddy beds on the Tiruvella-Kozencheri road. Thinking of the road calms me down. It runs between the two houses that have always been there for me, the Tiruvella and the Kozencheri houses, different as idli from dosa, plum pudding from peach pie, but akin nonetheless, with tiled roofs and cool floors and windows cut in teak and polished brass, no glass there. I am at home on the road that bumps a little as it passes the old wharf where at dawn the fishermen crowd, laying out their wares, crying out the prices of the catfish and swordfish and shrimps, all curled up on the granite slabs of Kerala.

So let me try again, let me lay it out. Laying it all out so that the housewife in me—I do that now, another skein in the tight ball—can step back in delight. Admire the order—plates, cups laid out in mass array, jug of water, orchids in the silver vessel—savour it before the knock at the door, the clip-clop of footsteps.

For a brief minute, there is no sign of the grubby little hand under the table, hunger under the floor, fault in the earth where my house stands, cries on the street. Here, here: take, eat, take your pleasure in these well-washed plates, these bowls of late orchids with petals as thick as fruit flesh, the colour of rare plums.

See, see my lover's lips. Quick, smooth the blouse down, tuck in the stray hair at the nape, at the cheek before he enters. Before he speaks words to me, words that in the inner chambers of my ear, resound.

O tympanum, most delicate soul. Who cries? Is it he or I?
Or she, listening perpetually?

I do not see her but she who once listened at the keyhole shrinks back against the outside wall as I enter the white room. Once I am in the white room we become one, fusing as water and sky in a child's eye as she gazes down into a pool from a great height, or even as fire and the wood it consumes on a funeral pyre become one, one and the same. Then we split again into two. She becomes me, I she. All around us, houses shatter and fall, shards of them, bits and pieces of them. Nothing sticks back together again, nothing holds in innumerable broken houses.

Inside the white room she picks up plums, piles them on a dish with markings of fish and rare fowl, a dish made of china so delicate, the painterly abstractions in indigo, the curve of the lower covert of the fowl's wing, the jut of the fin, cast into relief a pallor in the invisible bone no eye could have discerned without desire moving there, shaping, refining, burning up substances.

"What is desire?" she asks him.

"It is what I have."

"But isn't that instinct?"

"No, instinct is what they tell you you have."

She does not follow him. She does not glance at the door. Nor reflect on the sunlight from the street darting off a white wall of the room.

Outside the grill work of the tiny balcony where the window box stands empty, its soil dry, puffing a little in scabs as a slight wind blew, is the street. She knows the street is there, the street with its stench of dropped cabbages, and bits of rabbit fur from the nearby market, and radishes packed in immaculate heaps, their tails whisked up under the leaves.

It was in the street she heard the cries from the man from Eritrea who was brought in on refugee papers a month ago. He spent four years in the squalor of refugee camps in Khartoum. The Blue Nile, heat glinting off its brassy hood of water, burnt his eyelids raw. The White Nile by Sunt Forest, the acacia branches scratched like a mound of hair over the blistering sky, was no help at all. The water was all muddy. The mud made his ankles sore. Once or twice, wandering by the water, he tried to stuff half-dried acacia leaves down his throat, and gulp some water, but started to choke.

In another country, in a street just a stone's throw from the market he sees the sun on the metal railings of the subway stop. Water from a burst hydrant splatters his swollen feet. He walks to the subway stop. Holding onto the railings he starts to weep.

She saw the man in cast-off clothing, his whole body shaking. She could not make out his words. His cries seemed to be torn from inside him, as if someone had stuck fingers down the delicate passage of the throat and plucked the tender flesh of the sides, made music with that frail thing by stringing it on an oudh and playing.

When Hamza El Din plays the oudh the waters of Nubia burn as if angels had descended, casting golden crowns into the waves. Can Hamza El Din make sense of this poor man weeping? Or is the mind of the great musician set on the rhythms of a young lad sitting atop a waterwheel, rubbing sand into the shadow made by his knee, perfectly happy? A child who knows nothing of angels or djinns, who has learnt not to fear the sun?

She does not ask herself such questions. She is in the room now, not on the street. She composes herself, runs her hands lightly over her hair. Delicately, using forefinger and thumb she picks up plums, piles them on a dish with markings of rare fish and fowl. She stops a moment. Where did this room come from, with the white walls and the sunlight and the street below? Just where is she? In which land, which town, which turning of what street? She lays her fingers on the globes of mauve and vermilion tinged with green where the ripening stopped.

She recalls the vein in his forehead. It beat as he brushed his lips to her wrist, her throat. His lips were round, ivory brushed with red, filled with heat, an "O" made by the inmost circle of the oudh. When he kissed her throat she heard the breath in his chest, in his lungs. He examined the knuckles of her right hand. He kissed her there on the slight soreness above the knuckle of the index finger. Perhaps she will need to use the woollen gloves again, the red ones with the finger tips torn off. Her knuckles hurt with writing.

Everything hurts with writing but everything works with it too. She conjures up forms, figurations of desire. To be in any form, what is it, she wonders. She runs her fingers over and over on the whorls of a plum where the fruit flesh dips and the rough stalk starts.

That night she cannot sleep. Her head with the mess of black hair sinks into the pillow and she forgets where she is. Something whispers in her that the room was in another country, the white room with the grille work and the sunlight off the walls. Who was he, the man who came to her in the white room? What was his name? Where was he born? Who was his mother? How did she die? The questions crowd in.

She sees the man as a baby, just about a year old, seated upright on a woman's knee. Was it a dream that not so long ago, as they sat side by side on a roadside bench under the shade of a green tree he opened up a square of paper to show her a picture? His infant self on his mother's knee. A xerox of a photograph that itself was reproduced from a book. Who wrote the book? Who took the photo of this exquisite madonna and child?

The child in the photo was wary though, staring at the camera, frowning a little. His little feet were bare, the toes flexed. The mother's left hand was held firmly over the infant's foot, as if to stop it from kicking out as infants are apt to do. How lovely she was, with her two long black plaits and her downcast gaze, the embroidered robe she wore covering her knees and feet, her nose and chin perfectly aligned. She had large eyes, one could tell that even though her gaze was cast down at the child. The jewels on her forehead, pearls, rubies made into an intricate triangular shape, the shadow of the earrings on her ears were all visible. How still they sat, mother and child, a darkness visible, the figuration of desire in a perpetual elsewhere, another country. Where did they begin, the mother and child? Why does she dream this dream?

Back and back, I keep slipping back to the bed where she gave birth to me. Slipping back as if she were a hole in me, a gash where time started. Then suddenly it's all blurred, like a winter morning in February, the month in which I was born and I feel the light wind that blows off the Hudson, I feel the light wind that blows off the twin rivers, the Ganga and the Yamuna scraping the surface of water at the invisible line where the rivers meet. The wind gathers force, puffs out the curtains, awakening amma. She lies there utterly spent. She has just given birth to me in Allahabad, in the northern state of Uttar Pradesh in India in a room, a hospital, in a city, in a dry wintery plain to which I have never returned.

A beginning? Surely that is where the difficulty lies. The never-returning bit. What to do with a beginning to which you will never return? Conceive of a life, the story of a life in which the "I" keeps moving away from a womb, room, house verandah, balcony, street, city, province, nation, never returning. The "i" reduced in all her travels to the sheerest dot, black ink on a crumpled sheet, spilt menstrual blood, a spurt of semen, dribble of milk.

Consider the kurianna, dusty Kerala mole. She digs her head in, burrows into the soil. Microscopic legs toss up the dirt in a perfect circle. If a child were to blow on the dirt, lips very close to the soil, she could make the hind quarters of the tiny elephant of earth reappear. *Kuriaana* in Malayalam, my mother tongue, means hole elephant. *Kuri* is hole of pit; *aana* is elephant. The thing is so minute that to name it after lordly creatures that weigh a ton or two, seems the perfect pitch of tone. Ever so slightly askew as things turn beyond the range of eyesight.

Saying which I seem to feel a slight scrape on silk, a sliver of ivory as the craftsman with his monocle screwed on just right carves the outline of a minuscule elephant, trunk and all, out of the wafer-thin piece of ivory. The elephant he carves is half the size of a kurianna. No, a quarter of its size, one eighth surely. He straightens his back, then leans forward so he can reach the wooden bench without straining. He cuts one, two, three, four, ten tiny elephants and fits them into a manjadi kuru.

A manjadi kuru is a brilliant crimson nut, about half a centimetre in diameter. It grows on a green tree. There is a manjadi tree in front of my mother's house in Kurial. All I remember of the tree is that in spite of the dark gloss of leaf, and the profusion of red seeds that swell up against the blue air, the tree seems an austere thing. Nothing lush about it, or over-blown. The branches are akin to the dark brown of skin, raised as elbows might be, or wrists arced in a dancer's pose. Gazing at the tree, I sense a difficulty in the lift of those branches, a tension in how the joints are knotted under green leaf cover.

The uses to which such a jewel of a seed can be put still amazes me. The steps are simple. Cut out a tiny hole at the top, hollow the seed by scraping out the innards and fill it with miniature elephants all cut from a sliver of ivory. Pack in one, two, ten, twenty, thirty of these tiny elephants, each so light an infant's puff of breath would whisk it away. Then carve a little lid in ivory that fits into the eye-shaped hole. Insert the lid, and the artifact is complete.

As a child I loved to visit the handicrafts shop in Trivandrum and watch as the salesman laid out the tiny manjadi kuru elephants onto a piece of black velvet. I was allowed to buy three, four, sometimes even five of the manjadi kuru with elephants inside, to give to my friends in Khartoum. I recall one particular plane ride, the metal body we were travelling in at such high speed twirling as a cut blossom might in the monsoon winds that churned up a scary, rhythmic turbulence. All around in the thunder storm was darkness, slashes of light. Several times an electric current jagged at the window next to where I sat.

Amma in her dark red sari muttered prayers under her breath. "O Jesu Christu have mercy on us all, O Lamb of God." Appa's knuckles were almost black with the pressure he exerted on them, clenched over the seat. He was a meteorologist and spent much of his working hours predicting the courses of storms and mad currents of wind. As the seat dropped under me I sensed the coolness of the tiny seeds in my pocket. I imagined the darkness inside each seed, elephants prancing in their ivory skins, each snorting, racing in the minute cavity it was placed in. Somehow, it did not matter so very much that the plane was veering sharply to the left, then the right, like a mad dog with its head cut off. The delicate zigzag of the elephant's tail I had glimpsed earlier that day, when I laid the ten creatures end to end on Ilya's muslin handkerchief, filled my thoughts. As the metal capsule pitched from side to side, threatening to unseat us all, collapse inside and outside, even in my fear I felt a poise, a balance in extremity that I am hard put to explain, even to myself. It is a condition that has returned to me in the act of writing poetry, making words to fit the music in my head. I have learnt to recognize it. Now I recall how the cloud bank outside the plane window had the colour of those imagined elephants. A luminous milky thing, a session of opals, a tablet of pale bone.

In my bedroom in Khartoum, I tucked the manjadi kuru at the bottom of my drawer full of underclothes. I ran my fingers over the shiny surfaces of the seeds and watched eagerly as the elephants spilt out. Gradually, in the heat of Khartoum—or perhaps this would have happened anywhere with time, in Nottingham, in Minneapolis, even in Nome, Alaska—the seeds grew darker. Turned the colour of dried blood. And the brilliant white elephants yellowed a little.

Perhaps it wasn't the heat. Perhaps it was time, its tail snapping. Nowadays it is hard to find those manjadi kuru elephants. Who can make a living in today's world carving minute ivory elephants to fit into a bright red seed?

The manjadi tree in front of the Kurial house is no longer there. The land has been sold in parcels and the great house with mosaic floors and teak ceilings has been turned into a factory where they process and refine shiny strips of what looks like cellophane but is not. An expensive material imported from Japan, stored in the huge hangars at the back of the house —the original cowsheds—and processed in some fashion and then shipped out to Italy and France. The shiny stuff, I was shown bales of it, wrapped up in knobbly white paper, is immensely expensive and is used for electronic purposes.

A century ago when the Dutch windows were thrown open, standing in the mosaic-tiled drawing room one could see the great manjadi tree, and a little to its left a gnarled mulberry that even my grandmother saw as a small girl. I imagine the reddish, tangy fruit curled up as if the silk worms were still there, feasting inside the fruit flesh. There were roses too, all prickly and hot, and the spreading elegance of the lime trees. Now the four-part windows have been removed and the windows are all glassed in. The house needs airconditioning, since foreign visitors from France and Italy must be made to feel comfortable in the tropical heat of Kerala. With load shedding, quite frequent now with electricity in short supply, the airconditioning splutters and gasps. The music in the cinema theatre just down the road, where the large trucks park, stops, and in the sudden silence we hear the cries of dogs, buffaloes, elephants, and small children playing in the dirt.

The cottage at the side where my grandmother's brother Abraham brought back his English wife Hermione in the second decade of the century is rarely unlocked. The cottage as it is called, a little bungalow really, in the British colonial style with pillars and long open verandah, was built specially for the new couple. After all, how could an English daughter-in-law be expected to share in the communal living of the large house, with the prayers, the cooking, the early morning whispering and laughter? They lived there for seven long years before moving to Madras. I wonder what those years were like for them. All I know of Aunty Helen, as she was known, is from amma and from old photo albums. An immense lady with her hair combed back in the fashion of the day, she used to have a special armchair set up for her in Spencer's in Madras, next to the sweet counter, and from her seat she would dispense toffees and barfis and liquorice sticks to all the little children she knew. So the scent of sweets clung to my mother's memory of her English relative, a lady originally from the flats of Norfolk who made her way into the hearts of her Suriani in-laws through the exquisite duck-with-orange recipes she brought tucked into her bodice. The cottage where she lived with her new husband is now used to store the account books of Japanese transactions and of sales to France and Italy, which are slipping a little. This was explained to us by the new order, an elegant, efficient woman who showed us around.

She is Mariamma the sister-in-law of amma's cousin Roshni. In her late forties, dressed in an immaculate starched sari, hair drawn back in a neat bun, her one overt concession to her wealth are the diamond studs in her ears. Having raised her children, she told me, she felt she needed a career and found herself one, managing the import-export business that was being run from the Kurial house. The business was owned in part by her husband who wanted to diversify from cardamom estates. Mariamma's husband had inherited large holdings from his own father who had been able to increase them by shrewd speculation and sales of his own patrimony, mainly in paddy fields and rubber-growing properties. Mariamma is courteous to me. She knows that my grandmother and my mother grew up here. I explain to her that I spent long childhood days playing in the back courtyard of the old house, chasing the turkeys and my great-aunt's pet pekinese dogs, entangling myself in the long curtains that hung in the back wings of the house to read Zola's *Nanna* which one of my uncles had brought back with him from Bombay. I wonder what she thinks of me, married to a foreigner, living in North America. But she is a contemporary woman, she has travelled not just to Tokyo and Hong Kong, but also to Rome and Florence, Paris and Dijon, making little trips for business purposes and to see the world elsewhere.

Outside the old ancestral house the dust rises. It's the dry season and behind the hen coop brambles grow. There are no hens now, no turkeys, only crows and the odd myena circling round the well which is boarded over with a neat wooden lid. Metal pipes run from the boards, into the house, and further back into the water warehouse for the cooling system. The temperature must be controlled lest the valuable electronic sheets perish. Around the well, all around the warehouse, grows wild grass, the kind with ivory-coloured seeds. Seeds so sticky that they cling to your sari or trousers, even latch onto your legs like little burrs. A wild persistent grass.

The same grass grows in Kayamkulam, by the waters of Ashtamudi Lake where the train toppled, where young girls dressed in white sing an elegy for corpses unshriven, swarming in water. Two years ago today the train from Bangalore crashed here. No one knows if it was the bridge that caved in or if the driver, exhausted by the night journey, lost control. The villagers near the water were brave. They leapt in, rescuing those they could. When they emerged, their mouths and eyes were covered with the filthy water. One man well past middle age stooped, eyes shut, into the water. The body he touched, the body he lifted out, was that of his own son. At first he did not understand. Then he shuddered, touching dry land. On the wild grass he laid down his precious burden. Then he laid himself down, stretching out his old man's body, and tried to stop breathing.

The sky was very clear and blue the day of his son's death and there were water lilies by the edge of the water, utterly untouched by the metal carriages, and human flesh and blood in the lake. The water lilies were the colour of sulphur.

The old man shut his eyes. He covered his nose and mouth with his hands but felt the breath explode out. Next to him lay the waterlogged body of his son. With a hand, he touched the tangled hair. There was a crashing sound in the sky, he heard it in his innermost ear. He wondered if he was dead already, if he was holding his infant son in his arms again, in the darkness of a small hut, in the very hour of the child's birth.

When I was a child, when it came time to leave Tiruvella and return to Khartoum, I used to try and stop my breath—pinch my nostrils, tamp up my mouth with a fist. But I could never manage it for very long and as my head filled with blood, my breath burst outwards. Using that breath I raced to my hiding place down by the railway line where pink stalks of tapioca grew higher than a six-year-old child. Like a kurianna, I crouched, bottom up, trying to bury my face in the soil. The taste of black earth was on my tongue, the sharp scent of tapioca root, raw, hidden under my shut eyes. But even then I needed to go on breathing. I tried to be careful not to snort in dirt with the breath that kept coming and going, going and coming.

Tale-telling I think is like breathing. If you try to hold your breath it explodes outwards. Sometimes in my effort to stop I would think of what it would be like to turn into a stone or a rock in the front garden in Tiruvella. But what would that solve? If I were a stone, amma could so easily pick me up—and surely she would, surely she would come crying into her father's garden, under stalks of jasmine and mulberry, or stand under the manjadi tree in wild grass crying, where is my child, my first child, my Meena—surely she would come and catching sight of my half-buried form, a two-inch stone with streaks of red, just like the glinting one I had picked up near the quarry, she would grab hold of me, tuck me into her black handbag, the one appa bought her from Beirut, and make off with me in great haste, leaping into a metal body that travelled at great speed, over crossroads, boundaries of nations, oceans, cutting from garden to garden, house to house, state to state, never stopping, never resting, my stony self bound always in a metallic thing with wheels, wings or steam puffing as it coasted over earth, sky or water. And so I think of what it would have been like to begin, before motion was, before the first hiccupping breath, before the first sky, the dry Gangetic plain.

153

But I seem to have travelled always. After all Allahabad where I was born is eight hundred miles north of Tiruvella where I come from. Tiruvella is in the state of Kerala, Allahabad is in Uttar Pradesh. Allahabad is colder. There people eat wheat, wear kurta pyjamas and speak Hindi. The Ganga and the Yamuna flow there. Allahabad has real winters, dead cold, about thirty degrees though it never snows. Tiruvella on the other hand has seventy-degree winters. That's when the winter monsoon creeps in and those who can afford it huddle up in blankets. Old grandfathers cover up their nostrils and ears in wool and sit very straight in their rattan chairs to stare out over the wet gardens, the mist, the pepper vines clustering on the fruit trees.

Allahabad however is in the same country: the Republic of India. You need another language, other clothes to manage in the winter, or at least coverings for your Kerala cottons, but you don't need a passport and if a stranger asks, you can always point out that you come from a village, the distance of a crow's flight from Kanyakumari and it works, that geography, that shining water that binds in the land mass of India. Or at least you hope it works as you sit sipping chai in the dusty air, in a chai shop by the university where your old friend, the poet teaches. Does he have an office with white painted walls? What does he search out in the library? Elizabeth Bishop? Remember how in those days in Hyderabad, he read you out the poems of Elizabeth Bishop? You had never heard of her. He read out "Questions in Travelling" in a wonderful clear voice. The austerity of her lines, the etch as of old copper cut to a precise curve, made for a great delight. Later you two drank tea together in a chaishop much like this. You and he. He had just returned from Iowa, somewhere in the wheat fields of the American midwest and told you stories of snow and pool tables and poets with long hair and pink cheeks, dead drunk over the wheels of their automobiles.

Circum the Gesture

YASMIN LADHA

Muhammad is the Messenger of God, and those who are with him are hard against the unbelievers, merciful one to another. Thou seest them bowing, prostrating, seeking bounty from God and good pleasure. Their mark is on their faces, the trace of prostration. That is their likeness in the Torah, and their likeness in the Gospel: as a seed that puts forth its shoot, and strengthens it and it grows stout and rises straight upon its stalk, pleasing the sowers, that through them He may enrage the unbelievers. (Arthur J Arberry, trans. "Victory," *The Koran* (Oxford, 1983), p. 535.)

Baba, for me, you do not come first today, on this flight from Delhi to Cochin. Though at home, I have been well taught that *Baba* comes before anything. To always steer with prefix, "Only if *Baba* wills," on my lips. But today, flying to the south, to Cochin, from Delhi, almost leaving India, I would only meet strangers and I don't even speak Malayalam. This my thought as we land in Cochin, but when I raise my head after the "Fasten..." sign has been switched off, a man rises and rests his hands below his chest, impervious to the jostle of arms stretching inside coats or the smack-smack of the overhead cabins. *Baba,* in front of my seat, I see a knot of familiar quiescent hands resting below the chest, right in the

155

aisle! This gesture of countryside
hands looks beautiful then: vulnerable yet nourished: figs, yo-
gurt, fowl and grapes. The man's
shoulders spread wideout, solid,
nothing short of a sower's shoulders but right at the edge, they
droop (almost to soggy corners)
pouring arrogance to the floor.
Heart in this world and heart in
prayer is Muslim way. La Balance
in Islam.

(Cochin, September, 1992)

My Allah, why do You roar in the Book? Who-whom to explain my *Baba*'s
roar is instantly cool? Loud hot, then right away, cool. Even that my *Baba* is
womanly. Watch *Baba* beckon-ing, wash-ing, spill-ing, chor-ing like a
woman's fingers. A woman's fingers-ing constantly in aerobic rhythm:
skillet/iron/rest/pump. Now lifting a pot of dal on a winter stove (her ginger
root warm as toddy), then looping thread around a button until it is stiff:
tuck-and-a-snap! Clothes in wash, and

    much later
    at the kitchen table, woman,
    she bends over assignments
    a familiar burn right here
    between her shoulder blades
    waft of Bounce trailing up (curtains in dryer).

Like a woman's chores, *Baba*-ings forever: beckoning, washing, spilling. It
odd hours, I act up, break discipline of prayer five times a day and dinner punctua
At odd hours, I am starved for prayer and will not let such love to climb out o
mosque dome to the sleepy, washed and waiting, just at dawn. I mulch *azan*-pr
in bread or push it inside my soap crusted navel.

    I, *Baba*'s jugular vein
    I, *Baba*'s *jago*-roused vein
    I, *Baba*'s *jugnu*-firefly pretty
    I, *Baba*'s Jamun Purple fruit favourite
    I, *Baba*'s *Juma*-Friday moon
Baba whispers in my ear sweet j-j-j, jelly bean treats

jago   jugnu   Juma
rise   firefly   Friday

out of the earshot of the *mullah*/Khomeini/terse *mujahideen* and then *Baba*
is off to brandishing swords with the Torah-keepers and Christians, "Come
on you infidel!"

Sometimes, I overstay at the Plaza Cinema, then I am in for it with *Baba*,
when I hang around with Roberta outside the cinema. Unexpectedly, I see
her after the seven p.m. show. "Roberta!" and we are off arm-in-arm to the
Higher Ground Cafe. She and I (like women before us) chuck out barrister-
male-din of

"When women plaits meet, they break a verandah."
Translated:

Women are destroyers of dwellings, warpish gossipers.

Sometimes men sulk: They sulk and say:

"That only flies enter a dirty mouth."

Who is a dirty mouth? Never a man, always a woman who talk-talks,
ignoring man-the-monitor, be it husband, brother or *mullah*.

Men even threaten to chop off our tongues. But we chuck out the
barrister-male-din, anyway. Women brouhaha is always hymen closed to
men, even *Baba*.

When I head to Higher Ground opposite the Cinema, at home, there is a
raucous at the dinner table. But I am unhungry after tucking away layers of
azan-prayer (today, strudel layers before pre-rosy dawn). And when I am
ordered out of prayer once a month by tyrant *Baba* and His lot, that is when
I crave *azan*-prayer, oyster oily, slippery as warm clot. Indeed, I even report
on vigilant *fajr* time: precisely after dawn and before sunrise.

Outside Higher Ground, *Baba*'s car makes zoinky noises because "Why
is daughter not at home?" The *cafe au lait* drinkers being on higher ground
have a great seat and stare at the ethnic spectacle below. *Baba* and I   lend
to Kensington's folksy globe just like Dan Jenkins's green and red castles
opposite the Plaza, just like the two-storey decor of naive-abroad Harry's
Africa (*lot-ta* Zebras and ice-creams). All on the Kensington strip, carrier
of international papers, even *The Cochin Malabar News*.

But there is raucous at the dinner table, tonight. Who-whom to explain
that *Baba*'s musket sound is really carnival excess? "So you are an
apologist?" the media nutshells my dilemma. Go away, I am conversing
with my blustery father. Who-whom to explain that

mullahs have beefed up Allah.

Saudi eyes auction women.

And when *Baba* turns chauvinistic, He fits me into male hands, who in turn, banish me to the couch when I talk back:

I, Muslim woman
live in a mirror house
which does not break
instead
adheres to images
(as is business of mirrors)
fickle images of woman nature.
Spill on-and-on
about Prophet and women's charter of rights
in Mecca-Medina century.
The Prophet has passed away
my mirror house still endures
iron tough
as museum chastity belt.

In Urdu, to conjure up mirrors is to lose one's senses. Who has gone potty, *Baba?* Rabbits breed a barrage and mirrors are multiplied on women by the *mullah*-clan. In Arabic, she is *fitna*, one name for chaos and beauty. In Urdu, she is *rundi*, whore. She is *rundi*, widow. Only mother is woman and heaven is at a mother's feet the Prophet said. Contemporary *mujahideens* throw acid on purdah-naked woman. Then *Baba*, I want to denounce you thrice as is the solemn pronouncement in our Book

I divorce you once
I divorce you twice
I divorce you thrice

but I cannot discard like male, instead I, Muslim woman, follow my own cadence. It is true, so true

when Rushdie Babu comes home
I will knead flour with flying fingers.

My *Baba* has a girthy forehead. He is my jugular vein. I have mated with a new soil (many label it, this intercourse, immigration). My mate does not have a clue of *Baba*'s girth, or *Baba*'s revulsion to pig flesh, or that His Prophet was partial to perfume. Dominant in my new domicile is the media-jati caste and I cross the North American expanse shielding *Baba*'s forehead. If I am permitted to circum His forehead, I will matt my new soil in stories chubby as collarbones, that my *Baba* is not *mullah* blind but salt warm like the story mother tells me of her three sisters on her forehead, ''This is your Malek *Didi*, This is your Zarin *Didi*, this is your Dolly *Didi*.''

I caress my aunts on mother's forehead, two light and a dark mark. Never ask her which mark, who? Never matters. My *Didis*, a huge mass watch my eyes grow heavy. *Baba's* forehead this girthy. (*Baba-O-Baba*, when You of the girthy forehead advertise virgin-*houri* treats in heaven, it is so kith!) Let me shield Your woman forehead from the spicy eye of the media. (*Baba*, them media-caste are still locked in the entertainment of polygamy. Still holds saucer-eyed magic for them.) My gluttony with You, of mulching *azan*-prayer on bread, sometimes push it inside my soap-crusted navel who-who would understand?

Ooi Baba, come back! How *churro*-sure you are that you have won your daughter back! But I speak the language of rebellion underneath. I don't speak to you as a woman. What's the point? "Pah!" probably your response, *Baba*, and would shove me aside for Turkish coffee with the *mullahs*. But as daughter, I heat your heart, and I do what my *Didis* and Grandma*ji* have done before me, heat the heart of the matter in the process, come to the core this way and that, giving You time to warm up to woman-nosh. *Baba*, "nosh" out of "nourishment." A woman nourishes a word, learning its heart.

When I disobey You and the *mullah-jati*, then I am discarded as the first and second ugly sisters in a fairy tale because I refute woman-ban and take over male space/public space reserved for male. But my name is also *Niyyat*-sincere. Third and last daughter. I, *Niyyat*, create, errand, keep and nourish in relation to *Baba*, sister, brother, buddy, *Didi*, husband. *Relational to* is a woman-organ. Ask any *Niyyat*, ask any woman. Only this organ is without physical space, unlike breast and womb. (To her give her a physical geography, I name her in italics.)

Oof Baba, open the door this instant! Don't you know it is illegal to brandish sword in public! You are lending to C-grade pulp of another unshaven actor to play a Muslim terrorist, accomplishing a job of shoulder shrugs and Omar Sheriff accent.

To be a sower is to be Lakshmi benevolent. (*Baba* cringes because I am hued by the goddess.) Lotus Lakshmi who tolerates, lets others before her, be it fortune wooers who won't let her take a breath and mend. Or be it her Lord Vishnu, most polite and civilized of all gods, but husband-typical, he consumes all limelight, the goddess walks a few steps behind. Lakshmi's *Relational to,* most sincere. (When I circumambulate the Sacred Basil in my courtyard, I don't think of Lakshmi as Lotus-venus, but Basil-Lakshmi whose elbows are crusty tired. I lavish all water on her).

The man in the aisle is Lakshmi-sincere, and even, and even, old-fashioned chivalry prevails in his courtesy, but I have banned "gallant" and "chivalry" from woman language. For no matter how spread the chivalrous cloaks, woman crosses small. But neither do I want to discard his traits unequivocally as to lobotomize him of all manly celebration. So I embrace the man in Urdu *"adab"* ارب courtesy. Courtesy that is homey and palatial gallant. For me the shape of *adab* drips warm in my ear—let me in, I am home.

Grandmother had a fountain pen she dips in warm medicine ink (that's what she calls it)—"In the name of Allah, the most beneficent, the most merciful," and plotch! in goes the fluid in my ear. Warm, at the same time familiarly foreign. Plotch! My shoulders clench as collar bones angle outwards. Delicious. Neck in Grandmother's settled hands. *Baba,* You, on my jugular vein, even closer.

I *Baba's jugnu* - firefly pretty
I *Baba's Juma* - Friday moon

Soon I am asleep, all earache gone. There are even colours in this gesture of adab ارب :
    Mendicant ochre/ghat/basil
    But also formality of tribunal turquoise.
Good things in life, like You say, *Baba.*
    prostrate / pleasure
    homey / courtly
    inside / out
    Muslim / Allah
This is *La Balance* in Islam. Today I want to forget
    Sheikh from Gulf heaves on scrawny Bombay women
    rupees, rupees, rupaiya!
and to celebrate (salut) this *adab*-courtesy of a Muslim traveller, be it Bulgaria, Cochin or Calgary, this gesture of right hand over left wrist in rest-wait.

In the aisle on this plane, I play a child's game: I spy the Muslim man's four fingers and a thumb peep . . . at them, at the spaces between his gallant fingers. His thumb lax as a basking roof. This time, I am not afraid of Muslim male legs (in my imagination, they are even pressed together, not like the Arab sprawl in five star hotels). This time, as the Muslim man makes room for others to pass in the aisle, "Allah willing, my turn too." (Plotch! I hear him speak in my ear.) Elsewhere (let me forget)

The Arab with fierce hair admits
he thrust the bomb
in the bag
of his blonde girlfriend, pregnant.
The broadcaster's eyes turn enormous.
Back in Calgary, I can't stop circumambulating the gesture. I phone up
friends.

—"Sadru, you know why we stand this way?"
—"Your Grandfather, too!"
—"My Grandfather stepped out of the bathroom with his hands
folded!"
—"But isn't it a form of hierarchial respect? The hand maid presses her
eyes to the floor in front of her *Begum*-mistress."
—"On *Unsolved Mysteries*, yes, yes, that same guy with the fuzzy, sand
face. Yah, and the gray trench coat. In this episode, when the policewoman
comes to visit this Muslim taxi-driver at his home—she's the one who
rescues him after he has been shot. This guy stands with his hands folded
above his stomach, even with one eye popped out!"
—"Oh, I remember the gesture. When the Sultan of Zanzibar was driven
down Main Street, Prophet's green flag on the bonnet, and ten miles an hour
pomp, Zanzibaris folded their hands and dropped their eyes. Isn't this
gesture also one of the *namaaz* positions? Hang on, I have a *salat* book, I
will find out."
—"*Yaar*-Sadru, after all this circum brouhaha, tell me, tell me, does the
gesture move you?"
This gesture of hands folded below the chest leaves a mark on Muslim
shoulders. This time, as men lift a white sheeted body on their shoulders. I
always stop crying then, shifting all grief on their shoulders. Who-whom to
explain this giving over to grief to copious, abundant shoulders?
Oh, if it isn't the professional media nutsheller. No one shot the man Mr
Nutshell, you didn't miss a thing (as if all Muslims go to Allah this way,
bang, bang terrorism) but all Muslims are wrapped in white shroud and
lifted on a brother's shoulder.
There are stories:
A heroine's melancholy *filmi* line:

when my coffin is lifted
do not lend me your shoulder

how Sadru and I sobbed in the theatre, acidic salty tears wrung our jaws. And the story of the last Mogul, Zafar the poet, who is exiled to Burma by the British. Never to return to Delhi, not even to claim his final two yards of a burial plot. Agha Shahid Ali, a contemporary Kashmiri-American poet writes:

I think of Zafar
led through this street
By British soldiers, his feet in chains
to watch his sons hanged

In exile he wrote:
''Unfortunate Zafar
to spend half his life in hope,
the other half in waiting.
He begs for two yards of Delhi for Burial.''

Mr Media Nutsheller, broadcast this, bellow this: that the British buried him in Rangoon.

A Muslim's white-sheeted body is carried from shoulder to shoulder, uniting shoulders. (In Kashmir, I hear the same wood-*ka* coffin used to carry all departed.) Allah, yours we return to You. Give a shoulder, brother. Lend a shoulder, brother. Shoulder to shoulder, brother.

My stomach swells. In the aisle, I want to grasp this Muslim traveller's hand and press it to my right eye, then my left and bring it to my lips. My jugular vein shivers. There is a familiar stomping. Who is there? Today, *Baba* is an elegant mood of glittering sabres (not the makeshift swords or kukris in old black and white films). ''Infidels! My sowers will show you!''

Behind the Headlines

VIDYUT AKLUJKAR

The phone rang as Lakshmi was taking the weekender out from the closet. Lakshmi expected it to be from Hariharan's secretary, but it was from the Vancouver crisis centre. Old Mrs Mierhoff from the centre was on the phone asking whether Lakshmi would be able to fill in today from two o'clock onwards. They were rather short on volunteers that afternoon. Lakshmi looked at her watch, and consented right away. Hariharan's flight to Toronto was at eleven this morning, and after he left, Lakshmi's time was her own. Mrs Mierhoff thanked her heartily for coming to their aid on such short notice, and Lakshmi could hear a distinct sigh of relief in her aged voice. Somebody was going to be happy because of her being close by. Her mere presence was going to warm some hearts, heal some wounds. That was a rewarding thought.

Lakshmi placed the weekender on the bed and opened it. She had already laid out Hariharan's clothes beside the suitcase. Just as she was about to start packing, the phone rang again. This time it *was* Hariharan's secretary from the University. Lakshmi knew by heart what she was going to say. She did not have to hear it. She had taken identical phone calls for the last twelve years. She held the receiver to her ear and twisted her lips to mime the words of the secretary, while she watched her own reflection in the mirror of her bedroom. But today, she did not feel like laughing over the call as she used to do all these years. After the call was over, she turned back to the empty suitcase lying open on the bed, and stood staring at it for a while. She saw her own life yawning in front of her in the form of that empty suitcase. Lakshmi shuddered at that thought. She closed the lid of the suitcase and looked away.

Hariharan's secretary had conveyed the usual message. "Dr Hariharan has asked me to remind you to pack the morning newspapers. He will be home to pick up his suitcase on his way to the airport." Lakshmi should have been used to all this executive neatness by now. After all, she was married for twelve years. Wasn't one supposed to be reconciled to all such quirks in that much time? Her mother had seemed to be all her life. Somehow, they still bothered Lakshmi. She thought of the many times she had packed such weekenders for Hariharan's conferences. Not a single mistake ever. And still he kept on sending these unnecessary messages via his secretary. Such a lack of trust. But try as she would, she had not been able to convince Hariharan that there was a lack of trust in his sending these reminders to her through his secretary. He did not feel that he was insulting her intelligence in any sense. This was routine for him. He was a born executive. Memos, reminders, double-checking, all these predictable details of executive life were bread and butter to him. He never made any distinction between his home and his office. "Everything in its place, and a place for every little thing," he would say. Lakshmi had a place in his home just as his computer had a place on his desk. She had a specific job, specific duties. When those were taken care of, he had no complaint against her. She was free to do whatever she wanted with her time, as long as his needs and his routine were looked after scrupulously. What more freedom did a woman want?

In Tamil, her language, a twelve-year period was called a "tapas," a penance. Did I really serve a term of penance in Hariharan's company? Lakshmi wondered. What did I achieve in these twelve years? She was going over the balance sheet. There was not much to show on the side of profit. The daily routine was set here. She did not have to spend as much time on cooking or cleaning as her mother in Chidambaram. There were only the two of them in her house, so once Hariharan went to work, she had nothing much to do. Even when he was at home, he did not have a lot to say to her. What was there to talk about? Every once in a while, Lakshmi would start a conversation, but soon she would begin to sense the futility of it all. Her talk would invariably be about the people nearby, in her neighbourhood, or in her family, or in her life. She had nothing of international importance to convey to her husband. And Hariharan was interested in news of international importance. The dinner table was the only place where there was any occasion for conversation between the two, but even there, Hariharan would have a newspaper in his left hand and his ears would be tuned to the news on the radio. His hands would be busy putting in his mouth the delicacies prepared by Lakshmi, but that was by sheer force of habit. His mind was preoccupied with the World. So Lakshmi had learned to be quiet while he was around.

Hariharan had no complaints about Lakshmi. An onlooker would not have been able to accuse him of mistreating her. He was a prominent professor of economics in a respectable Canadian university. Over the years he had served on many executive committees on campus, and so had acquired a reputation for being a conscientious administrator as well. He was fulfilling his academic duties by attending and participating in a few conferences every year. She had a nice house, a respectable bank balance, and a car for her use as well. She had no children, but Hariharan had never harassed her about that. She could not be considered one of those abused or mistreated wives. Even though Hariharan would spend most of his time on campus, he never forgot to call his wife from his office. As soon as he came to his office at twelve thirty-five after his class, he would ring her up. Of course, there would not be anything other than the two predictable questions in his call. "Any phone calls for me? Any letters? All right then, see you later."

Lakshmi could recite Hariharan's routine by heart even in her sleep. There was not much change in it in the last twelve years. He did not ever fall sick. Jogging in the morning, breakfast with the morning newspaper, and "The World at Eight" on CBC. Then the morning classes at the University and office hours. The nap after two-thirty for exactly fifteen minutes on the divan in his office, coffee at the Faculty Club exactly at three, then the correspondence and committee work. Home by seven. Dinner at seven-thirty. Again the evening newspapers to read over dinner, research papers on the computer after dinner, and the national news at ten on the television. Everything was laid out just so for all these years. The dentist's appointments would be every six months apart, and the medical check-up every year. Lakshmi got tired just thinking about the predictability of her life and she sat down on the bed. The bed. Yes, even that was predictable. The only time that routine would be disturbed would be just before he went to such a conference.

She looked at the things she had laid out on the bed to pack in his suitcase. White shirts for two days, night clothes, a suit, the little shaving kit with its lotion and after-shave, the file of conference papers that Hariharan had packed himself, and the morning newspaper that he did not get to finish. Hariharan would forget his own name perhaps, but never the newspaper. There would be newspapers on the plane, but what if fellow passengers grabbed them all before him and never let go? Anticipating such adversities he would make sure he had the paper with him from home. Even at home, his newspapers and news hours covered Lakshmi's life like a shroud.

When Lakshmi was growing up in India, she would wake up to the sound of her grandmother singing the Venkatesha stotra from her temple room. Then there would be the shehnai of Bismillah at the end of the morning radio

165

program. And devotional songs, bhajans, to warm one's heart with a warm cup of coffee. Mornings begun thus with Sanskrit and Sangeet would make one feel warm and pure. When she got married to Hariharan and followed him to Canada, of course, she had to forget about all that. As soon as he woke up, Hariharan would stretch his hand towards the headboard, and turn the clock radio on. The world would rush into her bedroom before she even had a chance to wash her mouth. When he went to jog, he had his walkman stuck to his ears. Breakfast would be in the company of provincial and national news. She did not mind the sound of English so much, she liked English literature. But she hated to listen to news about how many died in the floods and how many were raped, the first thing in the morning. These news items would make her morning coffee all the more bitter. Not a single day passed when the morning news did not have either wars, fights, strikes, firing squads, or earthquakes, floods, robberies, drought, starvation, child abuse, and rapes. Let alone the shehnai, she would have settled for a little conversation just between the two of them before actually facing the world. She had talked about this to him in their early days of togetherness. But he did not think much of it. He was in the habit of carrying out as many little tasks as he could all at once. "This is economy of time, my dear," he had answered her in earnest. When Lakshmi had seen that the radio was not going to be turned off, she had acquired the habit of turning off her own ears.

It was not that Lakshmi was not interested in other people's lives. She liked to hear about the lives of people in a smaller circle, people in whose lives she had a certain say, where she could make a little difference. She would feel terribly helpless, utterly inconsequential when she had to listen to the akhand-paath, the constant chanting, of news items about places and people to which she had nothing to contribute.

Since she had come to the west coast, she had tried to get to know her neighbours, but everyone in her neighbourhood had young children and their lives revolved around the schools, kindergartens, carpools, and schedules checkered with swimming lessons and sports activities. Lakshmi had the whole day in front of her. Of course, Hariharan had no objection to her spending her time whichever way pleased her. Lakshmi used to go to the public library and borrow a heap of books to read, but then there was no one to discuss those books with. Hariharan used to declare with pride that he had not been able to read a single novel over the past several years. "No time for light reading," was his favourite sentence at the departmental parties. Some of his colleagues used to praise him when they heard that remark at the parties. Lakshmi was used to hearing praise for her husband's singleminded-ness and his academic productivity, but she could feel the emptiness in that praise. She was quite thrilled when she read Rushdie's *The Satanic Verses* long before it became known to the world, and wanted to share her thrill with Hariharan, but could not do so due to his being so preoccupied. Then almost a year later when Hariharan heard about the book and the fatwa in the news, he had exclaimed to her, "How can anyone get so excited about a mere naavel?" She had only smiled and let it pass. Their tracks ran parallel, without any hope of intersection. What could she do about it?

She was pausing again and again while packing that little suitcase today. She was thinking about the earlier phone call from the crisis centre. She had started to go there regularly as a volunteer for over a year now. Hariharan did not even know that. He never asked her what she did all day long. In the early days of their married life, she used to offer that information to him but as she sensed his utter lack of interest in the activities that seemed significant to her, she had developed a habit of not communicating anything about herself. His daily schedule was not altered in the least by her visits to the centre. After his midday call, she would go there, and even after a four-hour shift she would have enough time to come home and prepare his dinner. Her own life, however, was thoroughly altered due to this work. She was getting to know about the lives of people totally different from herself. She had entered into many lives that were down in the pits, due to childhood abuse, adult frustrations, and the miseries and loneliness of old age. However, she also was beginning to realize how strong a person's resilience could be in spite of all kinds of unimaginable adversities. There was something else. She was amazed at how effective she could be in someone's life by simply talking over the phone. She had found the strength in her own voice. She could actually communicate over the phone to the person at the end of the line, and share her caring feelings, her warmth with them. Some calls would be interrupted, and then she would feel frustrated, but most callers would simply want someone to listen to their plight. She was a sympathetic voice-companion in their lonely battles. Many injured minds were getting a breeze of concern blown on their sore spots thanks to her soft and soothing voice. Many were hanging on to that slender thread for support in total darkness.

She looked at her watch again. In a short while, Hariharan would start from his office and on his way to the airport, stop home to pick up his weekender. She had almost finished packing it. Only the newspaper to be placed on top now. She glanced at the front page. The headlines were of the Iraqi occupation of Kuwait along with pictures of wailing Kuwaiti women. Pity for the plight of that little nation that was about to lose its identity welled in her heart. On an impulse, she unpacked everything that she had packed in Hariharan's weekender. She emptied it altogether. She ran downstairs to the garage and brought up a pile of old newspapers. She filled the weekender with all those papers, unfolded and placed the latest one on top, closed it, brought it down and kept it ready by the door. "Prominent economist stranded due to wife's mischief," she imagined the headlines that might appear in some newspaper. She wondered which would be more hilarious, to see his face when he opened the weekender, or when he read about it in the local newspaper if it made the headlines.

Then she took out another suitcase from the closet, filled it with her own clothes and some of her favourite books, locked it, and placed it on the bed. She heard the sound of the garage door being opened downstairs. Hariharan must be at the cul-de-sac. Lakshmi took his newly filled weekender in her hand and stood by the garage door. She felt a strange affinity to that garage door which opened and shut automatically by a sheer flick of his fingers as and when he needed it so. The thought shook her to the core. Hariharan's car eased into the garage. He remained seated, waiting. As she opened the side door, he said, "Hope you didn't forget the papers." She nodded without a word and placed the weekender on the seat beside him. As she closed the car door, he backed out and turned to go to the airport.

She ran upstairs, picked up her suitcase, put it in her car, and was about to turn the key. She stopped, opened her purse, and took out the house keys. She got down, went to the front door, and carefully dropped the keys into the mail slot. She then went back to the car and set off towards the Crisis Centre.

Altered Dreams

LAKSHMI GILL

Dawn light was a hammered sheet of steel over the sleeping town; grey, silver flints streaking the horizon. Mr Singh appreciated it, even this not quite the golden haze over his village, but at least another dawn his dimming eyes could see. And these past seven months he did see it go through the changes of three seasons. March was not quite all winter—it whispered at spring. Or so he hoped, wishing for an early spring. Those icy roads . . . he had been dreaming . . .

This morning, as with every Tuesday morning, he needed only to put his faded brown pants and beige shirt over the underwear which he used to sleep in. It saved time from having to remove his pyjamas. He didn't bother with a cup of coffee either, because the noise in the kitchen would wake his insomniac wife. So he tiptoed around the dark living room and looked out the window again. He was always too early for his ride but never wanted his son-in-law to wait for him. When he saw the green Maverick pull up in front of the apartment building, he quickly turned around for the door.

Magdalena looked in on the children before she ran down to make a quick cup of coffee. It was no use, decaffeinated; she invariably fell asleep even before they got to Sussex or half-way to Fredericton. Six a.m. They'd just make it for her nine o'clock class. She had got through last term's three half-courses; she didn't know about these next three. Not well-organized. Between house chores and three children all under ten years . . . How did other women do it? Must have such energy or motivation. She wasn't getting all the reading done . . . and essays . . . She tried reading in the car but would get dizzy. There was never enough time—all of a sudden, it was Tuesday again, as night in a Dracula movie. How foolish of her to be

169

thinking of taking a doctorate now. Had she been swept up with the ardour of 1970s feminism? Except that, ironically, she couldn't drive herself (she had to rely on her husband) and her father had to babysit the children: two counts of dependency against her.

Was it her dream or her parents'? Her mother had wanted to be a lawyer but marriage prevented it. Her father would have made an excellent history professor but there were the British to oust, the war to fight, the business to run. He was prophetic. He could read the newspapers like seers read stars. But it was the usual road-not-taken. As with her. Yet here she was now. On slippery unsure roads.

She was dreaming. Dark trees on both sides of the dark road, sentinels to dense evil recesses. Only the high headlight beams beat the darkness back. Suddenly, blinding round and fiery eyes of a monster. Then nothing again. Just the suffocation. A few yards away, another monster, thundering at supersonic speed. Her husband jerks up from an overpowering sleepiness. The car veers towards the trees that lunge at them.

"They're sleeping," Magdalena offered her father a cup of coffee.

"Don't worry," he said. "Drive carefully," he repeated what he had said to his son-in-law outside. She had often mentioned the astonishing number of overturned trucks in the ditch.

She waved at his bulky figure peering at them from the high Victorian windows, white lace curtains pushed aside. Of course, he couldn't see her, it was so dark.

"Need a new car," her husband muttered as it shook in the cold.

It *was* old, the seat-belt buckles were useless, so she never bothered. As they rattled backwards on to the driveway, she watched her father watching them. He stooped somewhat to see them better, his head slightly bent forward to catch the last sight of the car. Standing there, watching them— even while she felt his anxiety, Magdalena felt reassured by that image—he was faithful, a lighted candle for the traveller lost in the dark woods. At nine in the evening her father at the window greeted their arrival, all of them exhausted, as though he had never moved from that spot all day.

"Maybe I should quit," Magdalena said as her husband sat in front of the TV set, a load of essays on the floor, beer glass on the lamp table. His red pen scratched at the effort of some unfortunate student. She remembered she had to get on with her own paper. He said nothing.

"It's such an imposition for you. You look so tired."

"Well. It *is* tiring. It's a long drive."

She waited for him to look up. Driving her had been his idea. While he was on his sabbatical in England, her parents, she and the children had rented a house in Fredericton so that she could begin her studies. But on his return he wanted them all back in the old homestead.

—It would only be a year of courses, she had said.

—We might as well get a divorce, he replied, staring ahead.

But that was so out-of-turn, she thought. She was only trying to get a PhD.

—I'll drive you back and forth, he said. Finances were not an issue; she had a grant.

—Does that not limit me, she wondered. She wouldn't be taking what she wanted or what she should in her field.

—He shrugged, then it's divorce. He sounded confident. He had had a good sabbatical, judging from the circuitous letters he received from a Japanese student who had billeted at his university residence. In the photographs she sent of their nights in the pub, the garish lighting cast an inane smile on his red beefy face.

Magdalena watched him now. Perhaps that was what he wanted, how stupid of her! He probably thought she would put her studies ahead of the family, as he would, and say, ok, go ahead. And now his words had entangled him. How one was caught by words like "I do"!

As his body encircled the essays, the tv, and the beer, Magdalena got up and left the room.

"Maybe I should quit," Magdalena said to her father the next day, as she sat by the open dryer, folding the warm clothes. Her father was washing dishes.

"Why?"

"Oh, Jeremy's so tired." And you, she thought. This was not the right way to get an education. The impositions! It was like stepping on dead bodies instead of going around them. A desecration. "He teaches three courses and has all those meetings to attend. He wastes a whole day at the library waiting for me."

"Doesn't he bring his work?"

"Of course he does. He's working all the time."

"Well then?"

"It's a long drive."

171

Was it her dream or her father's? If she had really wanted a PhD wouldn't she had gone for it before she got married? Or done it correctly, as her husband had in the early years of their marriage. They lived in the city where the university was—none of these Trans-Canada exercises—in a basement apartment, on student loan and a TA, with a baby and another on the way, and a library job for her five weeks after the second child was born. He had to have a PhD, no matter what. One took that for granted and carried on. She remembered those two years vividly, centred around the empty wooden easel in a neighbour's apartment across the parking lot on which she gazed through her darkened window until two in the morning, waiting for him to come home from the pub.

Should she have a PhD, no matter what? Once, she thought, a long time ago, in a different country, she had wanted to be a Dr Singh, but now . . . and anyway . . . she had acquired another name. Foreign.

"There's no sense," she mumbled. "It's too late now." At thirty-six. Acting out a childhood dream, acting childish in dragging others behind.

"Maybe I should quit," Magdalena said to her mother, who was altering her granddaughter's pants.

"Don't you need a doctorate to teach university?"

"Yes." There were so many young women now who had overtaken her.

"Should you not be equal to your husband?"

Had they not started out with MA's when they first met, teaching at the same university? "He's an academic. Maybe I'm not."

"We are here, supporting you," her mother said simply.

Magdalena clutched her head. Was it her dream or theirs?

Mr Singh slept fitfully. It was that dream again. Dark road, dark trees, his son-in-law falling asleep at the wheel . . .

And another one: his mother, across the river, calling him . . .

She could hardly believe that she made it to April, was four days into it! It was still winter—snowstorms still came up suddenly but by now they were used to it. The car held up. Her husband, though, showed the strain. Daily jogging (except Tuesday, ruefully) didn't help. Bags under his eyes were heavier than usual. She castigated herself for her inability to drive long distances. (She drove all around town, delivering and picking up children to and from school, doing groceries, chores, but these didn't count, they were short hops. She hadn't learned how to drive until she was thirty, and only because her husband insisted since someone had to do the chores.) How she admired the assertive sixteen-year-old Canadian girls behind wheels! They freed their parents from all that running around.

His own parents dropped by from Ontario with hints that he was doing far too much and for what? He had his job to attend to, which alone took away all his energy. Magdalena waited for him to say something, as his mother sighed, feeling sorry for her boy. He said nothing, felt so weary he could say nothing. She had thought that his parents, high-school graduates, would have at least appreciated her struggle or desire, whether she was a daughter-in-law or not. But his father, rushing to get to opening time at the Legion at the bottom of the street, said, what do you need it for? You've got a husband here to work for you. As he had worked for his wife, thirty years at the distillery, they'd be giving him his gold watch soon. After his parents flew back, her husband merely doubled his work nights at his office to catch up on his work. Not an alarming trend. He had acted similarly when he was writing his thesis.

"Do you know how much more I could have done?" He yelled as he packed a suitcase to fly to the Learneds Conference.

The unstated Compromise, *the* Canadian virtue, loomed before her eyes. The conferences he had not attended, the committee headships he had to decline, the parties he had to give up. Work was so demanding; he was so much in demand. This double-headed Ontario work ethic fascinated Magdalena. It gave guilt and resentment: guilt that so little time could be given to family life, and resentment that not enough time could be given to working life. Imagine, she imagined, how much he could do if he were single! And yet he didn't quite want that. It was a couple-oriented society— a family made one look respectable and solid. He liked to go to the Concert Series with her beside him, as his eyes checked out who was in the auditorium. There had been a rash of wives who had left their husbands and the abandoned men were shunned. The gossip! Professor Ding slept in his car. Professor Dong missed lectures.

"The thing to do," Janice, the part time nurse said, "is to find your own work (on top of the housework of course)—you wean yourself from your husband but be there when he comes home."

"What?" Magdalena gasped. "Like his coffee break?"

"Well, they can only do so much per day. They do need a break, even after the pub. There's sex, too, you know."

"What do you do while you wait?"

173

Janice showed off her firm buttocks. "I do a lot of yoga."

"I work at a job!" He yelled as he fixed his tie before going to a luncheon for the visiting professor from Australia.

All he wanted was to be left alone so that he could "work at a job," a phrase Magdalena found curious: it was redundant, almost distasteful, as though there were no pleasure to be had from this activity. But, of course, there must have been pleasure; why would anyone spend a lifetime at it? It must be like the endurance training of the runner, pushing to the limits for that Olympic medal and the roar of the crowd. What a high one could get, working at a job. And the achievement was the champion's alone. It was his name on the trophy, not the bucket-carrier's. What frontier ruggedness, what pioneer individualism. None of that old Asian community stuff, where relations were as long as the red ribbon around one's neck.

So, all he wanted was to be left alone so that he could work at his job; anything she wanted to do for herself she had to do by herself—this was called self-reliance, a virtue. Just as he was free to do what he wished, so she was free to do what she wished, if it didn't inconvenience him—this was called the democratic way, another virtue. If she could only apply these Canadian truths to her character, she too would endure in this country.

"He has been teaching the same courses for nine years and now he has tenure; does he have to go to his office every night?" Mrs Singh asked.

Magdalena kept trying to read but had to look up now and then to answer her mother. "He's changing his thesis into a book. At this point in his career he needs to publish at least one book, and he's got to have some articles. It's research, too, not just teaching." Publish or perish.

"Could these not wait until you're done with your courses?"

"No, I don't think so." He was, after all, thirty-eight. Was it not all a matter of timing—Ecclesiastes and all that? Who or what could alter this Law? Perhaps, she had misjudged her own timing, giving in to a dream that was still in gestation. He, on the other hand, shook dreams into existence, barrelling against the harsh winds that would deprive him. He was Canadian, a survivor of the wilderness. Woe to the wounded and the weak.

This vision never left her: they had known each other only for four months and as she was visiting Ontario for Christmas, he had invited her to meet his parents. One year in Canada and she was still wearing tropical clothes: thin red silk cheongsam, yellow cashmere Vicuna overcoat, short suede boots, no scarf, hat or gloves—the ensemble seemed adequate enough in Vancouver. The visit itself was not memorable: it was tinsel-and-plastic tinged. But the walk up to see his old university, his "stomping grounds": that supplied the vision. Raw wind. Night. Hills. On a bus route. But not for him, no, no bus ride. This was invigorating. He strode up, chest out, in his survival parka and hunter's boots. A taxi, perhaps? Ha-ha, he laughed. This is nothing. He made boot tracks like a tank's. If this was nothing, she dreaded the real Canadian winter. Or was this mediocre nothing-cold, given in daily doses, the measure of one's life here? His strength was awesome. Would she ever be that strong? He climbed those hills as though she were not with him, wrapped up in his memories, oblivious to her shivering. Was it just from the cold, her shivering, or also from a presentiment?

It was difficult all around, Magdalena thought. Tomorrow, thank God, was her last day.

Mr Singh got up wearily. It was nearly three in the afternoon. She would drop them off after she had collected the children from school. He was feeling the weight. His bad knee was buckling again, ten years after the pins were put in. When he got up, he felt dizzy. Magdalena saw him hold on to the wall. So old. How old was he? Seventy-five? Eighty? No one knew. His mother said he was born during the confluences of some planets but no one ever registered his birth or checked the year. Later on, for a passport, he settled on 1904.

"You should see a doctor for that dizziness."

He shrugged, "It's nothing."

In the car, with the children happily talking away at the same time in the back seat, Magdalena glanced at her father. She felt guilty, too, with him, as with her husband, and yet, it seemed all right. He shouldered her across the stream. She was fulfilling a dream, his or hers or maybe all of theirs, and it was joyous. Without him, she would not make it.

"Thank you, Papa," she said.

He seemed preoccupied. "It's still slippery," he noted as the car came to a stop. "Storm predicted tomorrow. If the roads are bad, you don't have to go."

"It's my last day."

She was dreaming. Dark roads, dark trees, dark white husband, dark lights . . .

175

The telephone's shrill ring cut through her dream. Midnight. And she'd have to get up in five hours.

"Magdalena," her mother sounded far away. "Papa!" Her cracked voice broke into a swoon that made Magdalena's body grow cold.

Her Mother's Ashes

GEETA KOTHARI

She hears the children at the front door before she sees them. They rush into the hall, a mass of slickers and rubber rain boots, squeaking and slipping across the floor. Lally remembers when raincoats came only in yellow, and suddenly, she feels old. From the room, Lally watches them tear their coats off, struggle with their outdoor shoes, grabbing onto each other or the wall for support, laughing and breathless. Joke trips into the classroom, still wearing her red galoshes.

When she started working at the afterschool program, Lally told the children that while growing up, she wasn't allowed to wear shoes in the house. The one exception was the time her parents went to Boston and brought back a pair of red Oxfords for her. They were new and clean, shiny and beautiful; she'd worn them to bed that night. Her parents didn't know they were called Oxfords; for years, the shoes were simply Boston shoes, the only shoes she ever wore indoors.

"Joke," Lally calls out, anxious to get her before she takes another step into the clean classroom.

Joke looks up.

"Don't you want to put on your slippers?" Lally asks. The children take their shoes off when they come in and put on the slippers lined up under their pegs in the hallway. She doesn't want to tell Joke what to do, but the order is implicit in her question, said in a tone used only with children.

Joke looks down at her feet, as if surprised to see her outdoor shoes still there.

Before Lally knows it, they are standing around her, their strange little voices trying to drown each other out. Some of them have surprisingly low

177

voices, as if they've been staying up late nights with a bottle of whiskey and a pack of cigarettes. They are short enough to trip her without trying. Looking down at them, she feels very tall and awkward, not old but young now, like an unsure teenager.

"Tell us about the thousand-ton man, again, please Lally, please?"

"Twelve-hundred-pound man," she says automatically, then wonders what difference accuracy makes to a story culled from *The National Enquirer* and the evening news.

"Whatever. Tell me what he eats."

"I told you yesterday, Davey."

Davey is giggling behind his hands. He loves this story as do his ten giggling cohorts, standing in a rough semicircle at her feet.

"Okay." She sighs. Why do children love to hear the same story again and again? "But only if you promise, all of you, not to get on my nerves."

They nod, sort of, and shuffle to the big low table in the middle of the room. Over the sound of chairs scraping the floor, a question:

"What's get on your nerves?"

As the afternoon progresses to dusk, they draw pictures of the twelve-hundred-pound man. His profile, his bedroom, his chins, his tummies. The man stuck in the bathroom doorway. What he eats for breakfast, what he will look like after his diet, what he eats on his diet. They draw his life inside out, and when she tries to show them a photo of the real fat man, they are dismissive, as if his existence could never measure up to their stories.

She has never considered herself a storyteller, a necessary skill for this job that fits her like her old school coat—several sizes too big, with the saleslady's assurance she'd grow into it. At first, she felt herself shrinking. When the children crowded around her feet, she'd pull into herself, like a flower closing up for the night. Eventually she reached a comfort zone where she no longer felt the automatic closing off. Now, however, when she tells the same story again and again, she moves neither forward nor back.

Lally tries to read while they draw, but they won't let her. All the attention goes to the fat man. The questions and comments are constant. Lally gives up on her book, drawn into their world in spite of herself. It amazes her how fresh their fascination is, how their incredulity grows each day. They greet the story like a long-favorite fairy tale.

Lally's mother didn't tell fairy tales. Instead, she would tell her, about the Partition, "We lost everything. We had so much, and then, one day, we had nothing but the clothes we wore.'' Independence Day did not mean freedom; it meant Partition, the day Lahore became part of Pakistan forever.

Lally wanted to hear more, but even at ten she knew that if she asked for a happy ending, her mother would clamp her lips tight and walk away. Instead, she imagines her mother, eighteen and frightened, holding onto her uncle's hand—the little boy her grandfather so desperately waited for, through five daughters and two miscarriages—as they board a train bound for Hoshiarpur. What would it feel like to travel without luggage? Now when Lally's mother travelled, she packed large, unwieldy suitcases, stuffing packs of dry cereal and powdered milk into the corners as if she would never see food again.

''Your great-grandfather was the richest man in Lahore. He had a big house—the joint family lived there—and he had his own shop. One day he saw two young men eyeing my fifteen-year-old cousin. He had two of his men kill them the next day.''

''Didn't anyone say or do anything?'' Lally was stalling, hoping to distract her mother, so that she would not have time before school to finish off the cold, milky dregs of oatmeal in her bowl.

''Nope.'' Her mother covered her toast in marmalade, thick and sickly sweet. The morning paper was spread over her half of the kitchen table, and she read while crunching her toast, occasionally brushing the crumbs from the page.

''Why not?''

Her mother shrugged, turning the page. ''That's the way it was. It's the parents' duty to take care of the girls, to protect them and make sure they are settled.''

Even then, Lally knew what ''settled'' meant. It meant a home. It meant a doctor or engineer husband, a house in Cherry Hill, and two children—a boy, first, for the family, and then a girl, for herself.

''Did that girl, your cousin, ever get married?''

Her mother sighed, and her lips tightened. She looked up from her paper. ''She ran off with a Muslim boy, a few years before the partition. Grandfather was so stupid; he thought everything would stay the same, that nothing would change. He let the girl go, and we never saw her again.''

''Why not? Where did she go?''

Her mother started clearing the dishes from the table, her toast half-eaten, Lally's oatmeal forgotten. "You're going to be late for school. Come on, now. You're making me late."

Later, on the corner of Elm Street, the point where Lally would walk to school by herself, her mother said, as if there had never been a pause, "We used to see that girl in the market sometimes. I wanted to speak to her, but grandmother wouldn't let me. By the time I found out where she lived, it was too late. It was 1947. We went on holiday, and never came back."

She hugged herself against the chilly autumn air, crunching dry leaves under her feet. When Lally turned back to wave, from half way down the block, she was gone, already around the corner.

When Lally's mother died a year ago, Lally was in India, waiting for her. In between her tears, Lally smiled at the irony of her mother dying in New York, visiting friends for a few days before her flight to Delhi, when her express wish had been to have her ashes scattered in the Ganges. Lally dutifully obliged her mother, making the round trip, hassling with customs officials who gave in only when she started to cry, trekking up to the Ganges for the first time in her life, and finally, mingling with pilgrims and hippies on the banks, surreptitiously slipping her mother's ashes into the water. Looking around self-consciously, she noticed a couple of men bathing upriver, while a man in white beat some clothes against the rocks. At first she was repulsed by the brown water with islands of foam and flecks of ash floating on its surface. A line of marigolds, rose petals, and lighted clay lamps bobbed past her. The smell from the nearby *ghats* bothered her—it felt like she was breathing the dust of the dead—but she had learned that actively resisting a smell only made it worse.

A long time ago, when she was nine, Lally watched her mother feed her father's ashes into the Connecticut River with equal surreptitiousness. He'd always been slightly perturbed by her mother's wish to be scattered in the Ganges—"This is your home now," he'd say, pointing to the Berkshires that encircled the small Massachusetts town he taught in. But that had been no more her mother's home than this was.

Lally looked around to see if anyone else was doing the same thing—she didn't know the proper ritual, the right prayers. She'd been too embarrassed to ask her aunt; the family already thought she hadn't been raised properly. All she had were her mother's stories. What did they mean? Lally hears her mother's voice. "Sarasvathi sits on your tongue once a day; she is the goddess who watches us for correct speech. When I was ten, I said, 'One day we're going to lose all of this.' We lost everything. No home, no business, no nothing. My parents had to start all over again.'' And that was it. She never said how she felt, and the harder Lally tried to remember, the less she knew.

Dusk fell, and Lally stood on the banks of the muddy river, waiting for someone to tell her what to do. The cawing of the crows grated her ears, and she hesitantly opened the urn. But as she became absorbed in her task, less concerned with everything around her, more concerned with the ashes, with saying goodbye to her mother, who she would never see again, who would probably not even be able to come back as a ghost now that she was ash, Lally slowly left her perch on the sandstone bank and waded into the water. When all the ashes were gone, and she was left with an empty urn, she realized she was crying.

Lally missed part of the fourteen-day grieving period, wanting to dispose of the ashes immediately, almost afraid she'd forget her mother's directive. Family and friends crowded into the living room, the women seated on the Indian rug, dominating the conversation, the men on the periphery of the overdecorated room, uncomfortably perched on the overstuffed couch. The room was dark, even during the day, built deliberately to avoid the hot summer sun. Lally's grandfather built this house after the partition, working two jobs to resettle his family. The house took two years to build, and by then Lally's mother had already left for the States.

Lally couldn't stay in New Delhi, with the family, because they reminded her too much of her mother. The way her two aunts cackled in Punjabi, the heavy, spicy smell of the food, the lingering scent of jasmine soap on her cousins' skin—it was uncomfortably familiar and unknown, both at the same time.

At the end of her last meal in New Delhi, she asked her youngest aunt about the missing cousin, the one who ran off with the Muslim. "I wouldn't know," her aunt said, getting up to clear the table. "Such things weren't discussed in my presence."

By the next day, the fat man is old news. The children are bored with his story, have exhausted it in their discussions and play. Lally tries to read to them from a book of fairy tales donated by one of the parents.

She is barely into the first paragraph, when Joke announces, "This story sucks. My mom's always trying to tell it to me."

"Yeah, it's stupid. No one reads it any more," Davey says.

181

The other children agree, in varying levels of disgust. Lally watches the class dissolve.

"Hey, Lally?" Davey shouts above the growing chaos.

"What?" She stands up, hoping to restore her authority.

"Tell us another story like the fat man."

"I can't."

The fat man seems inspired now, as if it came from nowhere. She has no idea why they liked him so much. She tries to think, to remember when she last read anything of interest.

"I don't know any more stories like the fat man."

Joke starts to pick her nose. "Make one up."

"Only if you take your finger out of your nose." She's been trying to break Joke and Missy of the habit, at least in public. "And the rest of you, sit down and be quiet for a few minutes so I can think."

The chairs scrape. After a few seconds, Davey raises his hand.

"Can I have some o's? I'm hungry."

Suddenly, everyone is hungry. She passes out bowls of sugarless Cheerios. Lally would give them cookies, but this is the only food the parents could agree on as a healthy snack.

"Okay. No interruptions, otherwise there won't be a story. You can draw if you want, but no talking while I talk, okay?"

Michael, the peewee of the bunch, settles his head down on the table. Joke does the same. Missy is sucking her thumb and Davey sits up straight, ready to draw.

"Well, my mother came from a huge family. Her mother was only sixteen when she was born and, somehow, in all the confusion, the family forgot when my mother was born. She never knew when her birthday really was, February 8, 14, or 28. All she knew for sure was the year and the place." What she doesn't say, what she can't say, is that the disappointment of having a first-born girl child was so keen, that her grandfather first asked the doctor if he was certain and then told him that maybe he should check again. It wasn't until her third birthday that it occurred to him to record the date of birth. Lally's grandmother used to tell this story, while bragging about her gone-to-America daughter, laughing at her dead husband's foolishness.

"Does that mean she had three birthdays?" Missy looks upset.

"Yup." For a long time, Lally gave her mother three birthday presents, as if to make up for her grandfather's neglect.

"Cool," Davey looks up from his o's. "Go on."

"Anyway, one day when my mother was four years old, her grandmother, who was my great-grandmother, took her to her cousin's wedding in the next town. Her mother was too sick to go, but she didn't mind going with her grandmother." Too late, Lally pauses, trying to invoke her mother's voice, the way the story was told.

"In those days, a wedding was a pretty big deal. My mother got a new pair of shoes and a new dress. All her other relatives were going and since they had to go early, it was arranged that great-grandmother would pick my mother up at five o'clock that day."

Everyone is looking at Lally, except Joke, who is asleep. She can hear them breathing, watching her, waiting. It's raining outside and the sound of the cars whooshing up the street is familiar and comforting.

"Back then, not many people had their own cars. The wedding guests decided to catch an early bus to the town, since it would take three hours to get there. When great-grandmother picked my mother up, she was dressed in her new outfit, with new ribbons in her hair."

"Was she wearing her new shoes?"

"Yes."

"What kind of shoes?" Davey wants to know.

"Red Boston shoes," Lally improvises, using a vague yet definite term. It is difficult for her to see the shoes, the dress, her mother younger than she ever knew her.

To her surprise, she remembers. Everyone has had a pair of special shoes at one time or another.

Lally continues the story. "On the bus, there were just tons of people, mostly relatives, but also some neighbours and friends, who happened to be on the same bus. Great-grandmother put my mother in a window seat, so she could watch the sun rise. When the bus started, she went off to the back to talk to her family.

"The last thing my mother remembers is the sun didn't rise quickly enough. The sky was purple and she could still see stars. She fell asleep."

Joke is awake now, her eyes wide and pinned to Lally. Davey is drawing a bus. He stops and looks up.

"Then what?" he says.

"Then the bus broke down in the middle of the road. A flat tire. So everyone got out to watch the driver change the tire. Then they got back on and were on their way. Somehow, my mother slept through it.

"Well, they're finally pulling into town and great-grandmother returns to her seat to find my mother. But she's not there any more. Great-grandmother figures one of the aunts took her but when she gets off the bus no one has her. Naturally, she's upset. Someone starts yelling at the driver, saying it's all his fault. One aunt is praying, several others are crying. Great-grandmother gets back on the bus with her nephew Biku. The bus is completely empty and they find my mother, curled up sound asleep under a seat. Her new shoes are gone. When great-grandmother asks her what happened, she can't remember; she was too fast asleep."

"And then?"

"And then they went to the wedding and had a great time."

"But what about her shoes?" Missy pulls her thumb out. Every time Lally tells her not to suck it, she cries.

"Well, the shoes were gone."

"But what did she do? Did she get a new pair? Where were they?" All questions Lally had asked, all unanswered. Either she was making her mother late for work or trying to avoid doing homework—her mother, who had never heard of dodge ball became an expert without even trying.

Several children look up. Davey is scribbling hard. Lally doesn't think he can help her this time.

"Well, she couldn't do anything. Someone had obviously taken them."

Lally remembers her mother telling the story as an example of how spoiled and loved she was by the elders in her family. She used to say that she'd lost the shoes.

"Who? Who took your mother's shoes?"

"Yeah, and how old was she again?"

"She was four years old and they never found the person who took her shoes. She was asleep when it happened."

"Did she cry?" Missy has to know.

"No. She never cried."

No, her mother never cried, not when she lost her shoes, not when she lost everything. Lally wants to ask her: did she lose her home or was it taken? Her mother tried so hard to tell only the good, as if Sarasvathi had taken permanent residence on her tongue, yet always, "We lost everything" reverberated under her words. Lally wants to answer their questions, to give them a happy ending, but she can't.

The fat man wanted to lose weight, to live an easy, unencumbered life. Lally knows only that her mother wanted a home. She hears her mother's single request: "Cremate me and throw my ashes in the Ganges. She is my home now."

"Poor little baby," Michael says to Joke, shaking his head.
  "Didn't anybody love her?" Davey wants to know.
  Lally sees Missy's face falling, in seconds, the droopy mouth, jutting lower lip, teary eyes. She cannot think of anything to say to make it better. This is the way her mother told the story, no more and no less. Lally can't imagine it told differently.

Lally turns on the evening news and wanders around the apartment. Photographs of her and her parents are scattered haphazardly between photos of friends and old faded photos of her mother's family, somehow rescued from falling into that gap that split India and Pakistan. When her grandfather died, his family put up a colour portrait above the dining table and hung fresh garlands of jasmine and marigolds from it. When Lally was at the house in New Delhi, she wondered how they could stand the pain of seeing him while they ate. Her aunt remarked, when she saw Lally staring, "It is the children's duty to love and honour the parents. If we don't, then our children will forget us."
  Lally comes out of her bedroom in time to hear a news item about the fat man, who has died from a heart attack. His heart couldn't take the fluctuations in weight and now his family is suing the doctor who put him on a diet. "If only we'd accepted his weight," the mother is saying, "he'd still be alive. We thought we were doing the right thing. All we wanted was for him to be happy."
  Lally hopes that none of the children find out.

It's raining the next morning when Lally wakes up. When she gets to school in the early afternoon, her mind is unfocused, scattered over the many things she should and must do beyond the walls of the classroom. She remembers that this is a temporary job, that she is unsettled and on her way elsewhere.
  A block from school, she breaks the rules and buys the children a pack of chocolate chip cookies. One won't hurt them.
  The children come in helter-skelter, more restless than usual. They have been indoors too much lately. If it weren't raining, Lally would take them to the park by the river, near Sutton Place, although she always worries about a lawsuit brought on by a broken arm and her irresponsibility.

They gather around the table, where Lally has set up some modelling clay. Missy is the last to come in, still wearing her rain boots and clutching her bunny slippers close.

"Hey Missy," Lally says, "you forgot to take your boots off. Come here, I'll help you with them." She nearly adds, "Silly goose," but something stops her.

"No. I have to keep them on."

Lally briefly wonders if this is an edict from Mr Kaputsy. "Well, then why don't we put your slippers back?"

"No. I want to keep them with me," Missy whines.

The other children toy with their clay, listening, watching.

"Missy," Lally says, "you really shouldn't wear rain boots inside. They're dirty."

"No they're not. The rain made them clean."

"Well, you need to let your feet breathe."

"No, I don't. I won't," she says loudly.

"Why?"

Missy is sniffing and gasping, about to cry.

"That's okay, Miss, keep your boots on. I just wanted to know why. You sit next to Davey, over here, okay?"

After much effort to get them settled with drawing paper and crayons as well as the clay that's already out, Davey breaks the tenuous silence, almost thinking out loud, his head still bent over his work.

"What happened to the fat man?"

"He's dead," Lally says, and instantly feels regret mingled with irritation. If Davey hadn't suddenly broken her daydreaming, she would not have been caught so unawares. She doesn't want to talk about the fat man or her mother any more.

"Yeah," Davey nods, sagely. "That's what my mom said, but I didn't believe her."

The other children are listening, as if the fat man's fate does not surprise them. They whisper quietly amongst themselves, with few questions. It is easier for people to mourn those they know, or think they know. The fat man never fooled the children into believing he was anything more, and the children knew him as well as they could. They have no regrets now; there was never any more to know about him once they'd answered all their questions.

Lally understands that she has become that storyteller she thought she never was, but there is no comfort in this. Her mother's stories concealed more than they revealed, and the regret that has been gnawing at her all this time now washes over her like the muddy waters of the Ganges. She should feel cleansed, refreshed; instead, a wave of nausea hits her and she has to bite her lip to hold herself still. Lally gets up to give the children their cookies.

Her mother has found her home now, but where has she left her daughter? Lally can finally see a face on the four-year-old forgotten under the seat of a bus. It is her own.

A Memory of Names

ROSHNI RUSTOMJI-KERNS

Katy Cooper had no memories of her birthplace, no memories of her mother. She had vague memories of travelling with her father, Freddy Cooper, through France and England and of their life in Mexico. Or may be it was in Guatemala. She couldn't remember. Her dependable memories began with New Hampshire when she had started her life as a ward of Gregory and Theresa Sanders at the age of nine years. Gregory Sanders had been her father's employer.

Katy had always thought that she was born somewhere in Europe, most probably in England, in 1934. She was certain about the date because it was on the papers naming the Sanderses as her guardians. The place of birth had "Unknown" in the space provided for that information. She had no birth certificate. Theresa Sanders had said that it had most probably been in Freddy's bag which was lost when he and Katy had flown from Chicago to Mexico City. Katy had been two years old.

Katy discovered that she was born in Devinagar, India, when the frame enclosing the one photograph she owned broke and she saw the back of the picture. She was living on the Pacific Coast at that time. In Half Moon Bay. A town surrounded by greenhouses filled with flowers, herbs and Mexican pottery, pumpkin fields which stretched to the ocean and Christmas tree farms which offered train and pony rides and were decorated with Santa Clauses, reindeer sleds and Snow White and the Seven Dwarfs. She had been told that her cottage used to be an old carriage house. She could hear the ocean on stormy nights and the creek across the dirt-paved road after a good winter rain. The stand of Eucalyptus trees on the banks of the creek shielded her from the cemetery which had its predictable quota of ghosts

188

and teenagers on dark and stormy nights. Katy had just turned forty-seven.

The photograph was of Freddy, an English woman Katy had always acknowledged as her mother and a baby. Her father had told her that the woman's name was Margaret. Katy had assumed that her parents were divorced. Her father's precise handwriting at the back of the photograph stated, "Freddy Cooper and Margaret Shriver with baby Katy born in Devinagar, India, October 29, 1934."

It was damp and foggy in Half Moon Bay when Katy found out that she was born in India. Her garden was dormant. She had recently sold a painting. And both her favorite restaurants, "Original Johnny's" and "The California Girls " were closed. "Original Johnny's " for remodelling and "The California Girls " because the owners had gone to the mud baths in Napa for a vacation after their Thanksgiving-Christmas baking marathon. Katy decided that it was a good time to go to Devinagar, India, to begin her long-deferred search for her mother.

Devinagar was a small town somewhere between the port cities of Bombay and Karachi. It had only one hotel, the Niketan. The Niketan had ten rooms, four bathrooms and a restaurant which served tea, pakoras and its own version of meat cutlets. Since most people who came to Devinagar were visiting family or friends, the hotel rooms were usually vacant. But the residents of Devinagar had discovered that outside of one's own family kitchen or dining room, the best place to gossip about other families was on the Niketan verandah.

Katy did not find her mother in Devinagar but she did find her aunt, Agnes Driver, whose maiden name had been Agnes Cooper. Katy found Agnes through the Devinagar lady lawyer, Roxanne Japanwallah, who had come to the hotel restaurant for her weekly dose of Devinagar's best pakoras. Roxanne had never been known to encounter a stranger in Devinagar without initiating a conversation. It usually began with a strong handshake which of course startled people unused to handshakes, especially from a woman. The handshake was accompanied by, "How do you do? I am Roxanne Japanwallah. I am from one of the oldest Devinagar families. If you need a lawyer, do please come to me. Even if you have no money. And if you need help in locating anyone in Devinagar, come to my house. My companion Nanibai will help you. She was, at one time, the founding president of the Devinagar Lady Thieves Union. She is quite reformed now but she still has a very useful network of friends and helpers." Most Indians did not find Roxanne's introduction too lengthy or overly disturbing. Katy was quite taken aback by it.

It was Roxanne who quickly understood that Agnes and Katy were related and it was also Roxanne who told Katy that her family name was not the English "Cooper" but the Parsi "Cooper." Katy was interested to learn that Freddy Cooper was not an Englishman who had lived in India. He had been an Indian. She could now explain to herself her own skin, eyes and hair. But she was surprised to learn that her father had not been a Catholic like the devout Sanderses but a Zoroastrian, a Parsi. Roxanne took Katy to the Cooper home, a large house with a deteriorating garden and a well-constructed ramp which started at the front door of the house, crossed the garden and ended at the iron gate which led to the road. She introduced Katy to Agnes with "How are you Agnesmai? Here is your niece from America. She has a photograph of herself with Freddy and Margaret and her name is Katy Cooper." And then she left.

It was Agnes Driver, sitting regally in her pink upholstered wheelchair, who told Katy that Katy stood not for Katherine or Catherine, not even for Kathleen. It was Katy from Katayun, Empress of Pars, Iran, and for Katayun Cooper, mother of Agnes and Freddy. Agnes went on to say that she was envious of Katy's real name. She had always wanted a Parsi name instead of her English grandmother's name. And when she had found out the meaning of her name she had felt doubly cheated. Katy had to agree that there was nothing lamblike about this woman who had invited her to live with her as long as she wanted.

Agnes was fascinated by American women. "They come in so many shapes, sizes, colours and dimensions. Look at you, Katayun. You and Ella Fitzgerald and Doris Day and Eleanor Roosevelt . . . all Americans! The only other place that happens is right here in India. Look at Devinagar . . . You and I and Roxanne and Nanibai and their friend Fatima and of course Margaret Shriver who used to live here. Amazing!" And then she told Katy about Eleanor Roosevelt's visit to Karachi, Pakistan.

When Agnes was eleven years old, her father Eddie Cooper decided to send Agnes away from Devinagar to Karachi for two years. He said that he could no longer live in the same house or even the same small town with an eleven-year-old daughter who never stopped running. She ran up and down the marble staircase, across the front lawn with the English roses, through the back vegetable garden with the peas, tomatoes, barren mango tree, lotus pond and three resident snakes and then throughout the town of Devinagar with its temples and churches and mosques and agiaries dedicated to conflicting religions haunted by strange female presences. And of course, everyone knew that Agnes Cooper collected an amazing amount of information as she moved from place to place. And so, when she was eleven years old she was sent off to the Mama Parsi Girls' High School in Karachi, Pakistan as a boarder. The Mama had nothing to do with a mother or a maternal uncle. It was the family name of the school's benevolent founder.

It was later, when Agnes was about seventeen, that she discovered why she had been sent off to Karachi. It was because Margaret Shriver was pregnant. Margaret was known to be Agnes's father's mistress and sus-pected to be Agnes's older brother Freddy's lover. It was a nasty situation. Eddie Cooper was worried that with all the ground his daughter covered and all the information she collected, she would discover the current Devinagar scandal. Margaret miscarried but Agnes had been sent off anyway.

Agnes assured Katy that there were only two highlights during her three years in Karachi. One was her introduction to camels and the other was Eleanor Roosevelt's visit to Karachi.

Camels, said Agnes, were like the region south of San Diego, California. They were made from the materials which were left over after the main creation of the world. Unusable rocks and mismatched bones. Agnes had seen the borderlands of southern California during her honeymoon trip to Los Angeles. As she grew older, she said that she did not remember much about her husband's relatives who had emigrated from Bombay to Los Angeles. She had a vague memory of one of the immigrant daughters wanting to be a film actress and arguing with her family that learning to recite the speeches of Shakespeare's heroines, with the correct English diction and much wringing of hands, would not make her a film star. In her more ridiculous moments, Agnes used to insist that she had recognized the young woman in the role of a junior harem wife years later in a Bombay film. Agnes blamed her hatred of travelling by air on the twenty-eight hour wait she had to endure those many years ago in the Los Angeles airport. She said that she survived the wait without driving her husband crazy because of a fellow-traveller with whom she had an interesting conversa-tion about various matters including viruses, politics, religion and opera. Dr Mary Mattson was a scientist. The first and only American woman scientist Agnes had met in her life. And Mary Mattson loved opera. Operas, accord-ing to Agnes, were created from leftover sounds. When Agnes discovered that Mary Mattson's mother had spent her life trying to navigate around the fact that the Virgin Mary had been known to appear disguised as a vagrant to test human faith and basic goodness, she had told the American woman that her mother was absolutely correct. Agnes described her own town, Devinagar. The citizens of Devinagar, Agnes explained, existed rather cheerfully with the knowledge that the goddess was constantly present among them, in and out of disguise. Agnes was delighted when Mary Mattson told her that her father had actually seen Eleanor Roosevelt one day on the steps of the Capitol in Washington, DC. He had even tipped his hat to her and said ''Good morning, Mrs Roosevelt.''

Agnes had a vested interest in Eleanor Roosevelt.

The Government of Pakistan was informed that Eleanor Roosevelt would be visiting Karachi when Agnes was attending the Mama Parsi Girls' High School in Karachi. The schools in Karachi were notified that the students were to line the route of Eleanor Roosevelt's motorcade from the airport to Government House. They were to be dressed in their school uniforms and were to be given a small green and white Pakistani flag and a small red, white and blue American flag. They were to wave both flags and smile as Eleanor Roosevelt's car passed by. It was known that Eleanor Roosevelt was most interested in the education of girls and therefore the girls' schools were allocated the more visible places along the motorcade route.

The Mama Parsi Girls' High School students were taken to their designated place on Victoria Road in front of the Bai Virbaiji Soparivala Parsi Boys' School on flat carts pulled by camels. According to Agnes, the camels were the only unexcited members of the trip.

Agnes found herself between Naseema Suleiman, the only Muslim girl in their class and Roshni Behram Rustomji who had recently been savagely hissed at by a camel as she crossed Bunder Road. Naseema's father was trying to persuade the women of his household to give up wearing the burqua. But Naseema had told Roshni that she would be safe from camels and other attacking creatures if she would cover herself with a burqua. Thrity Kerawallah was also in the vicinity of Agnes, Roshni and Naseema. Thrity Kerawallah did not speak very often but when she did, she made pronouncements. She spoke in headlines. She exclaimed. And she always won first prize in elocution competitions. She usually recited ''Captain, My Captain'' or Portia's speech.

Agnes, Roshni, Naseema and Thrity were not happy. They had been told to line up next to the younger girls. They wanted to be closer to the senior students. After all, Naseema, only a few months older than Agnes, Roshni and Thrity had already had her first period four months ago. But before the four could negotiate a more prestigious arrangement, they heard the motorcade. As Agnes described it to Katy, everything started to move faster and faster and yet everything seemed to have frozen into an off-focus photograph. The white uniforms of the school children, the flags being waved, the motor cycles thundering by, the first line of cars all began to blend together and then just as the car with a white American-looking lady drove towards the four friends, Thrity's voice was heard.

"Agnes, Roshni, Naseema look! LOOK! Even camels get it!"

Agnes, Roshni and Naseema followed Thrity's voice, eyes and finger pointing backwards, away from the motorcade, away from the American lady until they found themselves looking at the camel which had pulled their cart. She was bleeding and the camel driver was tying a rag around her nether regions. Thrity continued, "C-c-c-camels also get p-p-periods!" Agnes and her friends were amazed and educated.

Agnes said to Katy, "Katayun, don't you see? I was fated to meet Mary Mattson. Her mother believed in female deities descending and her father had looked Eleanor Roosevelt right in the eye and had tipped his hat to her. I look at the pictures of Eleanor Roosevelt whenever I get the chance. Magazines, books, old cinema newsreels. And really dear, she has the look of a camel about her. A benevolent camel. An endearing one. A most camel-like look. Don't you think so Katayun?"

Katy did not know what was expected of her. A "yes, " a "no," a "how interesting" or silence. Agnes as usual did not wait for an answer.

"Of course because we were looking at Thrity's bleeding camel we didn't see Eleanor Roosevelt. She rushed by so fast. And I was staring at Thrity. I had realized that she had stammered. Thrity who never stammered. My brother Freddy stammered whenever our father laughed at him. But to make my mother laugh, Freddy would call her Katy and sing that ridiculous K-k-k-katy song to her. Margaret named you Katy. For Katayun. Most probably she did not know who your father was. My father? My brother? My husband? So she named you Katy. For the wife or mother or mother-in-law. She could have easily named you after me. Agnes. For the daughter, sister or wife. But there you are. One never quite understands these things. You are named after my mother by your mother. That is of course if Margaret was your mother."

Katy did not hear Agnes's last statement. She was remembering her father singing "K-k-k-katy" to her. Whenever she needed comfort and solace. In her foggy memory of London, somewhere in New Hampshire in the summer humid heat, in the green regions of Mexico. She remembered the parrot who had learned to repeat the song. She thought she also remembered the last time her father had stammered her name. He had not been singing. He had been falling down, carrying her down with him, telling her to run, run for safety to his employer, Mr Sanders. But she was not sure of that memory.

Katy heard Agnes's story from Roxanne Japanwallah. Roxanne had been a very young girl when Agnes had taken to her bed never to walk again. Agnes had been about twenty-two years old.

Agnes's father had an Indian Parsi father, Peshotan Cooper, and an English Christian mother, Agnes Myers. Agnes had insisted that although her only child, her son, was to be initiated into the ancient Mazdayasni Zoroastrian faith, he would have a civilized name, Edward. Edward became Eddie to his friends, remained Edward to his mother, and was transformed into Edulji by the mobeds when they included his name in the family Jashan prayers of rejoicing and thanksgiving.

Eddie Cooper married Katayun Gandhi of Quetta. They had two children. Fareidun or Freddy as he liked to be called and Agnes, ten years younger than her brother.

Roxanne tried to explain Agnes's father and brother to Katy. "Eddie-Edulji Cooper disliked his son Freddy-Fareidun because he was not a healthy boy child, he tended to turn to others for protection, looked like his mother and was very intelligent. Father and son agreed on one point. The British. They revered their foreign masters."

Father and son also loved Agnes. She was beautiful and bright and noisy. She was in awe of her gentle mother and loved her father. But she loved her quiet, studious brother the most even though she could not understand his obsession with the sahibs and memsahibs. "They eat strange food . . . raw meat and mushed-up vegetables and they do not even look at us," she said. But she always gave her brother expensive and usually useless gifts which had come from England. Woolen scarves, ornamental ceramic dogs and shepherds and even walking sticks.

Agnes, according to Roxanne's informants, had made a "love match." She married Rohinton Driver who had come from Bombay as a partner in one of Eddie's business ventures. Roxanne remembered Rohinton as very charming and quite vacuous.

She told Katy, "My parents said that he loved to dance . . . waltzes, fox trots, rhumbas, tangos . . . and of course so did Agnes. I remember distinctly that he always wore white shoes and that as soon as he was married to Agnes he was called 'Roy' by everyone. Except by Agnes and her mother Katayun."

According to Roxanne, two years after her marriage, Agnes found out that her husband had a mistress. She shrugged, bought herself a baby cheetah, walked around Devinagar with her pet on a leash and said nothing. When she found out that the mistress was Margaret Shriver, her father's mistress, the cause of her banishment to Karachi and the endless pain in her proud mother's eyes, she still said nothing. She decided that the shock and the anger had made her grimly, seriously ill. The morning after she found out the name of her husband's mistress, she announced that she was unable to leave her bed. She refused to stand up, she refused to walk. She donated the cheetah to a zoo. She had her bed moved to the window facing the back vegetable garden and issued her orders for food, clothes, new furniture from the window. She refused to move out of her bed. Her father hired a special nurse for her. When Rohinton was killed in a car accident about two months after she took to her bed, she did not go downstairs for the funeral. When Katayun died ten months later she asked her brother to carry her downstairs for her mother's funeral. She heard rumours about a possible affair between Fareidun and Margaret. She heard the arguments between her father and brother. She said nothing even when her father announced that he was going on a vacation to England with Margaret who had announced that she was pregnant again.

Agnes found out that she had truly lost the use of her legs when she tried to run to her brother to stop him from shooting himself. When the cook came into her room screaming that Freddy had shut himself in the library with a gun, Agnes tried to get out of her bed. She couldn't stand up. She crawled towards the top of the stairs but when she tried to raise herself up, clutching the banisters, she fell down the marble staircase, a second before a shot was fired. The failure of Agnes' legs and her fall may have saved Freddy's life.

"But, " said Roxanne to Katy, "the bullet must have done some damage to Freddy's brain. Because of what he did next. He became a spy. For the British of course. Disgusting. "

Roxanne's family had been followers of Gandhi and her grandparents had participated in the salt march.

Katy was having trouble getting used to being Katayun and a Parsi. Her memories of her father were of a man who went out everyday to check on men and women as dark and short as herself as they worked among the sugarcane fields. He did not look like a spy. He was a kind man. And he had stammered her name when he had pushed her away from him and told her to leave him as he fell on the ground which was always covered with humid unflowering green growth.

Contributors

VIDYUT AKLUJKAR is a poet and writer, primarily in Marathi, who has lived as many years in India as in Canada. Her books include an anthology of essays (1990) and an anthology of travelogues (1991), both published in India. Numerous poems, short stories and essays have appeared in journals and periodicals in Marathi. She is a co-editor of *Ekata*, a Marathi quarterly published in Ontario. In English, her poems have appeared in journals in North America, her academic writing in several international journals, and she has written screenplays for television. She has also taught courses in philosophy, Hindi, and Indian literature at the University of British Columbia. She lives with her husband and two children in Richmond, British Columbia.

MEENA ALEXANDER was born in India and raised there and in North Africa. She lives and works in Manhattan. Her published books include a volume of poetry, *House of a Thousand Doors* (1988); a novel, *Nampally Road* (1991); and the memoir *Fault Lines* (1993). Selected poems and prose works by her have been translated into Malayalam, Arabic, Italian and German.

HIMANI BANNERJI was born in Bangladesh in 1942 and she came to Canada from India in 1969. She teaches at York University in the Department of Sociology. She has written poetry, short stories and essays on racism, feminism, culture and politics. Some of her works are *The Writing on the Wall: Essays on Culture and Politics* (TSAR, 1993), *Doing Time* (1986), and *Colored Pictures* (Sister Vision, 1992). She has also edited *Returning the Gaze* (Sister Vision, 1993), a collection of essays by women of colour.

CHITRA DIVAKARUNI is originally from India and now lives in the San Francisco Bay area with her husband. She teaches creative writing at Foothill College, where she is a director of the annual Multicultural Creative Writing Conference. Her work reflects her interest in travel, women's issues and the immigrant experience, and has appeared in a number of magazines including *Calyx, The California Quarterly, Ms., The Chicago Review* and *The Toronto Review*. Her poetry books include *Dark Like the River* (1987), *The Reason for Nasturtiums* (1990), and *Black Candle* (1991). She is the editor of *Multitude, Crosscultural Readings for Writers* (1993), and her first collection of fiction, *Arranged Marriage*, will appear from Doubleday in 1995.

RAMABAI ESPINET is Trinidadian by birth and has lived in Canada for many years. She obtained her PhD from the University of the West Indies in Trinidad and is currently Professor of English and Communications at Seneca College in Toronto. She is the editor of an anthology of poetry by Caribbean women, *Creation Fire* (1990), and the author of a collection of poems, *Nuclear Seasons* (Sister Vision, 1991).

LALITA GANDBHIR has lived in the greater Boston area since 1965. She has published stories and poems in several journals, including *The Toronto South Asian Review, The Massachusetts Review*, and *Journal of South Asian Literature*, and in the anthology *Our Feet Walk the Sky: Women of the South Asian Diaspora*. She has published four short-story collections in India. Gandbhir works as a physician.

LAKSHMI GILL was born in the Philippines of East Indian and Spanish/Filipina parents, and came to Canada in 1964 to pursue graduate studies at the University of British Columbia. She teaches in Vancouver. Her works include the collections of poems, *During Rain I Plant Chrysanthemums* (1966), *Novena to St Jude Thaddeus* (1979), and a novel, *The Third Infinitive* (TSAR, 1993).

FEROZA JUSSAWALLA has a doctorate in English and American literature from the University of Utah. She is the author of *Family Quarrels: Towards a Criticism of Indian Writing in English*, and co-author of *Interviews with Writers of the Postcolonial World*. She has written numerous articles and reviews of postcolonial literatures for publications such as *College Literature, The Journal of Indian Writing in English* and *The Johns Hopkins Guide to Literary Theory*. She is Associate Professor of English at the University of Texas at El Paso.

SURJEET KALSEY was born in India, came to Canada in 1974, and now lives in British Columbia. She received a master's degree in English and Punjabi literature from Punjab University, Chandigarh, and a master's in creative writing from the University of British Columbia. Kalsey edited the Punjabi issue of *Contemporary Literature in Translation* (1977), and has edited and translated an anthology of poetry, *Glimpses of Twentieth Century Punjabi Poetry* (1992). Her poems and short stories have appeared in many literary magazines. She has written and directed three plays on violence against women and currently works as a counsellor for battered women. Kalsey has published one book of poetry in Punjabi, *Paunan Nal Guftagoo* (1979), and two in English, *Speaking to the Winds* (1982) and *Foot Prints of Silence* (1988).

FARIDA KARODIA is a full-time writer living in Canada. She was born and raised in a small town in South Africa which provided the setting for her first novel, *Daughters of the Twilight* (The Women's Press, 1986), a runner-up in the Fawcett Prize. She has also published *Coming Home and Other Stories* (Heinemann, 1986) and most recently another novel, *A Shattering of Silence* (Heinemann, 1993), set in colonial Mozambique.

GEETA KOTHARI lives in Pittsburgh, Pennsylvania. Her writing has appeared in various newspapers and magazines, including *The New England Review* and *The Toronto South Asian Review*. She is the editor of *Did My Mama Like to Dance? and Other Stories About Mothers and Daughters*.

YASMIN LADHA is the author of *Lion's Granddaughter and Other Stories* (Newest Press, 1992) and *Bridal Hands on the Maple* (chapbook, Second Wednesday Press, 1992). Presently she is working on a book of multiple-genre fictions, *Circum the Gesture*. She lives in Calgary.

ARUN PRABHA MUKHERJEE was born in 1946 in Lahore, then a part of undivided India, and raised in Tikamgarh, Madhya Pradesh. She came to Canada in 1971 as a Commonwealth Scholar at the University of Toronto. An Associate Professor of English at York University, she

199

lives in Toronto with her husband and son. She is the author of *The Gospel of Wealth in the American Novel: The Rhetoric of Dreiser and His Contemporaries* (1987), *Towards an Aesthetic of Opposition: Essays on Literature, Criticism and Cultural Imperialism* (1988), and numerous articles on postcolonial literatures, women's writing and critical theory. Recently, she edited an anthology of writings by women of colour and aboriginal women entitled, *Sharing Our Experience* (1993), and contributed entries on several South Asian women writers to *A Feminist Companion to Literature in English* (1990). Her short stories have been published in *The Toronto South Asian Review, Tiger Lily* and *Asianadian* magazines as well as in anthologies published in Canada, India and the United States. Her most recent book is *Oppositional Aesthetics: Readings From a Hyphenated Space*, to appear from TSAR later in 1994.

HEMA NAIR was born in Jammu and raised in Pune, Bangalore, Vishakapatnam and New Delhi, among other cities. She graduated in 1978 with a bachelor's degree in education from Loreto House, Calcutta and in 1979 joined *The Times of India* and in 1988 *The Indian Post*. In 1989 she won the Best Woman Journalist of the Year award, an All-India prize for outstanding writing on women's issues. She came to the United States in 1990 and lives in Princeton, New Jersey. She has been published in *Ms., New Directions for Women* and *The Women's Review of Books* and is a founder member of the Princeton Arts Council Writers Group. She is currently a freelance journalist and working on her short-story collection.

TAHIRA NAQVI was born in 1945 and received her schooling in Lahore. She has an MA in psychology from Government College, Lahore and an MS in English Education from Western Connecticut State University, Danbury, where she is presently teaching English. Her work has appeared in journals and has been anthologized. She has also published translations of Urdu short stories and longer works by Manto, Hijab Imtiaz Ali, Ahmed Ali, Munshi Premchand and Ismat Chugtai. Her translation, with an introduction, of Ismat Chugtai's *The Quilt and Other Stories* has been published recently (Sheep Meadow Press, 1994). A collection of her short fiction, *Attar of Roses and Other Stories*, and her translation of Ismat Chugtai's novel *Terhi Lakir* (The Crooked Line) are to appear shortly.

UMA PARAMESWARAN was born in India and came to Canada in 1966. She lives in Winnipeg with her husband and daughter and teaches English at the University of Winnipeg. Her master's degree is from Indiana University and her PhD from Michigan State University. She is the author of four volumes of creative writing and numerous critical articles on postcolonial literature. "Freeze Frame" is one of a collection of linked short stories in progress entitled *Maru and the Maple Leaf.* Some of the characters who appear in this story appear not only in other stories in this collection but in her earlier works as well—*Trishanku* (TSAR) and *Rootless but Green Are the Boulevard Trees* (TSAR).

ROSHNI RUSTOMJI-KERNS has lived and studied in India, Pakistan, Lebanon, France, the United States and Mexico. Her academic background is in comparative literature and mythology. She has taught in Pakistan, Lebanon and the United States where she is Professor Emeritus from Sonoma State University, California. Her essays and short stories have been published in journals and anthologies such as *The Journal of South Asian Literature, The Toronto South Asian Review, The Massachusetts Review, The Literary Review* and *Our Feet Walk the Sky: Women of the South Asian Diaspora.* She guest-edited a special issue of *The Journal of South Asian Literature* on South Asian women's writings on the immigrant and expatriate experience and is the co-editor (with Miriam Cooke) of *Blood into Ink: South Asian and Middle-Eastern Women Write War* (Westview Press, 1994).

NAZNEEN SHEIKH was born in Kashmir and educated in Lahore and Texas, and immigrated to Canada in 1964. She has published a children's book, *Camels Can Make You Homesick and Other Stories* (1985), and two novels, *Ice Bangles* (1988) and *Chopin People* (1994). She lives in Toronto with her husband and is the mother of two daughters.

BAPSI SIDHWA was born in Karachi and grew up in Lahore. She resides in the United States but travels frequently to Pakistan. Sidhwa has published four novels, *An American Brat, Ice-Candy-Man, The Pakistani Bride* and *The Crow Eaters*, and she has been translated into German, French and Russian. She is the recipient of the 1993 Lila Wallace Reader's Digest Writers' Award, one of the largest awards in the United States. In 1991 she received the *Sitara-i-Imtiaz*, a Pakistan national honour, and the *LiBeraturepreis* in Germany for *Ice-Candy-*

Man. Sidhwa taught in the graduate program at Columbia University in 1989 and prior to that at Rice and at the University of Houston.

PERVIZ WALJI is a technical writer in the United States Agency for International Development (USAID) where she works on issues such as environmental technology cooperation, global efforts to stabilize greenhouse gas concentrations and promoting efficient private power technology in USAID countries. She has also written and produced documentaries on minority-related issues for radio broadcast. She has a master's degree in journalism. She lives in the United States with her husband and daughter.

About the Editor:

NURJEHAN AZIZ was born in Dar es Salaam, Tanzania, studied in Iran and the United States and immigrated to Canada in 1980. She is a cofounder of *The Toronto South Asian Review*, now *The Toronto Review*, of which she is an editorial board member. She is the publisher at TSAR Publications, a book publishing program which was set up as an extension of the activities of the magazine in 1985. She lives in Toronto with her husband and two children.